WRECKER

A JOHN CRANE ADVENTURE

MARK PARRAGH

Wrecker
by Mark Parragh

A Waterhaven Media Publication
First Edition – June 2017
Copyright © 2017 by Waterhaven Media, LLC. All rights reserved.
ISBN: 978-1-7339756-1-2

Cover Design by Kerry Jesberger, Aero Gallerie
Edited by Courtney Umphress
Production Coordination by Nina Sullivan

This book is a work of fiction. Names, characters, places, and incidents either are the product of the author's imagination or are used fictitiously, and any resemblance to actual persons, living or dead, or to events or locales is entirely coincidental. No part of this publication may be reproduced, stored in a retrieval system, or transmitted in any form or by any means, electronic, mechanical, photocopying, recording, or otherwise, without the prior permission of the publisher.

CONTENTS

Chapter 1	1
Chapter 2	8
Chapter 3	16
Chapter 4	24
Chapter 5	32
Chapter 6	41
Chapter 7	48
Chapter 8	53
Chapter 9	60
Chapter 10	68
Chapter 11	74
Chapter 12	79
Chapter 13	85
Chapter 14	93
Chapter 15	100
Chapter 16	106
Chapter 17	112
Chapter 18	120
Chapter 19	128
Chapter 20	135
Chapter 21	143
Chapter 22	150
Chapter 23	157
Chapter 24	165
Chapter 25	172
Chapter 26	179
Chapter 27	185
Chapter 28	190
Chapter 29	198
Chapter 30	205
Chapter 31	212
Chapter 32	219

Chapter 33	224
Chapter 34	230
Chapter 35	237
Chapter 36	244
Chapter 37	252
Chapter 38	256
Chapter 39	261
Chapter 40	268
Chapter 41	274
Chapter 42	282
Chapter 43	290
Chapter 44	298
John Crane Returns	305
Want even more?	307
Contact Mark Parragh	309

For Lara Quinn.
She knows why ...

CHAPTER 1

Tepehuanes Municipality, Durango, Mexico

Martin Cottrell pushed his stolen ATV down the dirt road as the stars blazed like fire overhead. He didn't think he'd ever seen a night sky so intense. It had been eight months since he'd seen the stars at all. Had they really changed so much, or was it him? He felt so alive in this moment. He'd made it! He'd kept his eyes and ears open, watched the guards. He'd gathered shreds of information and patiently fitted them together. When the time came, he knew how to get out of his room and up to the main shop floor without being seen. He knew door codes and how the alarm system was configured. He knew the layout of the grounds beyond the small compound where he was held, including where the ATVs the guards used to patrol the estate were kept at night. He'd disabled all but one of the four-wheelers and walked this one right out the main gate, unmanned this time of night as he'd suspected it would be.

Things were going his way at last.

Martin knew that the road he followed twisted its way down out of the Sierra Madre Occidental mountains for more than five miles, passing nothing but a few abandoned shacks. It would eventually take him to the highway, just a few miles from the town of Santa Catarina de Tepehuanes. There, Martin would find a phone and call for help.

I'll have a hell of a story to tell, he thought. He wouldn't have to buy his own drinks for the rest of his life.

Martin worked as a telecom engineer for his father's company, Cochise Broadband and Wireless, back home in Texas. Eight months ago, he'd gone on vacation to Cabo San Lucas at the southern tip of the Baja Peninsula. He'd enjoyed a couple days on the beach and nights in the clubs. One night in a bar, a stranger had struck up a conversation and was fascinated by Martin's work. Martin thought nothing of it at the time. But the next day, he'd rented an ATV not unlike this one and ridden out to explore the desert.

And everything had changed.

The cartel soldiers who took him drove him to a remote airstrip and packed him aboard a small plane. He'd ended up here, with a half-dozen other captives like himself. They were electrical and network engineers, spectrum planners, and programmers. To avoid police eavesdropping, Martin learned, the cartels had built their own illegal networks of cell sites and repeaters. The hardware was scattered across the country, hidden in remote locations and powered by solar panels. They gave the cartels their own secure communications, completely off the grid. Of course, the cartel's people were drug runners and killers, not engineers. They lacked the skills to even begin to design, build, and maintain a sprawling telecom network. But that was no problem. If the cartels needed something, they simply took it.

Martin's captors reassured him that someone would pay to get him home safely; they always did. In the meantime, his skills were needed, so he would be treated well.

His world became one building. The six men shared three

basement bedrooms, and by day they worked upstairs on the main floor. They built radios, designed point-to-point microwave links, and repaired equipment. As promised, they were treated well. Their rooms were comfortable, and the food was good. They had recreation time outside in the enclosed yard around the building. And, to Martin's surprise, he actually enjoyed the work. The technical challenges of an illicit hidden network were more interesting than those he'd faced back home. Eventually, Martin convinced himself that he would do his work for the cartel, and eventually they would ransom him back. Months went by this way.

And then Garza disappeared.

That wasn't unusual by itself. Every so often, someone would be gone in the morning, and someone new would arrive to take his place. They were told the missing men had been ransomed and sent home. But Garza had no family. Just an ex-wife who despised him. He used to joke about how she'd pay the cartel to keep him. And yet, he was gone.

That was when it occurred to Martin that he was now the senior man. He'd been here longer than anyone else. It was when the lies he'd used to calm his fears lost their power. Of course they weren't ransoming the engineers! What did the cartel need with the few thousand dollars these men's families could scrape together? If nothing else, they all knew where they'd been held. To do their work, they needed detailed maps and precise GPS data. Martin could locate the compound to within five meters. The cartel could never risk that information getting out.

They used their captives and then killed them. And he was next in line.

That was when he knew he had to escape. Thankfully, the guards thought they had their prisoners cowed, and security was sloppy. Martin had figured out how to get out, and tonight he'd done it.

He glanced back up the road. The hacienda was out of sight. He was probably far enough away now to start the engine without being heard. He climbed on, turned the key, and punched the starter button. The engine sputtered to life, and he released the brake and set off down the road. The ATV was louder than he liked, but it was a lot faster than walking. He needed to make it to the highway and into town before he was missed in the morning.

The night air was cool against his face. He slowed around a switchback, and soon he could see the hacienda again, well above him now. As he drove, he noticed lights coming on, more and more of them until the whole mountaintop lit up. *No*, he said voicelessly to himself. *No, no, no.*

A few moments later, a helicopter shot over the ridge, flying low. It followed the line of the road, sweeping it with a nose-mounted searchlight.

Martin did the only thing he could do. He switched off the headlights, and opened the throttle, speeding down the road and hoping he didn't collide with something in the night.

He could see the helicopter off to his left. They didn't know how much of a head start he had, so they were following the road from switchback to switchback. That was something, at least. If he could stay ahead of them ...

He took another sweeping turn, and the road opened up into a long, straight descent along the side of a ridge. The land rose up sharply to his right and fell away to his left. The land was stony and harsh, sparsely dotted with pines and scrub brush. There was enough moonlight to see by, and he accelerated to open up as much distance as he could from the helicopter.

Suddenly he saw something moving ahead of him. A figure ran into the road from a flat-roofed adobe shack. Then there were flashes of light, and something slammed hard into the ATV's fender.

Good God, they were shooting at him!

Martin reacted on instinct. He veered off the road and down the steep slope. The tires spun wildly, throwing up loose rock and sliding as he fought to control the ATV. He heard more gunfire behind him.

The shacks he'd seen on the satellite imagery weren't abandoned at all; they were the outer perimeter. That was why the main gate was unmanned. But it was too late for that knowledge to do him any good. The men firing at him would bring the helicopter down on him in moments.

Martin half steered, half slid the ATV between tree trunks until he came out on the road again. There was one more switchback below this one before the road descended into rolling hills. Take the road, or keep on down the slope?

The helicopter made his decision for him. It roared overhead, the searchlight sweeping across the road no more than fifty feet away. Martin gunned the engine, crossed the road, and soared over the bank. The ATV took to the air and then hit the ground hard and slewed sideways, throwing loose stones into the darkness. He steered into the skid, trying to bring it back under control, but a tree trunk swept into view as he spun, and Martin knew he was going to hit it. He let go of the handlebars and dove clear. He hit the ground hard as the ATV caromed off the pine and rolled away down the slope.

Martin ended up face down in a slide of loose stone shards. He hurt and he could taste blood, but he didn't think anything was broken. He had no idea where the ATV had ended up. The helicopter was almost overhead. Martin hauled his aching body across the loose stone, kicking up a few more small slides as he went, and plunged into a patch of dry brush.

Martin lay there, his heart racing, as the helicopter hovered and swept the landscape with its searchlight. The roar of its engines drowned out all thought. Martin lay still with his eyes closed, waiting for the light to pick him out. Finally, the helicopter moved on.

Martin found the ATV at the bottom of the slope. It lay on its side, battered and not running. But Martin managed to roll it over onto its wheels, and it complained when he hit the button, but it started. He turned the ATV around and set off down the road toward the highway.

He made it within minutes and turned onto the main road. By now, the ATV's engine was starting to complain. Something had been hit and was working its way loose, he guessed. But all it had to do was get him another few miles into Santa Catarina de Tepehuanes. From there, he could call home, and his father would have him out in no time. All during his captivity, Martin never doubted that his father was looking for him. If he knew his father, he'd have been tearing Mexico apart piece by piece since the day he didn't return from the desert. He had no doubt that a significant reward was being offered for anyone who helped bring him safely home.

Martin could still see the lights of the helicopter, but it was well behind him now, and he began to breathe a bit easier. He guessed he was about three miles outside Santa Catarina. Just a few more minutes and he'd be safe.

Then he saw headlights. A battered pickup heading north out of town. Martin pulled the ATV across the road and stood in front of it, waving his arms over his head until he was sure they'd seen him.

The truck stopped with a grinding of brakes, and two men got out.

"Are you crazy, man?" the driver shouted as Martin hurried to meet them. "What are you doing out here this time of night with no lights? You going to kill somebody like that!"

"I need help!" said Martin. "Please. I need to get to town. To a telephone!"

They glanced up at the helicopter in the distance. "What are you doing out here?"

"I'm an American," Martin said. "I was kidnapped."

The two men glanced at each other. Then the passenger stepped back around the truck's open door.

"Please. Take me into town and get me to a telephone. I have to call for help. There's a reward. A big reward."

"Yeah, man," said the passenger, "we know." He stepped back around the door, and Martin saw a heavy nickel-plated revolver in his hand.

"No!" Martin shouted, and then the gun roared, and he felt the cold impact punch through him. He stumbled backward, and the man fired again. Martin collapsed on the asphalt.

The passenger put his gun away while the driver retrieved a highway flare from the bed of the truck. Martin heard the snap and hiss as he ignited it. As darkness gathered around him, Martin saw only the baleful red eye of the flare waving back and forth, and heard only the growing clatter of the helicopter.

CHAPTER 2

Cannon Beach, Oregon

"Recalculating," said the GPS unit in a voice that sounded irritated that John Crane was ignoring its advice.

"You do that," said Crane.

The single lane of asphalt was cracked and pitted. A sign had warned him that the state didn't maintain this road, which explained why his GPS didn't know about it. But Crane had also spotted a faded wooden sign for the Fox Cove Inn.

He supposed he shouldn't be surprised. If anyone could drop so far out of sight that even the GPS satellites couldn't find him, it would be Malcolm Stoppard.

Malcolm had been Crane's mentor at the Hurricane Group. He'd been an agent in the old days. By the time Crane knew him, he was out of the field and training new agents. He'd retired and come to Oregon to run a bed and breakfast by the sea.

But Malcolm still had contacts. When Crane found himself needing support in the Czech Republic, it was Malcolm he'd called for introductions. He'd promised to come visit when he got back, and he'd put off that promise for too long. So finally

Crane had flown into Seattle, rented a 6 Series, and driven down the 101 to the Oregon coast.

He steered the BMW through stands of pine beneath a slate-gray October sky. After a mile or so, the road emerged into a clearing overlooking the sea, and there it was. The Fox Cove Inn consisted of a main building and two wings of guest rooms. Crane took in weather-beaten cedar shingles and driftwood, carefully tended grounds, and an empty gravel parking lot. The beaches here were mainly a weekend getaway for Portlanders, so it wasn't surprising that the place was empty on a weekday, especially in the off season. Or perhaps Malcolm was just a bad innkeeper. He found it hard to imagine the man he'd known serving tourists Willamette Valley wines and artisanal cheeses.

As he got out of the car, Crane heard frantic barking, and a huge black lab tore around the corner of the building.

"Molly!" Crane knelt down and let the dog dance around him, barking with joy. There were touches of gray fur around her chin now, Crane noticed.

"Good girl!" he said. "Yeah, I missed you too."

A woman looked at him from the front doorway, a striking brunette of perhaps fifty.

"Good morning," he called, patting Molly's head. "I'm John Crane. Malcolm's expecting me."

The woman said nothing but gestured for him to follow. Crane and Molly followed her into a large rustic dining room and found Malcolm Stoppard unloading a dishwasher silverware basket.

"John!" he said, wiping his hands on a towel. Molly jumped up on him, and Malcolm shooed her affectionately. "Yes, I know he's here!"

"It's good to see you, Malcolm," said Crane.

"Same here! Let me—yeah, I know, it's walk time. Go get your stick, then. Go on."

Molly bounded away, and Malcolm crossed the room to shake Crane's hand and slap his shoulder. "Too long, John, too long."

He said something to the woman in a language Crane didn't recognize. She nodded and stalked to the far end of the room where an island separated the dining area from a professionally equipped kitchen. She scowled back at Crane.

"You're looking good," said Crane. Malcolm Stoppard was in his sixties and still in shape, though there was more silver in his hair than the last time Crane had seen him. His eyes were deep blue and intense. Crane could still see the good looks that had supposedly made Malcolm a legendary womanizer back in his field agent days.

"See you're keeping fit," Malcolm replied. "What do you think of the place?"

"I love it," said Crane. "Very peaceful back here."

"You're staying the night, right?"

"I don't want to impose."

Malcolm sighed. "John, I've got a whole empty B&B here."

"I have been enjoying the scenery," Crane admitted. "I was thinking about keeping the car a few extra days and driving south."

"All right, then. It's settled."

Crane glanced over at the woman. She seemed even less pleased with him now.

Then Molly returned, dragging a well-chewed driftwood stick at least as long as she was.

Malcolm took it from her. "A million of these things lying around," he said, "but apparently this one's special. It'll be breezy down by the water, John. You got a jacket?"

"In the car."

Malcolm said something to the woman and headed for the

door, Molly dancing excitedly at his side. Crane followed, and the woman watched him go with the same dour expression.

Outside, Crane grabbed his Billy Reid pea coat from the passenger seat and buttoned it up. It was indeed cold here—a wet, persistent chill that would soak into the bones.

"I don't think your friend likes me," Crane said.

"Pari? She just doesn't like my old life popping in for a visit. She'll warm up to you."

They struck off on a trail that led down a grassy slope toward the sea. Molly ran into the grass, scaring up birds. Below them, the beach was a long, flat arc of sand and whitecaps. Offshore weathered stone fingers jutted up from the water.

"So what the hell happened at Hurricane, John?" Malcolm asked.

"I was hoping you could tell me! They yanked me out of the field, fired me, and then offered me a desk job in McLean."

"Which you turned down."

"Yeah. You know the funny part? I ran into Chris Parikh a while ago. He's back in the field. Someone came around to McLean a few months later, scooped up all those old Hurricane agents and built a whole new operation."

Malcolm nodded. "Different sign on the door, different people at the top, but the same business at the end of the day. It happens. You could have been there, if you'd stuck it out."

"I'm happy with how things turned out," Crane said. The trail deposited them on the beach, and they strolled near the tide line. Malcolm threw Molly's stick, and she gleefully took off after it, her paws churning up damp sand.

"You're not the only one," Malcolm said with a grin. "I heard from Alexey. He thanked me profusely for sending you his way. I gather you were the gunrunner's version of a Black Friday sale."

"So you heard what happened?"

"You burned down a vineyard," Malcolm said as Molly dragged her stick back again. "Take care of that, would you, John? And you wiped out half the Czech underworld. People notice that."

Crane hurled the stick down the beach, and Molly took off after it.

"Blowback?"

Malcolm shook his head. "Nobody knows who you are. Lot of rumors. But at the end of the day, nobody was all that upset to see Branislav Skala gone. And life goes on."

They stopped and looked out at the rocks and the white water swirling around them. Molly came back with her stick and was content to collapse at their feet and chew on it.

"So what the hell were you doing over there, John? Who are you working for?"

Crane knew the question was coming. And he knew he'd come here in part because he wanted Malcolm's approval. But he still didn't relish explaining Josh Sulenski and his one-man covert agency.

"A high-net-worth individual," he said at last. "The thing with Skala came up because it involved one of his charitable interests."

"Right," said Malcolm. "So that's why you had no support but plenty of money to throw around. So are you done?"

"I don't think I am," said Crane. "This is starting to look like a long-term deal."

"Okay. We'll take the part about how the government deals with loose cannons as read. You already know that. So what's this guy's agenda? What's the mission?"

Crane considered the question as Molly wandered off to investigate a group of plovers. He didn't see a pattern in the things he'd done for Josh so far, if that was what Malcolm was asking. "He wasn't always rich. Now he's got power, and I think he just wants to do some good with it."

Malcolm snorted. "That's not an agenda. That's a character trait. Vague one, at that. Everyone thinks they're doing good. What's that mean to him? What's the vision, John? If you're going to serve it, you've got to know."

Crane fumbled for an answer. "Help me," he said at last. "What vision were you serving at Hurricane?"

"Molly, leave those damn birds alone!" Malcolm shouted. Molly trotted back, with a last glance back at the agitated plovers.

"By the end, I didn't know anymore," he said. "That's why I retired. But when it began, I knew exactly what it was about—keeping the Cold War hitting on all cylinders. Fixing the bits that got out of joint. Making sure we got everything there was to get out of it."

"You make it sound like a machine."

"It was a machine. Damn good one, too. You knew the sides, who was in charge, who worked for who, what they wanted. Power got channeled to useful ends. The money moved like you needed it to move. People had jobs that mattered. We went to the freaking moon! We had the world running like a Swiss watch in the Cold War. Until the idiots had to go and win the damn thing. Look at us now. It's chaos."

Molly whined and leaned in against Malcolm's leg. He stopped and reached down to ruffle the back of her neck. "It's all right, girl."

He smiled at Crane. "We had it easier in our day, I guess. You've got to chart your own path. But there better be more to it than running around getting cats out of trees. That feels good, but it won't get you far in the end. That's my advice. If you're going to do this, figure out what the vision is and make sure it's one you're okay with."

They wandered back toward the inn, Molly alongside, dragging her stick. Crane wasn't sure Josh had any overriding vision.

He trusted Josh's motives, but ideas flew off him in all directions at once. And Malcolm was right that that wouldn't get them anywhere in the long run. It was something he'd have to take some time to consider.

Molly barked. "Come here, girl," Crane replied, bending down and grabbing at the stick. "Give me that."

After a bit of tugging and negotiation, Crane secured the stick and tossed it down the beach ahead of them. Molly took off after it once more. But she was tired now, and Crane noticed her gait seemed a bit off.

"Is Molly doing okay?" he asked.

Malcolm smiled. "Well, she doesn't run quite as fast as she used to," he said. "But then, I don't throw the stick quite as far as I used to, either. It all works out, John. Come on, let's see what Pari's got for lunch."

After he'd gotten Crane settled, Malcolm did his evening sweep of the property, with Molly at his heels. Lunch had given way to dinner, and then they'd holed up in the study and finished the last of the 2012 Seven Springs Pinot and gossiped about the old days.

Pari had gone to bed early. Malcolm had noticed that she hadn't spoken a word of English to him all day, a sure sign that she was angry. She'd get over it, and it was worth it. Crane was sort of like the son he'd never had. He knew he'd been something of a father figure during Crane's early days at Hurricane. Crane's relationship with his own father was complicated.

Like mine with Chloe, he thought suddenly. Then he corrected himself. No, his relationship with his daughter was its own unique kind of complicated. But both he and Crane got something they needed from their friendship.

Malcolm finished his circuit of the building and started up the stairs, Molly clicking her way up the hardwood steps in front of him. He noticed the aging crown moldings were starting to separate in the corner of the front hall. That would need attention soon.

Place was a goddamn money pit.

Halfway up the stairs, his phone rang. He checked the screen and saw "Chloe." He answered with a smile. "Hi, honey. How are you?"

Then he stopped.

"Honey ... Chloe, slow down. What? Wait, you what? Well, I don't think ... Chloe, start from the beginning. What happened?"

He let out a long, slow breath as he listened. *Oh, shit ...*

CHAPTER 3

Crane lay in bed, thinking about what Malcolm had said on the beach, when he heard a soft knock at his door.

"John, you awake?"

Crane got up and pulled on the robe he'd found in the wardrobe. He opened the door and realized something was wrong the moment he saw Malcolm's expression.

"Saw the light under the door," Malcolm said.

"I was just thinking about your advice," said Crane. "Come in."

Malcolm chuckled without any real humor. "Yeah. Two sides to that coin."

He sat in a wingback chair beside an arts and crafts side table by the window. "All that talk about it not being enough to go around getting cats out of trees? Feels different when it's your cat."

Crane sat on the edge of the bed. "What's going on, Malcolm?"

"I got a call from Chloe," Malcolm said. "She's all right," he quickly added, "but she's …"

"She's Chloe," said Crane.

When Crane had known Chloe, she'd been seventeen with a well-earned reputation for trouble. She'd been the sort of girl who stalked high-school boys' dreams and their parents' nightmares.

Crane didn't know the details, but there had been some kind of incident when she was around twelve, one that made it obvious exactly what her father's real job was and what he was capable of when his family was threatened. She hadn't reacted with post-traumatic stress or angry betrayal. Instead, she'd taken it as a life lesson. The rules were for those without the skill, wits, and audacity to break them. The proper response to any challenge was quick, decisive action. Adrenaline was the best high in the world.

"She wants me to blow up a yacht," said Malcolm.

Okay, that's different, Crane thought.

"Um ... any yacht, or does she have one in mind?"

"Crap," said Malcolm. "I'm doing just what she did. Let me back up. I told you she graduated UCLA back in the spring. Her mother went. That's okay. I got last summer and Christmas."

Malcolm's wife hadn't reacted to the truth about him the same way Chloe had, and Crane knew how much the end of the marriage had hurt him. He could still hear it in Malcolm's voice.

"She's been down in Baja," Malcolm was saying, "saving the ocean with some shoestring non-profit down there. There's this guy who hangs around. He keeps a boat anchored in the bay, and I guess he's got a reputation for creeping on the girls. So someone Chloe knows went missing, and she's convinced this guy took her. She thinks he's part of a trafficking ring."

"Did she go to the police?"

"Oh, yeah," said Malcolm. "They're incompetent, or they're corrupt, or maybe both. Either way, she's decided it's up to her. She wants the guy's boat blown up, and she knows I know people who can do it. If I don't deal with it, she says she'll do it herself."

So if Malcolm didn't want Chloe putting herself in harm's way, his only option was to keep her out of it by doing what she wanted done himself. It was a tactic she'd used before, and Malcolm had learned the hard way that Chloe wasn't bluffing.

"What are you going to do?"

"I'm just worried she'll get in trouble," said Malcolm. "She's not in the States, and she's not a minor. She's not going to get two hundred hours of driving old people to the doctor this time."

"I can check in on her," said Crane.

"I can't ask you to do that."

Of course, that was exactly what Malcolm was doing. He was just deeply uncomfortable with it.

"Don't be ridiculous," he said. "I'll fly down and see if there's anything to it. That should calm her down, right? You sent someone like she wanted. And I'll make sure she doesn't do anything crazy."

Malcolm let out a relieved sigh. "Thank you, John," he said quietly. "I don't know what to do with her anymore."

"Mind you, I'm not blowing up some guy's yacht for her."

Malcolm rolled his eyes. "Of course not. That's what you say now."

"She still as good at getting her way as she used to be?"

This time, Malcolm's chuckle was genuine. "What do you think? She's a thousand miles away, and look at us."

"Go to bed, Malcolm," said Crane. "Toss me my phone, will you? I'll see if I can get a flight out of Portland in the morning."

Malcolm pitched him his phone and then stopped with his hand on the doorknob. "Thank you, John," he said. "I owe you."

"Put it on my account." Crane smiled. "Come on, Malcolm, this is what we do for each other."

Of course, he would have some stern words for Chloe when he got to Baja, he told himself after Malcolm had left.

Not that they'd ever worked before.

Palo Alto, California

The Myria Group campus had been built by a dialup Internet service provider that drew venture capital like bees to honey back in the nineties. With so much cash, decadence set in. Their new headquarters covered what had once been several lots. They started by filling it with artificial hills to hide the cityscape. By the time they finished, the site looked like a piece of national park dropped into the middle of Palo Alto. All parking was underground. The buildings were glass fronts built into earth berms, or gleaming curves wrapped around the shore of a man-made lake.

The interior was equally extravagant, from the lobby's stone towers and waterfalls to the restaurant on the roof. The cavernous room Josh Sulenski sat in had been some kind of recreational facility. Josh had heard gossip around the office that suggested it had once held an ice-skating rink. Josh wasn't sure about that, but he knew the back wall had been an indoor climbing wall. It was full of holes for attaching movable holds. It must have been quite a party until the bubble burst.

Josh sat at a lone desk and looked up from his spreadsheets. For a moment, he imagined a sound system blaring out Pearl Jam while programmers climbed the wall, and the marketing department did the Jane Fonda workout on the floor.

Jane Fonda? That's more eighties. Where did that come from? Oh yeah, Rollover.

Josh liked end-of-the-world movies; he enjoyed the catharsis. A few weeks ago, he'd watched *Rollover*, from 1981. It wasn't a great movie, by any means. But it was fun to take a break from zombies, super flu, and rogue asteroids and have the world end through financial chicanery for once.

The Saudis murder Fonda's husband because he learns some big secret about their bank accounts. So she starts investigating, and she finds the big secret too. The Saudis try to kill her, but it doesn't work, so they panic and end up pulling down the global economy. By the end, people are rioting in the streets and burning their useless dollars.

But what struck him was something a minor character had said.

Hume Cronyn.

He played one of those obscure powerful people pulling the world's financial levers. Josh knew people like that in real life now. He knew better than to trust them.

Everything's spinning out of control, and he's freaking out. Before he kills himself, he tells Fonda, "Money has a life of its own. It's a force of nature like gravity, like the oceans. It flows where it wants to flow."

That was what had been coming back to Josh recently. He was digging through SEC filings, reading 10-Qs and 144As and 15-12Gs until he saw numbers in his sleep. And this was the easy part. Most of the companies on his radar were privately held and didn't have to file anything. He knew huge amounts of money were moving around Silicon Valley. And whether it was going where it wanted to go, or clever people were steering it, it was doing things it shouldn't be doing. But Josh was in way over his head. He needed a forensic accountant to go through all this. He needed cybersecurity people to sift through e-mail headers and untangle spoofed IP addresses. He needed ...

A ragtag bunch of misfit geniuses who solve mysteries and have adventures together!

He rolled the chair back across the floor in disgust. This was stupid. He scrolled through the contacts on his watch until he found Maggie Nguyen in HR. She'd been working on it until he'd given up a few weeks ago.

A general cattle call? Hey, who wants to work on a special project side by side with the billionaire founder of the company? What did you think was going to happen?

"Yeah, Josh?" Maggie said through his watch.

"Hey, remember that Special Projects thing I had you work up a while ago? Did you trash all those résumés?"

He heard her scoff, and then, "No, I categorized them by skill set, and then within each category, I ranked them by how likely you were to want to talk to them."

"Really? Based on what?"

"On a year and a half of you barging into my office unannounced with some totally new project that's like nothing we've ever done, but that you want stood up by the end of the month."

"Wow, okay," he said. "I guess that's why I pay you the big bucks."

"You pay me medium bucks."

Josh paused. "Really?"

"My salary's in the fifty-sixth percentile nationally for HR professionals with my experience and level of responsibility."

"Huh. Okay, well, when we finish this, bump yourself up to seventy. Can you shoot the résumés to my tablet? Wait. Maybe just the top ... three? From each category?"

"You got it, boss." And she hung up.

She really gets you. You should ask her out.

I can't do that. I'm her boss. That's creepy. Besides, I need her doing what she does.

He heard his tablet in the leather messenger bag beside his desk chime as it downloaded the résumés he'd asked for. Josh looked back at the monitors with their tables full of third-quarter terminations of registrations of classes of securities under Section 12(b) and amendments thereto.

Just shoot me now.

He spun through his watch contacts again and punched "Tim."

"Can you bring the car around, please?" he said.

"Sure thing," Tim answered.

Josh shut down the computers and collected his bag. His footsteps echoed in the large, empty space.

"Good night, war room," he said as he switched off the lights.

"Gentlemen! You can't fight in here!"

Tim waited in the lobby beside the statue of Einstein. He wore a suit that was well-tailored to his wedge-shaped torso but still hid the holster at his belt. His eyes swept the area as he walked Josh through the front doors to the Mercedes.

"How was your day, sir?" Tim asked as they drove out of the campus.

I'll probably skip over it when I'm writing my memoirs.

"Fine. Yourself?"

"Very good, sir."

"We know what Anna Louisa has on the menu tonight?"

Tim discreetly checked his phone. "Balsamic-porcini dry-rubbed chicken, buttermilk mashed potatoes, and charred Brussels sprouts with bacon."

"Sweet."

After a long silence, Josh said, "Plans this weekend?"

"Going up to Napa with my fiancée," said Tim.

Megan? Karen? Emma?

"Emily? Well, have a good time."

"We will, sir, thank you."

So how's that working out? Pretending he's something other than a guy with a gun who gets paid to make sure nobody kidnaps you?

No reason we can't be friendly.

Boss friendly. These people work for you. Are they supposed to pretend they're your old college buddies, and they put their lives on hold to help you deal with your daily crap? Why would they do that?

Because I'm a billionaire.

That's right. Nothing gets around that. You're not normal. You don't get normal life stuff. People told you this would happen.

Fine, the hell with it.

Josh opened his bag and took out his tablet as the car made its way across Palo Alto. He opened Maggie's package and looked for the résumés tagged "forensic accounting." If he couldn't have friends, at least he could have minions to sift through all those damn 10-Qs for him.

CHAPTER 4

Bahia Tortugas, Baja California Sur, Mexico

Crane had landed in San Diego that morning and taken a cab to the Cross-Border Terminal at Otay Mesa. He'd crossed into Mexico via a footbridge that deposited him in Tijuana International, where a charter was waiting. It was just after noon as the small plane descended toward an airstrip outside Bahia Tortugas.

Baja couldn't be more different from the Oregon coast. Crane saw bright blue water, desert landscapes, and a small dusty town perched beside a natural harbor.

The plane touched down and taxied into a paved parking area. The airstrip had no tower, hangars, or refueling facilities. There was nothing but asphalt and dust except for an airplane and an aging Toyota pickup parked at opposite ends of the turnoff. The airplane was an Embraer Phenom 100 jet that Crane thought looked rather out of place. A lone figure leaned against the truck, waiting.

Crane retrieved his bags. The temperature was around ninety, and this was October. He slipped on his Ray-Bans, thanked the pilot, and walked toward the truck.

The figure leaning against the fender was a young woman wearing denim shorts, cowboy boots, and a plaid shirt tied off above her midriff. Chloe Stoppard had cut her black hair short. She was taut and tan, and she pushed off from the truck with a languid motion meant to entice. Crane gathered she hadn't changed all that much.

She looked him over with approval. "Hey," she said at last.

"How are you, Chloe?"

"Doing all right," she said. "You've been taking care of yourself, I see. Toss your stuff in the back."

Crane put his bags in the bed of the pickup and got in. The door bore a circular logo, an ocean wave wrapped around a dark-haired woman's face, and the words "Namaka Foundation." Chloe started the engine and ground the truck into gear. A hot breeze swept over them as she bounced off down the dusty, unpaved road.

"Namaka Foundation," Crane said. "That the group your father said you're with?"

"She's a Hawaiian sea goddess," said Chloe. "She sends tidal waves to punish the wicked."

"Tidal waves? Sounds kind of indiscriminate."

Chloe flexed a tan thigh as she hit the clutch. "Maybe she figures nobody's really innocent."

Crane decided Namaka made a good muse for Chloe.

"We collect data for different research projects," she said. "Mapping water temp, salinity. It gets us some grant money. But mostly we're about education and activism. That's where you make a difference. We're halfway between San Diego and Cabo, so all the asshole cruisers stop here to refuel, and they dump their sewage in the bay. We give them a hard time about that. Try to get them to take better care of the ocean."

The airstrip wasn't far outside of town, and soon they were driving past single-story homes of wood and cinder block. They were painted in bright colors that stood out against the tan landscape and looked like they'd been slowly settling into the earth ever since construction was complete. Crane saw scrawny dogs roaming the streets, and aging cars coated in dust. A pair of orange and white radio towers marked the center of town.

"Couple thousand people," Chloe was saying. "It's quiet. Nobody much comes here except the cruisers. You can fly in like you did, but not many do. Overland, it's three and a half hours of bad road out to the highway at Vizcaino."

They reached a paved and divided road strung with power cables, the median lined with small palm trees. She hung a right and headed through the middle of town. Homes, shops, and offices shared the streets, jumbled together at random. Suddenly Chloe veered left onto another dirt road. From here, Crane caught a glimpse of the bay dotted with the white hulls of sailboats. Chloe turned along the waterfront and pulled up before a row of cinder-block garages with numbers on their rusting metal doors.

"You mind?" she said, tossing him a key on a carabiner clip. "Number four."

Crane got out and used the key to unlock a padlock and slid the door open. Chloe pulled the truck in alongside a couple rusting bicycles and a knobby-tired Yamaha dirt bike. They walked out and closed the door again.

"Dinghy's tied up at the pier," said Chloe. "Come on."

Chloe led the way past cinder block walls, and parked pickup trucks. A man sat outside a small cafe, picking out the chords of *House of the Rising Sun* on a guitar.

"You want to fill me in?" Crane said as they walked.

"You see what it's like here, right? People don't have much, and they're busy just getting by. It's the cruiser types that cause all the trouble. Weekends when the weather isn't too hot, it's like a bad frat party," she said. "On the boats, out at Punto

Dorado, or here on the beach. They get wasted, hassle the locals, leave trash everywhere. One of the worst is a guy who goes by Boz. I don't know his real name. He's a major creep. Likes to invite you out to his boat. All the booze and drugs you want. Word's out among the local girls; you don't go out to the *Gypsy*."

"He lives on this boat?"

"No, he just comes here to play. That's his shiny jet you saw. I don't know where he lives. He keeps an Escalade in town, and he's got a couple of goons to keep an eye on the boat when he's away."

"So he's a sleazeball. Why do you think he's trafficking?"

"Sometimes the boat just sails off. It'll be gone a few days, maybe a week. Thing is, he's not even on it most of the time. His plane leaves. Then the boat takes off for a few days."

They turned a corner, and the harbor lay spread out before them. Crane counted about a dozen pleasure boats. The locals used outboard-driven pangas. Crane saw several fishing at anchor, and a pair laden with fifty-five gallon drums heading toward a motor yacht. Across the bay, an automated light perched on an outcrop of rock.

"There's home," Chloe said, pointing to one of the boats. "That's the *Emma*."

The boat was a fifty-foot catamaran with a single mast, white with aqua trim, anchored well out from shore. Crane made out the Namaka Foundation logo on the bow.

They made their way down to the pier. The aging, weather-beaten planks shifted and creaked beneath their feet. Chloe led Crane to a ladder with a rigid-hulled inflatable motorboat tied up at the bottom. She climbed down, and Crane followed.

"I'm not sure how that gets you to sex trafficking," said Crane.

Chloe huffed at him. "The locals have all kinds of stories

about girls who got lured out to the *Gypsy* and didn't come back. But that was just stories. Then my friend disappeared."

Chloe untied the boat, and Crane pushed away from the pier. Chloe sat by the outboard but didn't start it yet.

"Her name's Amy Carpenter. I knew her from college. We weren't besties or anything, but she was vagabonding around Baja, and when she found out I was here, she came out. We hung out a few days. She dragged me to a party down on the beach, and Boz was there. Man, did he go for her. Laying it on thick about his private jet and his boat, all the famous people he knew, his uncut Molly. It just didn't stop. I told her about his rep, but I think she figured she'd just have some fun and walk. Last I saw her, she was going down the beach with him."

"When was this?" Crane asked.

"Little over a week now. I went to the cops. They're useless. They claim she took the bus to Vizcaino a couple days later. She wouldn't do that without saying goodbye."

"Has the boat moved since she went missing?"

"No," said Chloe. "I think she's still out there. That's why I wanted you here. To get her off that boat and burn it to the waterline."

She yanked the starter, and the boat's outboard roared to life. Chloe steered away from the pier.

Crane considered her story as they crossed the bay. It was far from convincing. Unless Chloe had more to tell him, he didn't see much to go on. Chloe wouldn't be happy about that.

When they reached the *Emma*, Chloe guided the boat to the stern, to a swim deck between the catamaran's twin hulls. She cut the engine and glided in. A black woman wearing a bikini top and an orange wrap around her hips tossed them a rope. They pulled in beside a second dinghy and tied off.

The woman looked Crane over as they climbed out onto the swim deck. "Who's your friend, Chloe?" she asked.

"This is John," said Chloe. "We used to date in college. John Crane, Carolyn Yates."

"Careful," said Carolyn. "You'll make Scott jealous. He's back, you know."

Chloe squealed with delight and ran forward, shouting, "Scotty!"

A figure stepped out of the main cabin, and Chloe launched herself at him, wrapping her arms and legs around him.

Carolyn traded a look with Crane. "Guess she's the one who got away, huh?" she said.

Crane smiled at her. "Chloe usually does."

"We won't see them for a while," she said. "Come on, I'll show you around."

Within a few minutes, Crane had gotten a tour of the *Emma*, met the crew, and managed to put together a reasonable picture of how the group worked and who was sleeping with whom.

Carolyn Yates was the daughter of successful Chicago attorneys. She was here to work on a doctoral thesis about grassroots organization and environmental policy. Chloe's boyfriend was Scott McCall, a radio engineer earning his keep by overhauling the *Emma*'s navigation and communications systems.

The ship's cook was a German named Max Brandt, and he definitely had eyes for Carolyn. Crane wasn't sure whether it was mutual.

Fleur Garraghty was the child of Hollywood royalty. Her father was a producer, and her mother had starred in a hit medical drama that Crane remembered hearing of but had never seen. He suspected Fleur's parents were the *Emma*'s major source of funding.

The last one Crane met was the captain. Allen Burch was in his late thirties, easily the oldest member of the crew. Crane gathered he was something of a legend in environmental activism circles. Carolyn mentioned he'd been the target of FBI harassment for years back in the States.

With the possible exception of Burch, who seemed to take his responsibilities seriously, they didn't strike Crane as a particularly effective crew. They seemed more like college students trying to avoid the real world. But at least they were friendly, and they seemed happy to have someone new to talk with.

Carolyn explained that Scott had left for Vizcaino several days ago to pick up some electronic parts he'd ordered, there being no secure package drop-off in Bahia Tortugas. The shipment had been delayed, and he'd just returned.

"He thinks he can get the satellite link working," she said with a hint of excitement in her voice. "Be nice to have phone service again."

Carolyn and Fleur both confirmed the reputation of the man they knew only as "Boz." They'd kept their distance, but they'd both been warned by local girls to watch out for him. They didn't seem to think he was especially dangerous, though. Fleur's impression of Amy Carpenter was that she was "kind of a flake." She didn't think it unlikely that Amy might have skipped town as quickly as she'd come, without saying goodbye to her friend Chloe.

As the sun began to graze the surface of the Pacific, Crane sat at the bow of the starboard hull with a pair of binoculars. Allen Burch stood nearby, nursing a bottle of beer.

"There's the *Gypsy*," said Burch, pointing out a long, boxy motor yacht. "Sixty-five-foot Hatteras. Twin diesels. She'll make about ten knots. You could outrun her on a bicycle. But she's got range. Twenty-five hundred miles on full tanks."

"So if you *were* trafficking women, she'd be well-suited to it."

"I suppose."

"You think he is?"

"I don't know the guy," said Burch. "We don't travel in the

same circles. I know he's a jackass. But beyond that ..." He shrugged.

Crane scanned the boat with the binoculars. On the rear deck was a davit for launching and recovering a boat, but the deck itself was empty.

"He's got to have a tender, right?"

"Sure," said Burch, "thirteen-foot Boston Whaler."

"Well, it's not there, so I guess he's not aboard. Any idea where he spends his time?"

"Punto Dorado, most likely," said Burch. "Private resort across the bay. Look left of the light."

Crane did and made out a dock and a seawall with some kind of building beyond it.

"Run by an old drug runner named Orly Wilde," said Burch. "Some of the yacht crowd hang out there, but mostly it's friends of the owner, guys with no visible means of support. You're taking this seriously, aren't you? I mean, if you used to date, you ought to know Chloe can go pretty far out on a limb before she stops and looks down."

Crane put down the binoculars and laughed. "Yeah, but she'll usually take you along with her, whether you want to go or not."

It is probably nothing, he thought. Chloe being Chloe. Still, while he was here, he might as well check the guy out.

CHAPTER 5

"Ah, come on, Orly, not this Creedence shit again! You're not that old!"

Across the courtyard, the woman looked up. Boz caught her eye, and she grinned.

Orly Wilde shook his head and tapped a button on the player, and *Born on the Bayou* cut out abruptly.

"All right, Boz," said Orly with a tired sigh. "What do you want to listen to?"

Boz glanced up at her again. Mid-thirties, but she'd taken care of herself. She was with a doughy, balding guy who looked like an insurance salesman and had to be pushing fifty. He'd be no trouble. *And I can go for a woman my own age once in a while.*

Yeah, he could definitely go for a slice of that.

"Something smooth," he said. "Bebel Gilberto?"

"Fine," said Orly, "fine." A few moments later, a samba began, slow and sensuous, and Gilberto's breathy voice flowed across the flagstones like honey. Oh yeah. That would work.

He closed his eyes and let himself feel the music. He was thirty-six years old, though he knew he looked younger. He was fit and tanned, with sun-bleached hair. Women liked him. They liked his cheekbones and the inguinal crease at the bottom of his torso. The guy she was with looked like someone who'd scrabbled and hustled all his life for his money. So now he finally had a boat, but he was so old and worn out, it was wasted on him.

Not him. His father had done that shit and then married a model, so he'd gotten a little genetic head start to go with the trust fund. He stood up, one arm clinching an invisible partner as he swayed. He could feel her eyes on him. He stepped around the table. Dancing was sex. And he was a good dancer; that was another thing women liked about him.

"That's better, Orly. Seriously, man, Creedence? On a day like this?" He opened his eyes and looked over to the couple. "Am I right?"

She smiled and nodded. The insurance salesman took notice of him now.

"You two came in with that Oceanis 38 yesterday afternoon, right?"

The man nodded. "*Second Wind*, yeah. You know your boats."

He called his boat *Second Wind*. Well, of course he did.

"Mine's *Gypsy*, the Hatteras 65."

The woman spoke for the first time. "Oh! I saw that! That's a nice boat."

Yeah, compared to insurance man's little hundred-and-fifty-thousand-dollar sailboat, it was a pretty nice boat.

"Thank you. I'm Brad, but folks call me Boz. Is this song sexy as hell or what?"

Then someone came in from the breezeway. The newcomer was young, tall and lean, black hair. He wore blue chinos, boat shoes, and a white linen shirt. Boz didn't recognize him; still, he thought he noticed a flash of recognition when the stranger's eyes fell on him. Then Orly showed the new guy to his table, and he returned his attention to the blonde.

At the end of the pier, Crane found an entrepreneur named Luis who ran a jitney cab. Luis drove him out on an unpaved road that hugged the coastline for a couple miles to a parking lot with a sign that read "The Beach Club at Punto Dorado."

It looked like Boz was here. Chloe had said he drove a black Escalade, and there it was. But it wasn't the stock model; this one had been heavily armored. Crane spotted a bulkhead behind the rear gate, run-flat tires, and heavy ballistic glass. Across the lot, two very large men lounged on the seawall. They eyed him with suspicion until he'd walked past the Escalade. Crane assumed they were part of the security package.

Crane could think of three reasons a man might own that vehicle. He could just be showing off. He could be seriously paranoid. Or he might actually have a legitimate need for that kind of security—like someone involved in trafficking women, for example.

Crane heard music coming from a breezeway, so he passed by the front doors and followed it through into a square courtyard dotted with tables and palm trees. Three sides were surrounded by a covered walkway lined with doors. The fourth looked out over the beach and the dock with a handful of motorboats tied alongside. A sound system played bossa nova, the music blending with the gentle, insistent roll of the surf.

An older man, thin, with gray dreadlocks, rose from his chair. This would be Orly Wilde. According to Captain Burch, Orly had been a serious drug smuggler back when the trade was beach bums with Jimmy Buffet tapes instead of cartel thugs with chainsaws. He'd gotten out when it got dangerous, or possibly been busted and done federal time in the States. Either way, he'd retired to Bahia Tortugas and built his place. Crane thought he looked the part.

"Hey, welcome to Punto Dorado," Wilde said. "I'm Orly."

"John Crane."

They shook hands, and then Orly showed him to a table with a view of the beach and went for a menu. There were three customers: a couple at a table and a man standing nearby. That one matched Chloe's description of Boz. He looked around thirty, average height and build, blond hair, blue eyes. He wore board shorts, blue canvas sneakers, and a muscle tee. As he swayed to the music, Crane watched the drape of the fabric, looking for a concealed weapon. He didn't see one. He pretended to study his phone while he zoomed in the camera and took several shots of Boz.

Boz was enticing the woman to dance now. She laughed nervously, glancing from him to her companion. What was going on was something ancient and primal. Boz was claiming dominance, shaming the weaker man, claiming his woman. Finally she took his hand and stood up. Tension hung in the air despite the smiles and the music.

Orly returned with a menu, and Crane nodded across the courtyard. "He always like this?"

"It'll blow over," Orly said softly. "It's nothing."

Crane stood and walked toward them. Boz had led the woman away from the table, still holding her hand in his outstretched arm.

Crane strode up and slapped Boz on the shoulder. "Todd Osterberg, you old pervert! I thought that was you!"

Boz whirled and dropped the woman's hand. Crane saw him trying to work through his confusion.

"Damn, buddy!" he added, ramping up his amazement at finding an old friend here. "Haven't seen you since Tijuana! Remember? You, me, and that asshole Carmichael fighting over who got which hooker? I think Carmichael's still on penicillin."

Boz still didn't know what to do. "I think you've mistaken me for someone ..." he said.

"Come on, pal, you weren't that wasted!"

The woman dropped back to her table, and her companion stood up. Together they headed for the exit.

Boz tensed, and Crane caught a sudden flash of hostility. He shifted his weight, prepared to deflect a punch and sweep Boz's legs. But then the moment broke, and Boz laughed. "Nice meeting you two!" he called over his shoulder. Then he laughed and shook his head at Crane. "Ah man. You cockblocked me! That's cold, dude!"

"She didn't look like she was into it," said Crane.

Boz shrugged. "Eh, just passing time. I'm Brad Zahn. Call me Boz."

"John Crane." Boz grinned as they shook hands, but his eyes were cold.

"Well, John Crane, least you can do after that is buy me a beer."

Crane gestured to Orly for two beers and joined Boz at his table.

"So you're new here," said Boz. "What brings you?"

"Just visiting a friend."

"Haven't seen many new boats lately," Boz said. "You drive in?"

"Flew in yesterday," said Crane.

"Ah, so you saw my jet, then."

"The Embraer. You got the original model or the 100E?"

Boz looked confused. "What's the difference?"

"The 100 had some issues with the brake-by-wire system. There were some runway overruns, blown tires. The E's got new spoilers to make it more stable on the ground."

Boz suddenly slapped the table. "Shit, I'm bored already. You do any shooting, John?"

Crane shrugged. "Sometimes."

"I keep some shotguns here. We shoot pigeons off the end of the pier. What do you say? Come on and throw for us, Orly."

Boz led the way to a side room that turned out to contain several wheeled racks of clay pigeons. A locker held a half-dozen Remington 1100 semi-auto shotguns and several green and gold boxes of 12-gauge STS shells. Boz handed Crane a gun and a box of shells, and they headed out to the pier, Orly following with a rack of pigeons and a hand thrower.

"This isn't formal skeet or anything," Boz explained. "Way we play, Orly throws one or two targets, your call. He throws from different angles, but we each get a throw from the same place. Dozen throws each, so anywhere from twelve to twenty-four targets, depending on how you call them. Your score's hits minus misses."

"Got it," said Crane.

The pier ended in a large "T," giving them room to spread out. Crane loaded his gun while Orly windmilled his arms to warm up.

"What do you say, John?" said Boz. "Twenty bucks a point?"

"Works for me," said Crane.

"All right. I'll shoot first, show you how it works. Give me two, Orly."

Boz readied his gun. Behind him, Orly loaded two pigeons into the thrower, cocked his arm, and sent them out over the water in close parallel arcs. Boz raised his gun, tracked them for an instant, and then fired one shot that shattered both targets.

"Oh yeah," he said. "Two points." He stepped back and let Crane move into position.

"I'll take two," Crane told Orly. Crane brought the gun quickly to his shoulder a couple times to get used to the weight. He'd trained with combat shotguns. He hadn't shot clays in a while, but the movements came back easily. He placed his finger inside the trigger guard.

"Go."

Orly hurled the two pigeons over the water. Crane held his breath, focused on a point directly between them, brought up the gun, and fired.

Both targets fell into the water intact.

"Oh!" Boz crowed. "Too bad, John. Minus two there. Might want to stick to single birds until you get the hang of it."

Orly moved to another throwing position, and Boz held up two fingers.

This time the targets' arcs took them farther apart. Boz fired and shattered one, and then snapped off a second shot but missed. Crane saw him swear under his breath.

"Still plus two minus two," he said.

"Give me one this time, please, Orly," Crane said as he took position. This time, as the target flew, Crane aimed directly at it and paid attention to the feel of the gun and the recoil against his shoulder. He pulled the trigger and shattered the disc.

He was right. He took a couple shells from his box and studied them as he loaded the gun. The casings were labeled as #9 shot, but Crane knew they weren't. They weren't slugs, either. The recoil wasn't *that* far off, and the end wasn't open as a slug would be. But they acted like slugs.

The answer came to him as Boz squeezed off two more shots and took out both his targets. They were wax slugs. It was an old hunter's trick for saving on ammo. They would open a regular shell, pour hot wax in around the shot, and let it solidify. Instead of spreading into a pattern when fired, the wax and shot remained a single mass. It was like shooting at clays with a rifle.

But as it happened, Crane was very good with a rifle.

"I'll take two this time," he told Orly.

"Sure about that, John?" Boz interjected. "Just digging yourself in deeper."

Crane nodded to Orly. Whoever made these—Crane couldn't see Boz doing it himself—had done a good job. Someone without Crane's experience might never have realized why they kept missing. So Boz had gone to quite a bit of trouble just to cheat at his target shooting game. He obviously didn't need the couple hundred dollars he'd get from a mark. He did it because he liked winning. No, not just winning—beating someone else.

That was a valuable clue to his character, Crane decided.

Orly threw the pigeons. Crane swung the gun up, nailed the first, and then quickly altered his motion and squeezed off another shot to shatter the second.

Boz looked stunned. "Nice," he finally said.

Now that he knew where he stood, Crane consistently fired two shots, each taking a target dead center. Boz was a decent shooter, and he could take both targets with one shot if they stayed within his shot pattern. But he was inconsistent, and Crane's steady, methodical shots unnerved him. He began to miss.

By the sixth round, the score was even. By the time Crane finished with two last clean shots, he was up by six.

Boz thrust a wad of cash at Crane without counting it. Then he put his gun over his shoulder and stalked off up the pier.

"Not a fucking word, Orly," he snapped as they passed.

Crane slipped Orly a twenty. "Would you mind calling the payphone down at the harbor? Tell Luis to come pick me up."

As the jitney drove off with John Crane, Boz stood in the

doorway and watched it go. Then he summoned Arturo and Juan Manuel with a shrill whistle.

"Everything okay?" asked Arturo.

Boz pointed at the departing car. "That guy," he said. "His name's John Crane. Find out who the son of a bitch is and what he's doing here. I want to know all about him." He spat on the pavement. "And then mess him up."

CHAPTER 6

When Luis let him off at the pier, Crane caught a panga and had it run him back out to the *Emma*. As it pulled up to the stern, he heard muffled shouting and noticed most of the crew were milling around on the rear deck. Burch came down to the swim deck and helped him out of the panga.

"What's going on?" Crane asked.

Burch shook his head. "Scott and Chloe are getting into it. They took over the saloon."

"What's it about?"

"He took a job somewhere, and she's not taking it well," said Burch. "So I guess Scott will be leaving us. At least he got the electronics back up to spec."

Crane had hoped for a quiet place to think, but it sounded like that was out. He headed toward the *Emma*'s bow. As he passed the main saloon, he heard Chloe shouting, "You didn't even ask me!"

"What was I supposed to do? Not take it? " Scott shouted back.

"You could have talked to me first! You're supposed to care what I think!"

Crane left them to it and headed forward. He took a pair of binoculars from a cabinet, sat cross-legged on the canvas sheet stretched tightly between the boat's forward hulls, and scanned the *Gypsy*. The tender was still gone, so Boz wasn't aboard. *Where did he go when he left Punto Dorado?* Crane wondered. Did he have a place in town? That was worth looking into.

But what had he learned from his encounter with Boz, besides that it was short for Brad Zahn and that he cheated at target shooting?

He could certainly see why people avoided the man. After the initial flush of charm wore off, he was vain, crude, misogynistic, and untrustworthy. He had a need to dominate those around him, and he was very thin-skinned when he failed. Crane was no psychiatrist, but words like narcissist and sociopath came to mind.

But was he trafficking women?

Crane didn't know what to think. In some ways, he seemed the type. The two thugs and the armored Escalade fit with a criminal lifestyle. Down here, they suggested narco cartels. But Crane wasn't convinced. For one thing, Boz just didn't seem that competent. And he was an outsider here. It would be very difficult, if not impossible, for an American to talk his way into the kind of high-status position with one of the cartels that would explain the boat and the jet. And Boz didn't strike him as someone who made friends easily.

If not a cartel, then where did his money come from? That was probably the best avenue of investigation.

His phone rang. Crane took it from his pocket in mild surprise and saw it was connected to a satellite uplink. Apparently Scott was as good as his word.

"Hello?"

"John!" said Josh Sulenski. "Where are you, man? You're going to miss it!"

"Miss what?"

"Dude! Don't you check your messages? The new Batman! I've got it. We'll be the first people to see it who aren't in I.A.T.S.E."

"I don't know what that is, Josh."

"It's a union for film crews, but that's not important now. The point is, brand new Batman! Not in theaters yet. One night only on the big screen at my place. Drop whatever you're doing and get over here."

"Josh, I can't just run over there. I'm in Baja."

Josh paused. He sounded confused as he finally said, "Do you need me to send the plane?"

"No! I'm in Mexico. But while I've got you, I need you to run down some information."

Somehow, this seemed to get through. "All right," said Josh. "I'm with you, John. What's going on?"

Crane gave him a quick rundown of what he'd found in Bahia Tortugas. By the time he was done, Josh said, "Okay, I'm at my desktop. What do you need?"

"Anything you can find about a Bradley Zahn, middle initial possibly 'O.' Caucasian male, early thirties, American, maybe Canadian."

"Hang on, going to put you on speaker."

Crane heard keystrokes, and then there was a pause before Josh said, "Couple dozen Bradley Zahns in the United States. Though a bunch of these are duplicates. And most of them are too old to be your guy."

"Could be an alias, of course," said Crane. He tapped a few buttons on his screen. "I just sent you some pictures."

"Not a lot to go on, John, but okay. These are loading pretty slow. You on a satellite connection or something?"

Crane took the phone away from his ear for a moment and gave the water an exasperated look. "Yes! I'm not down the street in a Starbucks! I'm on a boat in the middle of the Baja Peninsula with the Pacific Ocean to my right and a couple hundred miles of empty desert on my left. I'm on a satellite uplink, and I'm lucky to have that!"

He realized Josh had gone silent. "What is it?"

There was no reply.

"Josh? Everything okay?"

When Josh came back, his voice suddenly seemed hushed. "I don't need to run these. John, I know this guy."

Josh was standing, leaning over his desk to look at the screen as Crane's photos downloaded. Crane was ranting about how far out in the middle of nowhere he was, like that was his fault. Not this time.

An image slowly resolved out of large blocks of color. Josh made out tables, flagstones, a beach and the ocean in the distance, a palm frond out of focus at the edge of the frame, and a man. Blond hair, something about his face. *Oh my God ...*

There were other photos resolving in windows behind that one. Josh flipped through them. *It's him. Jesus. He dyed his hair, but that's him.*

He edged around the corner of the desk and settled heavily into his chair. "I don't need to run these. John, I know this guy."

He really did skip the country. Hiding out in Mexico with a fake name and that ridiculous haircut. The rest of it must be true too. God ...

"His name's Jason Tate."

"Seriously?" said Crane. "Who is he?"

The prodigal son.

"Someone I ran into when I first made it big out here. His father's Alexander Tate. He's the one who got rich. Jason's a trust fund baby. Alex was a high roller back in the PC boom in the eighties. He was an angel investor. Backed the right startups and hit the jackpot. We hooked up not long after the stock market thing. Suddenly there were people coming out of the woodwork, throwing money at me, wanting to partner, wanting a piece of me. The sharks could smell blood. Alex helped me out, showed me the ropes, warned me off a few bad deals. He kind of watched out for me until I figured out what I was doing."

"That's the father," said Crane. "What about the son?"

Josh sighed. *This is going to be fun.* "I met him a few times. He and Alex had kind of a strained relationship, but there was money to go around, so they mostly kept out of each other's way. Jason was pushing a startup with some weird name. Dig something. Digara. Diganna. I don't remember. But at one point, he wanted me to join the board."

"Did you do it?"

"Oh, no. He had some kind of Vision Document, but it was just buzzwords about paradigms and disrupting everything and generational synergy. Half the names were deeply connected, like retired admirals, ambassadors. I think one of them was a national security advisor from the Bush administration. The other half was teenage pop stars and actresses. It was deeply weird."

"I'm getting that," said Crane.

"I never did get a coherent explanation of what this thing was meant to actually do, but I remember one time he was bouncing off the walls about how Taylor Swift was coming to something he set up, and he was going to pitch it to her. I finally decided the whole thing was about him trying to pick up celebrities."

"That doesn't seem inconsistent with the guy I met," said Crane.

"By then I was starting to figure things out for myself, and I kind of backed away. I saw Alex a few times after that, at functions mostly. But I steered clear of Jason."

"So why's he living in Mexico under an assumed name?"

Josh closed the windows with Jason's photos and leaned back in his chair. *He won't stop until he drags it all out. That's what John does. That's why you picked him.*

"Not long after all this, everyone was suddenly whispering about him. Anywhere you went, the gossip was all about Jason."

"The tech billionaire's grapevine?"

"You've noticed how we all go to the bathroom together? That's what we're doing." Josh paused and rubbed his temples with his fingertips. "That's all I know from here out—gossip. But word was he took out this girl from a big-deal financial family, and he got aggressive. Some people said there'd been a couple incidents in college that his father had to cover up—I don't know about that—but I guess this was too big to sweep under the rug. She and her family were out for blood. They were tight with the district attorney. The press was starting to get wind of something. Then suddenly, Jason was just gone."

"Was there an arrest warrant?"

"I don't know if it got that far," Josh answered. "Is it important?"

"Could be," said Crane. "If he's a fugitive, it opens up some avenues. What happened after he disappeared?"

Here we go. "It was hard on Alex. Maybe six months later, he drank too much one night and ran his Maserati down a hillside outside LA. He suffered a traumatic brain injury, and he's been in a private hospital up here ever since. He's not who he used to be."

"I'm sorry," said Crane.

You didn't do a very good job of keeping it out of your voice, did you?

"Alex had his flaws. Drinking wasn't the only one. But he was good to me. When I was vulnerable, he looked out for me and made sure I got on my feet. I don't like how things turned out for him."

He paused for a moment, then, "John, what's this about? What are you doing in Baja, anyway?"

"I'm doing a favor for a friend. I just ran across this guy, and things didn't add up," Crane continued. "I had no idea you had a connection."

"Of course not. All right. I can put out some feelers, see what I can find out. Check back in a day or two, okay?"

"Yeah. Thanks, Josh."

After Crane hung up, Josh sat alone in the darkened room, lit by the glow of his screen.

Alex isn't who he used to be. Well, who is? The world always finds a way to grind you down.

Dude. Cheer up. Remember? New Batman.

Josh checked his phone. No new replies. Everyone he'd invited over was out of town or busy or just didn't get back to him.

It was pretty short notice. You're not hanging out in the dorm with the rest of the comics nerds anymore. Type A people are busy taking on the world.

They could drop what they're doing, if they wanted to. Back at Stanford, this would make me a god. People would literally worship me.

But your friends don't like Batman, and if they don't like Batman, well, they're no friends of mine ...

Which is exactly why you don't have any friends.

He didn't have an argument for that. And now he was in no mood for the movie himself.

Josh sighed and shut down the screen. He sat alone in the dark for a moment, then he got up and wandered down the hall to see what was in those catering trays he'd had brought in.

CHAPTER 7

Chloe and Scott's fight had apparently run its course by the time Crane hung up. At least, he didn't hear them shouting any longer.

He noticed a small boat approaching the *Gypsy* and watched through the binoculars as it pulled up to the stern. Someone, presumably Boz, or Jason Tate, he guessed, climbed onto the platform and went up to the deck. Then two other figures swung the davit out and got to work raising the tender out of the water.

"You working out how to do it?" Chloe said behind him.

Crane put down the binoculars. She'd been crying, but she was putting on her stiff upper lip now.

"Are you okay?"

"Yeah. Sure. Scott left a while ago. He's going to get a motel room in town."

"Burch said this was about a job?"

"Yeah. With the phone company or something," she said. "His family isn't rich. He's got student loans, and his parents are after him. I get it. But he could have talked to me."

She shook her head. "Anyway, that's over. Who needs him? Are you going to sink the *Gypsy* or not?"

Crane got to his feet. Chloe wore jeans and a cutoff black T-shirt. Her eyes were red from crying, but she stood with a defiant posture, as if she were challenging him to call her on it.

"Boz's real name is Jason Tate," Crane said. "He's a trust fund bro from the States. Apparently the locals' read on him is spot on. He's a real piece of work. But trafficking? I'm not sold."

She was only half listening to him, he realized. She stared at the water as the waves gently slapped against the hull. The breakup with Scott had hurt her more than she was admitting.

"Chloe," he said. She looked up at him. "I don't think your friend's on that boat. There's no reason to think she didn't just take the bus out of town like the police say."

"Amy didn't leave town," said Chloe. "I know she didn't."

"Okay, what makes you so certain?"

She considered for a moment, and then said, "Come on."

She led him across to the other hull and then below decks to the small cabin she'd shared with Scott. The place looked like it had been tossed. Scott had packed and left in a hurry. Chloe opened a compartment over the bunk and removed a small metal box. She knelt down to place it on the mattress.

"Amy was sleeping on the beach," she said. "I told her we could find a place for her here, but I guess she was used to it or something. But she did give me some things to keep for her while she was here. She never came back for them."

Crane squatted down beside her as she flipped open the latches and opened the box. The first thing Crane noted was a Browning .32 automatic. Alongside it were a roll of Mexican banknotes, a plastic bag with a couple joints and assorted pills, a small Moleskine notebook with a pen clipped to the cover, and a US passport.

"She wouldn't have left without this," said Chloe. "Where's she going without her passport?"

Crane checked the Browning. The magazine was full.

"Don't let anyone see this," he said. "It's very illegal down here, and the sentences are harsh."

"Duh," she said.

The passport appeared to be real. The battered notebook was full of sketches from Amy's travels, phone numbers, various other notes Crane couldn't interpret. It ended before she arrived in Bahia Tortugas. A dog-eared photo was stuck between the pages. Three young women on the beach, arms around each other, mugging for the camera. Crane picked out Amy from her passport photo. She gave off a kind of neo-hippie vibe that fit with what Chloe had told him. *Wherever she is now*, Crane thought, *she's a real person with friends she loves, and parents somewhere. And she's probably in trouble.*

He stuck the photo back into the notebook and put everything back in the box except Amy's passport. That he slipped into his shirt pocket.

"Okay," he said. "That suggests she didn't just leave town. I'll see what I can get out of the police in the morning. If anyone asks after this, I'm a private detective working for Amy's parents, all right?"

She nodded, and Crane stood up to leave.

"I've got some tequila here," she said suddenly. "You want to hang out?"

She stood up and fished the bottle out of a small locker against the bulkhead.

"Nobody's going to want to be around me for a while after that whole scene," she said. "I don't want to just sit here alone and brood."

"Okay," he said after a moment. He could use some distraction himself.

She found a couple of plastic cups and poured a slug into each.

Crane sat back on the bunk, and Chloe sat beside him, legs

crossed and facing him. They touched rims and drank. It was cheap tequila, but decent enough, Crane decided.

"So how'd you end up getting the call?" she asked. "From my dad?"

"I was at the inn when you called," said Crane. "Just visiting."

"Coincidence, huh?" she said. "Funny how things turn out."

She took a long swallow of tequila and said, "That's how Scott and I met."

"You didn't meet here?"

"No," she said. "We came down together. We met last semester at UCLA. I was looking for a book in the library, but I messed up the call number and ended up in the totally wrong section. We ran into each other, and he helped me find where I wanted to be. We got talking, and he told me he was going to come down here after graduation. Hadn't been for that ..."

She finished the tequila and poured herself some more. She held up the bottle with a questioning look, and Crane held out his cup for a refill.

"What about you?" she asked. "I remember you being around from time to time. I guess my dad trained you. Stuff you can't talk about. Do you still work for the government?"

"Not anymore," said Crane. "But yeah, your father helped me get through training. He taught me a lot. And most of it I still can't talk about."

"That's okay," she said. "I've seen what he can do, remember? So that's what you do."

Crane said nothing.

"Keeps you in good shape, at least," she said, and she reached out to run her fingertips down the side of his torso. He looked up in surprise, and she met his eyes with a distinct look of lust.

"Chloe." He caught her wrist and gently returned her hand. He shook his head. "That can't happen."

"Right," she said. "Because Dad's like your father figure, and that makes me your sister or something."

"No," said Crane. "It would cause problems with Malcolm, and I don't want that. But you're not like my sister."

"Someone else?"

Crane shook his head.

"All right, fine," she said. "I'm sorry. I just ... Look, I get that I can be ... intense. I thought maybe for someone like you, that would be okay."

He had to admit that Hurricane Group training would be useful in trying to keep up with Chloe.

"But you don't want to be my rebound. I get it," she said. "Bad timing." She stood up and put the last of the tequila back in the storage locker where she'd found it. "Probably don't need any more of that, either."

Crane took the hint and stood up. "And I should go," he said. "You're going to be all right, Chloe. In my experience, nothing holds you back for long."

She smiled at that, stepped across the cabin, and hugged him with her head on his shoulder. "You're right," she said as she released him. "That's very true. Thank you."

When he left, Crane headed back up on deck. Across the bay, the *Gypsy*'s lights were on. Crane stood and pondered the boat. Chloe would be all right. She'd find some new avenue for her energy soon enough.

But Jason Tate was starting to worry him. In the back of his mind, he was already working through what he had learned, turning facts over and fitting them together. Whatever was going on here still didn't add up. Something was missing. There was something he didn't know, and he needed to find out what it was.

CHAPTER 8

The next morning, Crane got up early and worked out on deck. People were beginning to stir as he got a quick breakfast from the galley. He dressed in a charcoal Kent Wang polo shirt over Prana hiking pants, and his black duty boots. Then he borrowed one of the tenders and headed in toward the municipal pier.

If he was going to do this, he decided, he needed to lay down some smoke to cover what he was really after, and leave an obvious trail to follow. So he spent most of the morning strolling through town, asking the locals if they'd seen Amy Carpenter. He showed her passport photo around, and found a couple people who recalled seeing her. Mostly they remembered that she didn't dress like the yachters who were the bulk of the outsiders passing through Bahia Tortugas, and that her Spanish, like his, was unusually good for an American.

After an hour or so, Crane found a shopkeeper who insisted that he'd seen her boarding the morning bus for Vizcaino outside his store five days ago. Crane thought it sounded like a speech he'd practiced in front of a mirror.

Eventually, Crane decided he'd done enough. Anyone asking about him would find plenty of anecdotal evidence to support the idea that he was a private investigator searching for a missing American girl. So Crane made his way to the local police *comandancia* and found himself talking with the chief, a man named Moreno. Chief Moreno was a simple man with a simple job. There wasn't a lot for him and his three officers to do in Bahia Tortugas beyond the occasional drunk and disorderly call. Moreno was certainly not a graduate of any police academy, but Crane felt his fondness for his hometown, and his desire to protect it.

For his part, Moreno seemed happy just to have a visitor. "Most of the boats come through, they refuel, maybe they stay a night or two," he said, "but they stay aboard. They just talk to each other. They don't really get to know Bahia Tortugas. We have so much to offer."

Crane asked him about Amy Carpenter. Moreno confirmed that Chloe had reported her missing, and he'd investigated. Several witnesses had claimed to see her leaving town. Were they lying? It was possible, but he had no evidence to contradict them.

Crane took Amy's passport from his pocket and flipped it open. Moreno looked at it in silence for a long moment.

"Well," he said, "it's possible she lost it." Crane didn't think Moreno believed that.

"Can I ask how you come to have her passport?" Moreno asked. "And why are you here in Bahia Tortugas?"

"I'm a private detective," said Crane. "Her parents have been worried about her, and they hired me to find her. The trail ends here."

"Well, thank you for coming in and letting me know," said Moreno. "We wouldn't want any misunderstandings."

"No," said Crane. "Certainly not."

"I'll get in touch with Vizcaino," Moreno said with a sigh.

"We'll see if she turned up there. If you learn anything more, I'd appreciate it if you'd let us know."

Crane promised he would. Then he turned the conversation to the club at Punto Dorado, and to Boz, saying that the last time Amy's friend saw her, she was leaving a party with him.

Moreno grew more circumspect. He was definitely aware of Boz's reputation and had heard many stories of goings-on at Punto Dorado. But, he told Crane, his superiors had made it very clear that his was a municipal police force. His jurisdiction didn't extend to Punto Dorado. Nor did it cover Boz, no matter where he happened to be.

The message was clear to both Moreno and Crane. Boz was protected from on high. Crane gathered Moreno didn't care for this but knew he could do nothing about it.

The discussion had stopped being a pleasant distraction for Moreno, and Crane had learned all he was going to learn here. They shook hands, and Crane stepped out again into the heat of the afternoon.

He headed down toward the water and wandered until he found a bar on the beach called, appropriately enough, La Playa. It had a patio covered in palm fronds that offered a decent view over the bay and proved to have a friendly bartender named Hector. He had time to kill; the *Emma* was cruising deeper water today, collecting their water samples and salinity data. Chloe had said they'd be back before sunset.

So Crane relaxed with a couple cold beers, listening to Mexican pop music on the bar's tinny radio, watching the sailboats, and going through what little he knew, trying to fit the pieces together. Chief Moreno seemed like a decent enough man, but international fugitives, missing Americans, big money, and what looked like some kind of cartel connection put all of this well out of his league. If nothing else, his promise to contact the police in Vizcaino meant he hadn't already done so. That seemed an obvious first step to Crane. So the local police were keeping out of it. Crane wondered if that extended to him now that he was getting involved.

And of course, Chloe brought a whole other angle to things. She seemed to have calmed down, which was supposedly his goal in coming here. But he didn't know how long her patience would last if he didn't produce Amy or sink the *Gypsy*.

And her instincts aren't bad, he thought. Everything about Tate was skeevy, from his odd background and assumed name to the two big, well-armed men watching over him. It was possible they were former cartel soldiers who Tate had hired as muscle. But someone with Tate's combination of money and need to keep his head down would have to come to the attention of the cartels sooner or later, if only as a ripe target. But it didn't seem as though he was being extorted. No, there had to be something else.

Crane spent the rest of the afternoon rolling the pieces around in his mind, fitting them together in different ways. But he never found a picture that made sense to him. Finally, he noticed the *Emma* sailing back into the bay.

He dropped a few notes on the table and headed down to the pier. Perhaps Josh had learned something useful.

Two figures sat waiting near the end of the pier as Crane returned to where he'd tied up the tender. They stood up as he approached, and Crane recognized Tate's two bodyguards from Punto Dorado. He sighed. So his questions around town had hit a nerve. Or else Boz was just pissed off about losing his shooting match.

Crane tagged them as Groucho and Harpo, and scanned the area to nail down the tactical situation. There was nobody else within a hundred yards or so. The dock was about eight feet wide and fifteen feet above the water here. The boards were warped and creaked as he stepped on them.

As Crane came closer, they walked toward him, moving to either side as if to pass by him. But then they whipped out collapsible batons in unison and came at him fast. Groucho looked stronger, so Crane pivoted toward him. He slid inside the baton's arc and blunted the impact, but Harpo's baton hit him hard on the right side of his back. Crane grunted as a searing jolt of pain shot through him. He trapped Groucho's arm and pulled him into a tight clinch. He used Groucho's momentum to swing him around and shield himself as Harpo moved in for a second hit. Groucho punched Crane hard in the temple with his free hand. Then Crane head-butted him and thrust forward, throwing him off balance.

They staggered forward and slammed into Harpo, who went windmilling backward over the edge of the dock with a startled cry. That was one down. Groucho tried to get a grip on Crane's collar to pull him off himself. Crane stamped on his instep, pushed him away, and threw three quick kidney punches that put him down on the dock.

Crane realized he hadn't heard a splash. He leaned over the side and saw that Harpo hadn't hit the water. He'd fallen into an empty panga. It looked like he'd hit on the gunwale and was now lying on his back, groaning, with his legs hanging over the side. He could well have broken his back.

Crane kicked Groucho's baton into the water. They hadn't pulled guns. Their orders had probably been to just rough him up as payback for humiliating Tate. It was just a job for them. Maybe he could turn this to his advantage.

He knelt beside Groucho and helped him sit up. "Deep breath," he said. "Deep breath. You're okay."

As Groucho came to his senses, he started and threw up a fist. Crane caught it in his free hand and pushed it aside.

"Whoa! Whoa there. Truce. We can always fight more later, all right? Right now we need to make sure your friend's okay. He landed hard in somebody's boat. You understand?"

Groucho looked over the side of the dock, saw his friend lying below, and nodded. Crane led the way down the ladder.

"Arturo," Groucho called out. "Arturo! You okay?"

Harpo—apparently named Arturo—groaned and rolled onto his side.

"Don't try to move," said Crane as he stepped off the ladder into the boat. He felt Arturo's side and didn't feel any broken ribs. He didn't think his back was broken. He was probably mostly stunned. He bent Arturo's leg up and helped him roll into a semi-seated position. The other one looked on in confusion.

"Juan Manuel? What's happening?" Arturo said in confusion.

"It's okay," Juan Manuel said quickly. "Fight's over. Be cool."

"Sorry, man," said Crane. "I thought you were going in the water. Here, look at me."

He quickly determined that Arturo could move all his limbs and didn't have a concussion. He'd be sore for a while, but then, so would Crane himself.

"What's going on?" Arturo asked. "Why are you being this way?"

"That was a bad fall, man," said Crane. "This could have gotten serious. Nobody was supposed to go home in a box today. Your boss just told you to teach me a lesson, right? So I don't see where we've got any beef. He's the one's got a problem with me. Here, sit up. Slow. That's right. I have to say, he seems like a real pain in the ass to work for."

They traded a look, and Juan Manuel snorted. That hurt his side, and he winced. "Damn, man, that hurts!"

"You got some licks in too," Crane said. "That's what I'm saying. You guys have skills. Seems like you could be doing better, you know? So why him?"

"*Pinche idiota*," Arturo spit. "A donkey knows more. We work for a captain. *He* tells us to keep an eye on this guy, keep him out of trouble, give him what he wants."

"Well, no disrespect to your captain," said Crane. "I'm sure he's got good reasons. You ready to try standing up?"

He got Arturo on his feet and helped him to the ladder. Arturo moved slowly and winced with each rung, but they eventually made it back to the dock.

Crane turned as if to leave, but Arturo said, "We can't just let you go, man."

"Yeah," Juan Manuel added. "You got to give us something. We didn't beat you up. We've got to at least know what you're doing here."

Crane nodded. "I get it. Tell him you couldn't find me. But you found out I'm a private detective. I've been asking all over town about a girl named Amy Carpenter. Will that do?"

Juan Manuel nodded, and Crane walked away down the pier.

"Watch yourself," Arturo shouted after him, "next time, man."

"I won't take it personally," Crane called back.

CHAPTER 9

Marin County, California

Josh's Mercedes drove down a long approach road that wound between gently rolling hills. Fallon Landing was a spit of land on the north shore of Marin County, overlooking Tomales Bay and the Point Reyes Peninsula beyond it. It had been a ranch once. Now it was a very exclusive private hospital. For the last two years or so, it had been the home of Alexander Tate.

Josh sat silently in the back of the car, looking out across the hillsides at windblown grass and scattered trees. Tim was quiet in the front, having long since given up on engaging his boss in conversation. Josh had nothing to say today. Even his sarcastic inner voice was uncharacteristically quiet.

Josh didn't really want to be here. He didn't know what he would find at the end of this road. He wasn't sure this was the right thing to do. But if Alexander could still understand and connect to the outside world, and if he had spent the last two years here, not knowing if his son was alive or dead, then perhaps Josh could bring him some measure of peace. He owed Alex that much, anyway.

Eventually, the road emerged from a stand of trees and

descended a grassy slope toward the hospital itself. Josh saw carefully manicured grounds, discreet signage, and security personnel in black pants and white polo shirts. The building itself was long and low, all horizontal lines and planes of pale stone.

Tim drove around a grassy circle and parked in a visitor space. Josh let himself out and picked up the leather portfolio he'd brought. Tim followed as he headed inside.

It was all very tasteful, very expensive, very quiet.

Just the place for the super-rich to warehouse their deranged relatives.

Josh smiled briefly. *There you are. Good to know that, even under the circumstances, I can still find some way to be a jackass.*

Oh, always. Always.

A very efficient woman smiled up at him from the main counter.

"Good afternoon, sir," she said. "How can I help you?"

"My name's Joshua Sulenski," he said. "I'm here to see a patient. Alexander Tate."

"Yes, sir." She typed a burst of keystrokes on her computer. "I'm sorry, sir, I don't see you on the list of approved visitors."

Why would he be on restricted access? Who's making decisions about his care? Well, when in doubt, try lying.

"I'm on the board of the Thomas Kingsolver Foundation," he said. "It's a private charitable trust that funds cancer research. Mr. Tate's still technically a member of the board. After the accident, no one had the heart to call a vote to remove him."

That's actually true.

Mere corroborative detail, intended to give artistic verisimilitude to an otherwise bald and unconvincing narrative. Here, here comes a lie.

"But a situation's arisen that requires action from all members, so that compassion has rather backfired, I'm afraid." He took a page of legalese from his portfolio and showed it to her. "I need to either secure his proxy or affirm that I saw him personally and agree that he is unable to fulfill his duties to the foundation."

"That may be, sir, but without authorization, I can't let you see Mr. Tate."

Okay, you prepared for this. Who is on the list?

Josh took another piece of paper from his portfolio, an official-looking authorization to see Alexander Tate. On the signature line was an incomprehensible scrawl that could have been anyone's name. As she showed it to her, a sudden idea struck him.

"I've an authorization from his son, Jason Tate."

Her fingers fired off another burst of keystrokes, and she glanced at the screen. "Very well. I'll have someone take you to Mr. Tate's room."

So Jason's on the approved list. Interesting. Has he ever been here?

She pressed a call button, and a few moments later, an orderly appeared through a side door. He was a large, dark-skinned man, with Polynesian features, wearing neatly pressed scrubs.

"Mr. Tate in seventeen," said the woman.

The orderly nodded. "If you'll come with me, sir."

Josh followed him down the empty, silent corridor with Tim following a couple steps behind. The place was like a tomb.

No, he corrected himself. *A five-star hotel where they bury pharaohs.*

Shut up, internal monolog.

Humor is a fundamental coping mechanism.

But that wasn't funny.

The orderly stopped at a door and used a keycard clipped to his breast pocket to open it. The room was large, furnished minimally but expensively in tile, glass, and Scandinavian woods.

Open windows looked out over the water, and the breeze billowed the gauzy white curtains.

In the center of the room was a heavy hospital bed, tilted up so the figure lying in it could look out the windows. Behind it stood gleaming racks of monitoring equipment quietly hissing and beeping. As the orderly left them, Josh forced himself to move forward. The figure in the bed took no notice.

"Alex?" Josh said timidly. "Alex, it's me. Josh Sulenski."

The man in the bed turned his head. Alexander Tate was a shell of the man Josh had known. His skin was pale and seemed to sag from his skull. He struggled to focus his deeply sunken eyes. Josh remembered him with a full head of sandy-blond hair, but now it was thin and gray. He could see through it to Alexander's liver-spotted scalp.

Tate's eyes widened into an expression of fear, and he moaned softly.

Dear God, does he even know who I am?

"Josh Sulenski, do you remember?"

It was as if he'd aged forty years. Alexander Tate had been one of the princes of Silicon Valley. Now his world was a view of the water, an adjustable bed, and a mahogany side table that held a plastic bedpan and a Styrofoam cup with a straw sticking out of its plastic lid.

With difficulty, Alexander pulled a frail, bony arm from beneath the covers. His forearm was taped up with injection ports and sensor pads. He waved it in Josh's direction and made an "aaah" sound that stretched and modulated.

Josh realized he was afraid. Of Tate?

No, not of him, of this. This is death staring you in the face, saying your turn's coming. Just tell him what you came to tell him and get out of here.

"I don't know if you know this or not, but in case you don't, I wanted to tell you that Jason's all right. A friend of mine saw him in Mexico a couple days ago."

At the mention of his son's name, Tate grew more agitated. His keening grew louder, more insistent, and he shook his head with an irregular twitch.

All right, you told him. Let's get the hell out of here.

But Josh couldn't move. He stood rooted to the spot, pinned there by the old man's eyes. There was something there. Desperation? Some shred of the man he'd once been fighting to break out?

Trauma-induced dementia. He's probably terrified of you. Just go already!

Josh didn't move.

"I'm sorry, Alex," he said softly. "I'm sorry this happened to you. I'm sorry I didn't come see you after the accident."

"Nah! Nah! Nah! Nah!"

Tate began to thrash in the bed, grimacing and slapping the bedcovers. The consoles behind him beeped more urgently. Josh backed away a step.

This was a mistake.

"I'm sorry," he said. "I'll go."

Tate stopped moving. With what appeared to be a supreme effort, he calmed himself and beckoned Josh closer. Josh hesitated, but finally stepped up to the edge of the bed.

Tate took a deep breath. Then he reached out and clutched Josh's wrist. Josh flinched but didn't pull away.

Tate made a sound that seemed less like speech than noises leaking from his mouth. His expression sank, and he released Josh's wrist with a moaning sigh.

"I'm sorry, Alex. I don't understand."

Tate pointed to the Styrofoam cup on the side table.

"Gah."

"You want water?" Josh said in confusion.

Alexander shook his head. He took several deep, wheezing breaths. On the screens behind him, Josh could see the green phosphor trace of his heartbeat trending upward.

"Gah," he repeated, and then he slapped his chest with his fingertips. "Nahn gah."

He's trying to tell you something. He's desperate to tell you. What's important to him here?

"Okay, I'm trying, Alex. What is it? What is it about the cup?"

Tate pointed at the cup. "Gah." Then he made a new sound, a drone from the back of his throat. He varied the pitch, looking at Josh in frustration. The tone went up and down. He stopped to take a breath and then began again.

Come on, you remember that sound. Where have you heard that before?

It hit him suddenly.

Kids playing racecars. Engine noise. Shifting gears.

"A car?"

"Gah! Gah!" Punctuated by jabs at the cup with his bony fingers.

"Okay, the cup is a car?"

"Ahh!" He reached over and, with effort, pulled the straw from the lid with a faint, plastic screech.

He repeated the same sound and clutched the straw to his chest.

If the cup represents a car, what's the straw?

"The driver?"

"Ahhhh!" Alexander gripped the straw in his fist and pounded his breastbone.

Not just a driver. Him.

Josh heard footsteps hurrying down the hall. The nurse must have checked out his story, and the gig was up. Alexander heard it as well. He moved the straw to his left hand, holding it against his chest and looking intently into Josh's eyes. Then he turned, and with a guttural cry, he swept the cup from the table. It hit the floor, and the snap-on lid flew off, spraying water and crushed ice across the tile.

"Sir, you need to leave right *now*!"

Two security men with batons on their belts accompanied the front desk nurse. They moved toward him, but Tim dropped his hand to the butt of his pistol and snapped, "Keep back!"

Tim didn't draw the gun, but he made sure they knew he had it. For a moment, there was a standoff as Josh felt a wave of horror sweep over him.

The accident. He's ... he's telling you it wasn't an accident ... that he wasn't in the car when it happened!

"We're leaving!" he said. "It's okay; we're going."

If he wasn't in the car, then ... Go! Get the hell out of here now!

"You heard him," Tim said in a loud, commanding voice. "We're leaving. Clear a path!"

Tim led the way past the security men and the nurse while Josh backed out behind him. Tate's eyes were locked on his, pleading.

He mouthed, *You weren't in the car?*

Tate shook his head fiercely and repeated, "Nahn gah." He kept repeating it as the machines monitoring his status grew more frantic. An alarm started to chime, and the nurse took a handset from her pocket and thumbed the mic button. "I need a doctor, room seventeen. Now!"

Josh couldn't look away from the raw fear and desperation in Tate's sunken eyes until he'd rounded the corner into the hallway. Then he turned to see Tim hurrying him back toward the lobby with one hand on the butt of his gun and his eyes sweeping the doorways as they passed.

If he wasn't in the car, how'd he get injured?

Josh had a sudden flash, a roadside at night. Two men holding a third by the shoulders while two more pushed a sleek,

Italian sports car off the pavement. One at the rear, one at the open driver's side door. The car vanished over the bank, and he imagined the sound of it plunging through brush and slamming hard into a tree trunk.

Then the man in the middle, terrified, helpless. The two holding him moved a step away, stretching out his arms and holding him in place, while the others picked up wooden baseball bats. Movement. Screams. The sound of breaking bones.

They stepped out the front doors of the hospital, and Tim hurried him into the back of the Mercedes. Then they sped away.

Oh my God. Oh my God. What do I do?

"You're okay," Tim was saying. "It's all right."

But it wasn't. It was very far from all right.

CHAPTER 10

Early the next morning, Crane took one of the *Emma*'s two tenders across the bay to Punto Dorado. He cut the engine and coasted in to the dock. He didn't see any movement as he approached and tied up the boat.

As he walked down the pier toward the empty courtyard, he caught a sudden flash of black hair and brown skin. A naked girl ran away across the flagstones, moving silently on the balls of her feet. She disappeared through the breezeway arch. Crane moved quietly to the large outdoor chaise she'd come from and found Orly Wilde fast asleep beneath a rumpled linen sheet. The remains of a serious bender—empty bottles, torn condom wrappers, alligator clips—surrounded the chaise. The scent of marijuana lingered in the air.

He watched Orly for nearly a minute before deciding he was still fast asleep. Crane shrugged and looked around at the doors lining the courtyard. Some clearly led into the restaurant space or its kitchen. One he'd already seen; it was where Tate kept his guns and clay pigeons. He would just have to check the others in order. He took a slim brace of lockpicks from inside his sleeve and got to work.

The rooms were forgotten guest rooms with dusty furniture, storage rooms full of junk, a utility room with a water heater and electrical junction boxes. The fifth room had a different lock on the door, considerably more substantial than the cheap locks on the others. *Should have checked this one first*, Crane chided himself.

He opened the lock, and the door opened smoothly on well-oiled hinges. The room held stacked wooden shipping crates and some kind of machine on a table. He checked the topmost crates and found miscellaneous parts for AR-15 rifles. Now he was getting somewhere. The machine was connected to an old PC, and Crane realized it was a computer-controlled milling machine. Specifically, it was set up to mill AR-15 lower receivers out of metal blanks he found nearby.

In the eyes of the Bureau of Alcohol, Tobacco, and Firearms, the lower receiver was what made a gun. The barrels, trigger assemblies, stocks, and other components that filled the crates were just parts. Orly could buy those with no more trouble or official interest than he'd draw buying shoes. It was the receiver that was regulated. So Orly was buying AR-15 parts and then milling the receivers himself and building untraceable automatic rifles.

The legality of all this was dubious in the United States. In Mexico, there was no doubt at all.

That wasn't all, though, Crane discovered as he went through the rest of the crates. One was loaded with pistols, blocky, with sand-colored polymer frames. Crane took one out and let out a low whistle. They were 9 mm Sig Sauer P320s, the US Military MHS version. *Orly must have a friend in the service somewhere*, Crane thought.

So he wasn't just making illegal guns; he was running them across the border as well. If he got caught, the Mexican government would bury him. That ought to make it easier to talk to him.

Crane loaded the Sig Sauer from a stack of full magazines and stuck a few more in his pocket. Then he walked back out to the courtyard and dragged a chair next to the chaise where Orly lay. The noise woke Orly, but he was still languid and yawning with his eyes closed when Crane said, "We need to talk, Orly."

Orly opened his eyes to see Crane sitting a couple feet from him, the pistol hanging from one hand so that it filled his field of view.

"Whoa!" Orly cried. He jumped back and nearly fell off the chaise. "What the hell, man?"

"Calm down," said Crane. "You want to be careful around these. They're dangerous. That's why the Mexican government takes such a dim view of those AR-15s you're making in there."

"What? I don't know about any guns. I rent out those rooms!"

"You might be able to sell that to a judge down here, if you've got the right friends. But the Sigs are US government property. Gossip around town is that you already did one stretch in federal prison. You remember it that fondly?"

Orly gathered the sheet around himself. "What do you want?"

"What's your story?" said Crane. "You running guns for the cartels?"

"Oh, no way, man. You can get killed real fast that way. Besides, they've got their own channels. I stay under their radar. I deal to small buyers, local groups, sometimes just farmers looking for home defense. I'm just nickel and diming to keep the lights on. That's it, I swear."

Crane doubted that, given the crate of US Army pistols in his back room. But he wasn't here to worry about Orly. Then a thought occurred to him.

"So you're something of a gunsmith too. Did you reload Boz's wax slugs for him?"

Orly swallowed. "Hey, that was just a gag, man. Boz just likes messing with people. You saw. Besides, you turned it around on him. That was some great shooting, bro."

"Let's talk about your friend Boz," said Crane. "I met Arturo and Juan Manuel yesterday. You might not be cartel material, but they sure are. So how did Boz end up tied up with them?"

Orly took this in. Then he nodded toward a discarded pair of shorts balled up on the stones a couple feet away.

"Hey, do you mind if I ... ?"

"By all means," said Crane. "Boz's cartel connections?"

Orly reached for the shorts and pulled them on beneath the sheet. "We don't talk about that, you know. But he's here a lot. And I hear things. He's not part of the drugs side. He's a special case. I think he's like HR for them. He lines up people who can do things the cartel can't do for themselves."

That makes sense, Crane thought. Tate had money, social connections, and he wasn't someone you'd expect to be involved with a narco cartel. He could be useful in laundering money, connecting them to legitimate financial channels in the States, opening all kinds of doors that would be closed to Mexican gangsters. In return, they helped him keep his low profile, protecting him from things like the indictment hanging over his head. He could see it now. That might be a good trade for the cartel, assuming Tate was capable of acting like a professional when he had to.

"So he flies into town. You know from where?"

Orly shook his head. "He doesn't talk about it."

"And he's got his boat in the bay, and he's got his fancy Cadillac. Where's he garage that thing, by the way?"

"He bought a place in town," said Orly. "Used to be a bar, but it closed down a while ago. For a while he was saying he was going to fix it up and open it again, but I guess he lost interest. But he has some rooms upstairs, and he keeps the Escalade there."

"Where is this?"

"I don't know the address," said Orly. "I only went there once. It's a couple blocks east of the radio towers somewhere. There was a little cantina, I remember. It was blue, light blue, with the name painted in red. And we passed a house with a chicken coop ..."

"Okay, okay," Crane said, "I'll find it. Next question. He brings a lot of women here?"

"Well, yeah."

"What happens to them? Is he trafficking women for the cartel?"

Orly seemed genuinely shocked. "No! No, nothing like that. He meets people here for business sometimes, but they're men. When he's got a girl here, it's just social."

Crane considered that. If Orly was right about what Tate did for the cartel, then it wouldn't make sense to have him running women across the border in his yacht. Sooner or later, that kind of thing would get noticed and ruin their asset. And as Orly had said about the guns, they had their own channels for that sort of thing. They wouldn't need to involve an amateur.

"What's Boz to you, anyway, man?" Orly asked suddenly. "You homed in on him the moment you saw him. What's it about?"

With his left hand, Crane plucked Amy Carpenter's passport from his shirt pocket and flipped it open to the photo page. "You ever see her here? Ever see her with Boz?"

Orly leaned in to study the photo, and Crane caught a whiff of his body odor. He held his breath while Orly peered at the passport.

"Yeah," Orly said at last. "I think she was here a couple times. Yeah, I remember her. Girl could drink, man."

"Twice? She look like she was having a good time?"

"Oh yeah. Boz and her were getting along fine. Haven't seen her in a while. They come and go. You think Boz is kidnapping girls for like white slavery and shit? No, man, he's not into anything like that."

Crane closed Amy's passport and put it away.

Orly stretched a kink out of his shoulder. "I mean, sure, he likes pussy, but ... you know?"

Crane sighed. "Thanks, Orly. That's great to know. On that note, I think I'll be going." He stuffed the gun into his waistband. "I'm going to hang on to this, okay? And I think we should never speak of this again. What do you say?"

Orly seemed to grab on to his good fortune like a drowning man seizing a lifeline. "Yeah, man. Nobody needs to know about any of this."

Crane left him there, walking back toward the dock and his boat.

"Come back any time," Orly called after him. "Just be cool, right? Right?"

Crane untied the boat and sped back across the bay. He tried to fit Orly's new information into his picture of Tate. He was increasingly convinced that whatever Tate was involved in, it wasn't what Chloe thought. Amy Carpenter seemed to have been spending time with Tate by choice. But then, what had happened to her?

Regardless, Chloe wasn't going to be happy. He didn't fully understand the dynamic between Chloe and her father, but once she'd told Malcolm her theory about Tate's human trafficking ring, and played her dangerous-daughter card to force his involvement, she'd been committed. It would be very hard to talk her out of it.

CHAPTER 11

When he returned to the *Emma*, Crane found Chloe waiting for him, clutching a bundle of fabric shopping bags in her hands.

"The hell have you been?" she said as he came up the steps from the swim deck. "I've got grocery run today. I need the boat."

"Where's the other one?"

She sighed in exasperation. "Max and Carolyn took it. They've got some ... thing down the coast. I don't know."

"All right," he said. "I'll go with you, then. I can help carry stuff. You ready?"

She pushed past him and down to the swim deck. "I've been waiting for you for half an hour." She threw the bags into the bottom of the boat and climbed in.

Okay, then. He followed her back down, and they got the tender launched. Chloe sat up front and let Crane steer from the back.

"Sorry," she said when they were about halfway back to shore. "I'm just in a really shitty mood today."

"Don't worry about it," said Crane.

"It's this thing with Scott," she explained. "I don't know what's going on with him. He was supposed to call me, but he's ducking me. He's being a jackass." She paused and then said, "What's going on over there?"

Crane looked up and saw a crowd gathered on the beach. People were clustered in a tight pack, held back by men Crane assumed were police officers. Two cruisers were parked up the beach with their lights flashing. Another group of figures stood inside the circle, near the waterline.

In Crane's experience, a scene like that never meant anything good.

He veered away from the pier and headed up the shoreline toward the scene. The boat ground gently onto the beach about fifty yards behind the crowd. As he and Chloe walked up the sand, Crane caught a glimpse of something covered by a tarp near the waterline. He was pretty sure he knew what was under it. Chloe was picking it up as well, he realized. She'd gone very quiet suddenly.

Then one of the officers pushed his way through the crowd and headed toward them. "Mr. Crane," he called out as the crowd made way. "Mr. Crane, Chief Moreno wants you."

"Oh no," said Chloe, her voice becoming a half wail. "No, no."

Crane turned her toward him and held her by her shoulders. "Wait here," he said. "You shouldn't go any closer."

He saw the horrified look in her eyes, and then he followed the officer back through the crowd. The officer passed him through the cordon and remained there to keep the crowd back.

Chief Moreno stood at the waterline with two other officers and a man in civilian clothes. The surf was washing up just far enough to soak his pants cuffs. As Crane approached, he made eye contact and simply nodded.

Crane joined them, and Moreno knelt down. Crane knelt beside him, and Moreno moved the tarp back long enough to reveal the face of Amy Carpenter.

She had been beautiful. She still was, but in a different way. From her pictures, Crane could imagine her dancing on the beach, twirling by firelight, her eyes flashing, her arms beckoning. Now she was still. Her eyes were closed, and her skin was pale and matted with tendrils of dark hair. Now she looked like something carved from marble.

The last confirmed time she'd been seen alive was almost a week ago. He didn't think she'd been dead that long, but a coroner would know better, if Bahia Tortugas had one. Perhaps the civilian?

"No apparent injuries," said Moreno as he covered her face with the tarp once more. "I'd say she drowned."

"Can you test for drugs or alcohol?" Crane asked. Glancing up at the civilian, he asked, "Are you the coroner?"

"Miguel's a doctor," said Moreno, "with the local clinic."

Crane and the doctor shook hands. "I'm no specialist," Miguel said. "I can give you a general report, but a drug or blood alcohol screen? No. For a proper autopsy, she'd have to be flown out to Ensenada, or maybe La Paz."

"You know her family," Moreno said to Crane. "Can you tell them, find out what they want done?"

Crane realized his lie had taken on new dimensions. He had no idea how to contact her family. But someone had to. He had her passport number. Josh would be able to track her down and put him in touch with her family.

He nodded. "I'll make sure they know."

As Miguel knelt to examine the body more closely, Moreno took Crane's arm, and they walked a few yards back up the beach.

"She was with Mr. Zahn on the beach, at Punto Dorado, maybe on his boat," said Moreno. "They were together three days at least before she dropped out of sight. The last time I know she was alive, she was with him."

"I think he'd be the first one I'd question," said Crane.

"But we won't question him," Moreno answered.

"Because he's protected."

Moreno laughed. It was a short, bitter laugh without humor. "Because we're out of our depth, Mr. Crane. We're country rubes here. We give out tickets and sweep up the drunks on Saturday night. That's what we're here for. Something like this, we wouldn't know where to begin."

He took a breath and met Crane's eyes. Crane could see the anger boiling inside him.

"I bet someone could put a bullet in Mr. Zahn's skull in the middle of a busy street in broad daylight, and we'd be lost, chasing our tails. We'd never figure out who did it."

"You really think so?"

"I know it," Moreno said. "We're a terrible police department. No good for anything."

Crane nodded. "I'll keep that in mind."

He passed back through the police cordon and through the crowd who now kept a respectful distance and watched him closely. He was no longer just an onlooker like themselves, but part of the incident. Crane heard murmurs debating his role, apparently from people who didn't realize he spoke Spanish. Was he the dead girl's brother? Did he work for the American who killed her?

Crane made his way back down the beach, looking for Chloe, but he didn't see her. He looked for the boat and saw that it was gone.

He swore and ran down the beach toward the pier. A panga was beached another hundred yards down the shore, its owner leaning back against his boat and watching. Crane ran to the boat and had it run him back out to the *Emma*.

When they arrived, the tender wasn't there. Crane told the

boatman to wait while he went aboard. He found Captain Burch in the main salon.

"Has Chloe been here?"

"Yeah," said Burch. "You just missed her. She came back without any food, she went below, and then she took off again. What's going on?"

Crane thought for a moment. "I need the keys to the garage where you keep the truck."

Burch looked confused.

"Now!"

"All right, all right," said Burch. "I'll go get them."

"Meet me back here," said Crane. Then he headed below to Chloe's cabin, though he had a good idea what he would find there.

He was right, he discovered as he entered the tiny cabin. The storage compartment was open, and the metal box holding Amy Carpenter's things lay open on Chloe's bunk, her items strewn across the thin brown blanket.

Amy's .32 pistol was missing.

CHAPTER 12

The air was still and oppressive as Crane climbed the ladder to the public pier. The breeze had died down, and it seemed the whole town had gone inside for a nap. Amy Carpenter's body had been removed from the beach, and the crowd had dispersed. The *Emma*'s tender was tied up nearby.

Crane hurried to the foundation's garage and unlocked number four. The pickup and the Yamaha dirt bike were as he remembered them. He pushed the bike out into the light and checked it over. There was gas in the tank, and the engine roared to life as Crane rolled over the kickstarter and stomped it. He put the bike in gear and took off.

Almost immediately, he reached an intersection and stopped. Where was he going? He'd ridden through town with Chloe and he'd walked around parts of it, but he didn't really know his way around. Bahia Tortugas was a maze of mostly unpaved streets that followed no apparent pattern and had few street signs.

Chloe must know where she was going. Orly had mentioned an old bar that Tate had bought and renovated into a local apartment. But Crane still didn't know where that was. Finally, he spun the bike to the left and headed toward the center of town. The radio towers provided a handy reference point. He could halfway navigate by them, unless a street took a sudden turn and didn't go where he wanted it to.

He spent nearly twenty minutes riding around, kicking up great clouds of dust and sending the engine's poorly muffled roar through the streets. The heat and the heavy air had driven most of the locals inside. Sweat caked dust to Crane's forehead.

Then he caught a flash of gleaming black in his peripheral vision. He braked hard, spun the bike beneath him, and rode back a few yards. To his right, the land fell away in a steep bank. The street crossed what looked like an old storm gully here, and they'd packed in dirt to make it level. Crane looked over a backyard fence shared by two brightly colored houses. Between them, he could see that they fronted onto the end of a street that headed straight away from him. A couple hundred yards down that street, Tate's armored Escalade was parked in front of what looked like it could have been the old bar Orly had mentioned.

How did he get there from here?

He was mentally tracing his route, trying to picture streets that would connect with that street, when two figures emerged from the bar and crossed to the Escalade. Crane recognized one of Tate's goons in front, and Tate himself behind him. Then another figure emerged from behind the corner of the building. Chloe. She raised the pistol in both hands and opened fire.

Tate's man was opening the rear passenger door when the first shot went off. He dove to the ground and scrambled back toward the building as Tate dashed behind the door and climbed in. Chloe kept firing, splattering .32 caliber rounds off the Escalade's ballistic glass until the gun was empty.

Meanwhile, the Escalade started up and lurched forward, one door still hanging open. When Chloe ran out, the man on the ground sprang to his feet and charged her. He tackled her, hitting her low and knocking her off her feet. He grabbed her by her collar and dragged her toward the approaching Escalade. She screamed and flailed at him, but then arms reached out and dragged her into the back seat.

Crane gunned the engine and circled the bike around to the far side of the street to give himself as much run as he could. Then he revved the engine, dropped it into gear, and soared off the bank.

The bike cleared the fence by inches and hit the ground with a jarring impact. An old woman ran out of a side door and shouted after Crane as he shot between the houses and out onto the street. The Escalade was already disappearing around a corner, leaving a billowing trail of dust. Crane gunned the engine and roared after it.

A helmet would have been a good idea, he thought. *Or a dust mask, at least.* He breathed in grit as he slid around the corner and raced down another unpaved street. He made out the Escalade in flashes of black through the dust cloud it kicked up. Random obstacles appeared on the side of the road—a parked truck, a stack of rusting oil drums. Once a stray dog dashed out of his way.

He followed the Escalade onto one of the town's few paved roads and gunned the bike forward. He quickly closed with the SUV. The windows were shaded and Chloe's bullets had scarred them. He couldn't see inside, but they knew he was there. The Escalade jigged sharply and forced him to veer to his left. He jumped the curb and leaped over the sidewalk, ending up in someone's front yard. Crane spotted an open space and steered for it as he fought to keep the bike upright. He shot between two houses and through a backyard, fishtailed around the trunk of a parked car, and roared down a dirt street.

Ahead, he could see the street angling to the right, taking him back toward the Escalade. He gunned the engine and sped forward, catching flashes of black between the houses as he went. He raced past it to where the streets converged, and skidded to a stop at the corner.

The Escalade roared toward him at the head of a column of dust. As it flew past, Crane drew the MHS, steadied his aim, and put two rounds into the windshield. They spider-webbed the outer layer of ballistic glass around two bright white circles. Then the Escalade was past him, speeding away. Crane stuck the gun back in his belt, spun the bike around, and followed them.

Now they knew he had a weapon, and the situation had become a standoff. Tate was protected inside his armored SUV. But unless he managed to elude Crane somehow, he was trapped inside it.

Crane kept back, following from a distance and letting them lead the way wherever they thought they were going.

That turned out to be out of town. The buildings grew sparser, and eventually the Escalade turned onto the road that led out of town to the airfield.

Crane followed, dropping back slightly to get out of the worst of the SUV's dust. He wasn't likely to lose them out here.

Then, as the Escalade rounded a curve ahead, Crane saw brake lights. A rear door flew open, and a shape fell out. Crane saw Chloe hit the dirt and tumble as the Escalade accelerated away.

Crane braked hard, laid the bike down in the dirt, and ran to her. Chloe had rolled off the edge of the road and was on her side in a stand of small green plants with bright purple flowers. For a moment, he felt a gut-twisting fear that she was dead, either before she left the SUV or in the fall. But then he saw her move, reaching for her right knee with both hands and groaning in pain.

"Don't move!" he said as he knelt beside her. "You're okay. Stay still."

He automatically went through the checklist they'd taught him in the Hurricane Group. She was breathing, conscious, and responsive. No major broken bones, but the knee didn't look great. She was going to be in a lot of pain for a while, but she'd be all right.

She was trembling and breathing fast, looking at him with fear in her eyes. Crane could see her imagining all the things that could have happened. She was used to using her tactics against normal people, overpowering them with shock and awe. This was something different.

"How do you do it?" she asked him as she struggled to slow her breathing. "How do you not be afraid?"

"You don't," he said. "You learn to channel it so it doesn't paralyze you. That takes time and training."

"Look at me," she said. "I'm supposed to be tough."

"Believe me," said Crane. "Tough isn't your problem. That was just stupid."

She pulled back and looked at him with a quick flash of anger. Then it melted away, and she lay back in the dirt. "I hurt."

"It's okay," said Crane. "We'll get you back to town and have a doctor look at that knee."

She nodded toward the dirt bike still lying in the middle of the dirt road. "How? On that?"

Okay, Crane thought, *that is a good point.* How was he going to get her back to town?

He was still considering it when he heard the growing scream of jet engines. Then Tate's jet shot by overhead and climbed into the deep blue sky.

"I'm not sorry I did it," said Chloe. "He killed Amy."

"He had something to do with her death, at least," said Crane. Crane didn't know what. Perhaps he'd literally killed her. Maybe she'd overdosed on his boat, and he'd dumped the body. Maybe he'd gotten her high, and she'd fallen overboard and drowned. Whatever happened, Jason Tate's hands were far from clean. That was one more thing to add to his bill.

Crane looked up at the jet, a small dot fading rapidly out of view. The roar of its engines grew fainter and was gone. That bill was well past due. But Tate was gone with the plane, and Crane didn't even know where he was going. Worse, given his probable involvement in Amy Carpenter's death, there was little reason for him to come back this way. If Crane wanted another crack at Tate, he needed to lure him back from whatever bolt hole he was running to.

Actually, he realized, there was something still tying Tate to Bahia Tortugas, one way he could get his attention. He had to admit there would be a certain amount of personal satisfaction involved as well.

Crane shook his head. "How do you do it?" he asked Chloe.

"Do what?"

"We all talk a good game, but at the end of the day, you always get your way, don't you?"

"What are you talking about?"

Crane sighed. "I think I'm actually going to sink his damn boat."

CHAPTER 13

The warm blue water closed over Crane, and he swam toward the bottom with powerful strokes of his flippers. He'd borrowed the wet suit, flippers, and breathing gear from the crew. Strapped to his chest was the one thing he'd brought with him: a small IP 68 submersible bag full of tools and equipment.

He'd taken a bearing on the *Gypsy* before he stepped off *Emma*'s swim deck into the Pacific. Now he checked the dive compass on his wrist and followed it. Sunlight filtered down from above, and the bottom shimmered as Crane glided over the stones and sand.

As he swam, he considered for the hundredth time what he was doing. Chloe was back on the *Emma*, with her knee taped up and her other scrapes and bruises treated. She'd lost much of her taste for violence, at least temporarily. If he did end up sinking the *Gypsy*, he wouldn't be doing it for her. He'd be doing it to start a war with Jason Tate. He didn't find Tate especially worrisome. The idea of taking on a cartel was a bit more concerning. He supposed it came down to just how valuable Tate was to the cartel, and how committed they were to keeping him happy.

A few minutes later, Crane saw the *Gypsy*'s bow looming overhead. He hung in the water and looked up at the dark outline of the hull, silhouetted against the gleam of sunlight. They were well away from the other boats anchored in the bay. *Gypsy*'s tender had been absent when he left the *Emma*. He didn't expect to encounter anyone aboard, but he couldn't be sure.

Crane rose slowly toward the *Gypsy*'s stern. He broke the surface, took the regulator from his mouth, and removed his mask. He listened for nearly a minute and heard nothing. Finally he climbed up the diving ladder to the stern cockpit. There he found a pair of folding canvas chairs and a large plastic cooler. He took off his tank and hid it, along with the mask and regulator, behind the cooler.

Crane had researched the model's stock layout. Tate might have made some changes, but there was only so much he could do to the boat. There would be two enclosed decks. The lower deck would have the master's cabin aft, the engine room amidships, and guest cabins forward. The main deck had two covered walk-around side-decks leading forward to the bow. They wrapped around the deckhouse, which would hold the main saloon, the galley, and the forward pilothouse. On the roof of the deckhouse was the storage deck for the tender and a flybridge from which the boat could be operated in the open air.

The main saloon was the heart of the yacht. That was the place to start. Crane quietly let himself in through the aft door.

The place had obviously hosted a party. Sofa cushions lay strewn across the deck, along with empty bottles and plastic cups full of stale beer and cigarette butts. A painting on the forward bulkhead had been skewed to one side. Crane moved quickly and quietly, inventorying the remains as his wetsuit dripped on the carpet. A woman's shoe—the left one. A portable boom box on the coffee table, with CDs scattered around it.

There was nothing of interest, and nothing to suggest that Tate did anything here but entertain.

At the aft end of the saloon was a staircase leading down. At the bottom, Crane found two doors, an insulated metal one to the engine room, and a wooden one that led aft to the master suite. Crane opened that door and found himself in Jason Tate's private sex den.

The king-size bed took up most of the available space. It was unmade, a tangle of sheets and scattered pillows with a metal-framed headboard. The place was spangled with sex toys, bottles of lubricant, and bags of marijuana. Crane saw at least four pairs of handcuffs, including one still cuffed to the headboard. There were clothes scattered around, including a woman's shoe that matched the one upstairs. Crane suspected they had belonged to Amy Carpenter.

He checked the drawers and found Tate's clothes, a plentiful supply of recreational drugs, more sex toys. He was getting the distinct impression that the *Gypsy* was Tate's party barge and nothing more. If Tate conducted any other business here, he certainly hadn't left any evidence of it behind. Then he spotted a small action camera on a high shelf, aimed down at the bed. He pulled it down and found that a USB cable connected it to a laptop.

Crane unsealed the bag on his chest. He took out a small screwdriver, opened the laptop's case, and removed the solid state drive. He put it back in the bag, along with the screwdriver. That was something at least. The last time he'd brought home a laptop, Crane reminded himself, it had proved very informative. This one might finally provide real evidence to connect Tate with Amy Carpenter.

He took a quick look through the engine-room door on his way back up and decided it looked normal enough. Then he went back to the main deck and headed forward. The galley was as much of a mess as the main saloon, but the party had been kept out of the pilothouse. It was neat and well equipped. Crane glanced over the controls and the navigational instruments, and satisfied himself that he could operate the yacht. Then he took the stairs down to the lower deck.

Crane found himself in a short corridor that ran from two cabin doors amidships to the single small cabin tucked into the bow. The first of the aft cabins was tidy but empty, probably used for guests. The other had two bunks, one low and a higher one perpendicular to it. This looked to be where Tate's two goons lived. Crane found clothes, magazines, dirty dishes, nothing of interest.

The forward cabin was different, he realized as he approached the door. This one had a heavy, reinforced wooden door, locked from the outside with two heavy bolts. Crane knew there would be a windowless triangular space on the other side. If Tate was using the boat to smuggle women, this was where he would keep them. The faint sound of metal on metal came from behind the door. Someone was locked inside.

Crane unsnapped the sheath holding the dive knife on his forearm, just in case. He slowly opened the two bolts, took a deep breath, and yanked the door open. He heard a gasp, the figure on the bunk turned in surprise, and Crane found himself looking into the shocked face of Scott McCall.

For a moment, Crane simply stared at him, dumbfounded. Scott seemed just as stunned to see him.

"What the hell are you doing here?" Crane said at last.

Scott was seated on the bunk that filled one side of the chamber, with his back to the hull and his knees drawn up to his chest. His left wrist was handcuffed to a lead pipe fastened to the hull.

"You have to get out of here!" Scott stammered. "Before they get back! Call the police!"

"I don't think the police will be much help. Why are you here?"

"They kidnapped me! Right after I left the *Emma*. Two guys threw a bag over my head, and here I am!"

"All right, we'll sort it out later," said Crane. The cuffs were Smith and Wesson Model 100s. Getting out of them was more or less a party trick. Crane slipped a pick into the lock and released the tension on the jaw. Scott pulled his wrist free and rubbed the circulation back into it.

Crane looked around. There wasn't much in the tiny cabin beyond a pair of shoes in the corner. Scott put them on while Crane double-checked the empty storage cabinets.

"Stay behind me and close," said Crane. He led Scott back up the stairs to the pilothouse.

Crane had still been ambivalent about this, even as he swam over. But he was feeling better about going hard after Tate all the time. Tate might not be trafficking women, but he was up to something bad. It was time to do some damage and see what happened.

Crane powered up the GPS system and the radar. According to the screens, if he turned the yacht a few degrees to port, there was a straight course that went nowhere near any of the other anchored yachts and ended at a jagged shelf of rocks just off the southern shore. At full speed, Crane was pretty sure those rocks would rip the bottom out of the hull. All he needed then was a little accelerant.

"Can you swim?" he asked Scott.

"Yeah. What are you doing here, anyway? Were you looking for me?"

"I don't think anybody even knew you were missing. Just your lucky day, I guess. Come on."

He led Scott back through the saloon. Then he heard an outboard approaching. He peered out a rear window and saw the yacht's tender. Arturo cut the motor and let the boat coast up to the stern, while Juan Manuel perched in the bow, ready to jump aboard. From the bags stacked in the boat, Crane gathered they'd been grocery shopping.

"They've got guns!" Scott whispered. "What do we do?"

Crane moved him around the railing that surrounded the stairwell and pushed him back against the bulkhead. "Stay right there."

Crane could hear Arturo and Juan Manuel talking outside, heard someone come up the ladder to the stern cockpit. He saw a shadow fall across the doorway, and then Juan Manuel stepped through, loaded down with grocery bags.

Crane grabbed two great handfuls of his shirt and pulled him inside before he knew what was happening. Produce and junk food tumbled to the deck. Crane threw a quick series of punches and bounced Juan Manuel's head off the bulkhead. Then he ran him back to the stair railing and threw him backward over it and down the stairwell.

As Juan Manuel was going over the railing, Crane saw a heavy revolver in his belt. He grabbed the butt as Juan Manuel went over and then quickly stepped into the doorway and leveled the pistol into Arturo's face.

Arturo stopped cold. Crane stepped back into the saloon and beckoned him to follow. Arturo took in the gun, the groceries on the floor, Scott trembling in fear against the bulkhead. "Hey, be cool, man. It's nothing personal, right? We can cut our own deal here. You want him, you go, right? Hey, take the boat, and we'll just stay here."

"We'll all go," he said. He gestured for Arturo to walk back out the door. As soon as Arturo had turned around, Crane struck him hard with the butt of the revolver, and he fell to the deck.

"Who *are* you?" asked Scott.

"Let's just say I'm not really Chloe's ex-boyfriend," said Crane. "Here, help me get him out to the boat."

They dumped Arturo and Juan Manuel in the bottom of the boat and cuffed them together with cuffs from Tate's cabin. Then Crane went to work in the engine room. He disabled the fire suppression system. He checked the fuel tanks and filters, disconnected hoses, opened stopcocks, and turned on the engine block heaters. The smell of diesel fuel began to fill the room.

Back in the pilothouse, he started up the engines. *Gypsy* laboriously came about to the heading he'd programmed into the autopilot. Through the forward windows, Crane could see the rocks in the distance sliding out of the water at rakish angles. He opened up the throttles, and the yacht started forward.

By the time he made it back to the stern, *Gypsy* was already starting to pick up speed. The tender was pulled along behind by its mooring rope. Scott was in the bow, pulling the tender forward by the rope until it was close enough for Crane to leap into. Then Crane cut the rope with his dive knife, and they fell back as the *Gypsy* accelerated away to her doom.

Arturo and Juan Manuel had regained consciousness. They said nothing but only watched in horror as Crane made his way past them to the stern and started up the outboard.

Crane put them ashore on a flat stretch of coastline about a mile past Punto Dorado. He left Arturo and Juan Manuel in the boat while he and Scott sat on a rock and watched the *Gypsy* close the distance to the rocks. The engine room had already caught fire, and tendrils of black smoke were starting to escape from the saloon.

Then there was a horrible grinding sound, and the *Gypsy* heeled over to starboard as it drove itself up and over the rocks, ripping a fatal gash into the bottom of the hull.

A few moments later, an explosion ripped away the back half

of the main deckhouse. *Gypsy* made it a few dozen yards past the rocks on momentum, spewing fire and smoke, and then began to settle into the water as fire engulfed the main deck. By the time anybody from Bahia Tortugas reached the yacht, there would be nothing left of her.

"Well, that ought to get a reaction," said Crane. "Come on, let's get out of here, and then you can tell me what the hell's going on." They walked up the coast toward Punto Dorado as the wreck of the *Gypsy* sent up a thick column of smoke behind them.

CHAPTER 14

It was nearly sunset by the time Crane and Scott caught a panga back to the *Emma*. There was nothing left to see of the *Gypsy*. What hadn't burned had sunk behind the rocks. A handful of boats remained on the scene, but there was nothing left for them to do.

"Not a word to anybody," Crane said as they approached the *Emma*. "For their sake as much as yours. Do you understand?"

Scott blanched. He obviously wanted to think his ordeal was over, but it wasn't quite over yet. "I understand," he said after a moment. "It's not safe here."

"They'll want to know where you've been, where you got the bruises. Just say you don't want to talk about it. I'll give them a story to chew on."

Scott nodded. "Right, I don't want to talk about it. Thank you."

It had been a big day in Bahia Tortugas. Between the death of Amy Carpenter, Chloe's adventure ashore, and the wreck of a yacht in the bay, the crew would have plenty to talk about without digging into Scott's movements.

Still, everyone gathered around when the panga dropped

them off, treating Scott like the prodigal son returned and peppering him with questions. Chloe was in a chaise on the rear deck, her leg wrapped in an orthotic brace. An uneasy silence fell as she and Scott faced each other again.

"Hey," Scott finally said.

"Hey."

He glanced at the leg brace. "Are you okay?"

"I'll be all right. How about you?"

Scott nodded.

"I'm glad," Chloe said at last.

"Me too," Scott replied. "That you're okay, too, I mean."

Crane got Scott below decks and back into his old cabin. "Stay aboard until I can get you out," Crane said. He didn't think that would be a problem. When it came up, he would tell the others Scott had been waiting in a motel to hear about his job. It had somehow fallen through, and Scott was upset. He drank too much, found himself wandering the dark streets late at night, and got jumped. It was believable enough.

In the meantime, he still had Scott's real story, which made no sense to him.

When he returned to the main deck, everyone was still gathered near the stern. So he went forward and sat in a bow pulpit. He connected his phone to the boat's satellite uplink and dialed Josh's number.

When Josh picked up, Crane heard voices in the background. It sounded like some kind of boardroom presentation. "Give me a second," said Josh. The voices faded, and Crane heard a door closing.

"I've got to tell you something," Josh said when he came back. "I don't know what to make of it."

"Well, that's a coincidence," said Crane. "I've got to tell you something, and I don't know what to make of mine."

"Okay," Josh said, "let's swap the one-sentence versions and maybe that will make it clear who should go first. I think Alexander Tate's being held prisoner so someone can control his fortune."

"I blew up Jason's yacht."

There was a long pause until Josh finally said, "Jesus, you want to just flip for it?"

"No, no. You're putting up the funding. You go first."

"Wait, I get perks just for being rich? Sweet! All right, here's what I've got."

Josh told Crane about his visit to Fallon Landing, and Alexander's insistence that the accident had been staged.

"Someone needed him out of the way, but not dead," Crane mused. "If he dies in the crash, then his will goes into effect. Maybe that was the problem. Faking the car crash is easy enough. But then they'd have to give him injuries, including a traumatic brain injury if they want him declared legally incompetent. That sounds risky. Way too easy to end up killing him, and then they're back to square one with the will."

"That's what I've been thinking," said Josh. "I'm wondering if the brain injury's fake too. They've got him locked away under heavy guard in this little private hospital. They could be doing anything to him in there. Could the right drugs do what I saw? Is that even possible?"

Crane thought for a moment. "Well, as it happens, I know someone who used to consult for the Hurricane Group on ... very specialized medical issues. If it's possible, she'll have some ideas about how to do it, and maybe how to counteract it. I'll give her a call, ask a few carefully worded hypothetical questions."

"Okay, let me know if you learn anything useful. Now what's this about sinking Jason's yacht?"

Now it was his turn. Crane told Josh about the death of Amy

Carpenter, Chloe's attack on Jason, and what he'd discovered aboard the *Gypsy*.

"So they're not trafficking women; they're trafficking radio engineers?" Crane could hear the frustration in Josh's voice. "Who does that?"

"They were looking for very specific skills. Scott was reworking the foundation's radios, navigation gear, satellite uplinks. He was ordering a lot of specialized parts. Somebody noticed and asked if he was interested in a regular job. He was. The next day, he found himself getting interviewed by Jason Tate."

"That's ... odd. What did he ask about?"

"Point to point microwave links, DC power applications, software-defined radios. I gather it was pretty thorough."

"And Jason knew about this stuff?"

Crane shrugged. "Enough to do a credible job interview, I guess."

"Well, that's new," said Josh. "Did he say what the job was?"

"He claimed he consults to Telcel on talent acquisition. I'm assuming that was a lie."

"So this Scott guy aced the interview and got the job."

"He's got student loans hanging over him," said Crane, "and lying out on a boat with his girlfriend wasn't going to solve that. So yeah, he took the offer and went back to the boat to collect his things. Walked into a hell of a fight with the girlfriend. And then the next thing he knows, two thugs are stuffing him into a bag and hauling him out to Tate's yacht."

"He's lucky you found him. Where do you think Jason was taking him?"

"No idea," said Crane. "I'll ask Jason that when I find him. What are you doing up there? What happens if Alexander Tate's alive but incapacitated? Who's handling his finances? Can't be

Jason. He'd have to show up in court, sign things in front of notaries, give depositions."

"I'm trying to find out," said Josh. "The court papers list a law firm as conservator, but I can't find them. It's owned by a holding company, which is a partnership of about a dozen other LLCs registered all over the world. I haven't gotten very deep yet."

That all sounded very familiar to Crane. It had all the hallmarks of the illegal financial structures they'd been trying to investigate for months now. Someone had built a complicated and confusing maze in which to corral Alexander Tate's fortune. And apparently that required imprisoning him as well, in a shattered body and a fractured mind.

"I've got my people trying to follow the money," Josh was saying. "I'll keep turning over rocks until we find something."

"If they've got some spare time, I'm going to send you a drive," said Crane. "I think it's got video of Jason's bedroom."

Josh groaned. "Really? We're going there?"

"Might link him to Amy Carpenter's death."

"Okay, I'll watch his amateur porn. Actually, no, I'll make someone else watch it. One of those rich guy perks you were telling me about."

Crane laughed. "In the meantime, I'm going to see if I can get the foundation people out of town, which means I'll have to find a place to stay ashore, and this satellite link will go away. I'll be in touch when I've got myself repositioned."

There was silence, with only the soft crackle of static on the connection. Then Josh said, "So you're staying down there?"

"Until it's finished," Crane said with a grim determination. "Your friend Jason is causing a lot of trouble for a lot of people. And he's seriously pissed me off."

Josh paused and then said, "Good. That's where I want you. There's something shady going on with Alexander up here, and Jason's caught up in something shady down there. I don't like the coincidence. I'm guessing there's something we don't know that ties them both into one big shady thing. Either way, I'm not letting my end go, and you're not letting go of yours, so we're in this now. All resources brought to bear."

"Agreed," said Crane. "Whatever's going on, it needs to stop."

"Be careful down there, John," said Josh. "Whatever this is, it's weird, and it's too close to home, and I don't like it."

"You do the same," said Crane. Then they hung up.

Crane lay back on the deck as the sky grew a darker indigo and the sun sank into the Pacific. It had been a long day by any measure. He was tired. But he couldn't stop thinking about Josh's words. *It's weird, and it's too close to home, and I don't like it.* This was very close to home for Josh. He knew the people involved. He apparently had emotional ties to Alexander Tate. It reminded Crane of his own relationship with Malcolm. If that was leading Josh to action, then Josh was the one who should be careful.

But Josh was surrounded by staff and a full-time bodyguard. He had all the security that came with being a multi-billionaire. Josh would be fine.

Then, as the sun became a red sliver floating on the water, Crane suddenly remembered something Orly Wilde had said. He'd said Boz was like the cartel's HR department. He found people who could do things they couldn't. At the time, he'd assumed that meant money launderers and other financial resources in the United States. What if it didn't? What if they weren't trafficking technicians but forcibly recruiting them?

Why would a narco cartel want a radio engineer?

Josh sat cross-legged on a conference table in an empty meeting room. He put down his phone.

That was stupid, warning Crane to be careful. What does he have to worry about? He probably knows thirty-two ways to kill a man with his own socks.

Well, he still needed support. This was supposed to be a simple trip to check up on a friend's daughter. Josh didn't know what kind of things Crane would pack for something like that, but it probably wasn't the kind of things he'd need to take on a drug cartel.

When he got back in touch, Crane would have the usual shopping list of odd things he needed, and most of it would be illegal. He should start getting the ground work in place.

Josh tapped his watch and called one of his assistants. "Mary," he said, "find out where Jessie Diamond is right now, please."

CHAPTER 15

Tepehuanes Municipality, Durango, Mexico

Jason Tate lay in the sun beside his pool and looked out at the mountains. It surprised him how quickly this place had become home. He'd hated the idea when it became clear he was going to have to leave the United States and drop off the radar. He'd imagined some dusty hole with an escape tunnel lined with cinder blocks, a toothless old woman to cook rabbit stew, and a cartel bodyguard with gold teeth and terrible breath.

But in fact, the hacienda was a sprawling enclave of luxury deep in the mountains. He had all he needed here. The compound had its own water and solar power. A fiber line ran to a dedicated microwave link on a nearby mountaintop, giving him ultra-fast broadband even out here. The main house was thirty lavishly furnished rooms, and the grounds were designed by a prize-winning landscape architect. He'd done the ivy-encrusted archways along the far side of the pool, which Tate especially liked.

The airstrip was a couple miles away on the other side of the mountain. If he wanted something, he could easily go and get it, or it could just as easily be brought to him. The naked woman swimming in his pool, for example, was a model he'd seen in magazine ads and showing off prizes on a Mexican game show. Tate reached into the cooler beside his lounge chair and grabbed a fresh Tecate. Ice cold. He took a lime wedge from a bowl on the table and stuffed it down the neck. *All in all*, he thought, *I should have fled the country sooner*.

But he couldn't cut ties completely. The money was still generated in California, and managing it while keeping his own role hidden took some ingenuity. Fortunately, he had partners to take care of that. One was scheduled to call this afternoon, which was why there was a scrambled voiceover IP handset on the table beside the limes.

When it chirped at him, Tate picked it up and found himself speaking to a man named William Kim, who did the grunt work in a law office in San Francisco. They traded the usual pleasantries, and then Kim updated him on a few ongoing matters. It was routine. And then it wasn't routine anymore.

"Last thing," said Kim. "It's nothing to worry about, but it's unusual. I believe you know Joshua Sulenski?"

"Yeah, what about him?"

"He visited your father at Fallon Landing. Apparently he bluffed his way past the front desk and made it to his room. He was with your father for about five minutes before they figured out he wasn't supposed to be there."

Tate stood up, his mind racing. "Did he tell him anything? Do we have a problem here?"

"No," Kim reassured him. "No, your father's in no condition to communicate, and Sulenski didn't have access to his chart or any other information about him. But it's odd."

"You're damn right it's odd," said Tate. He realized he was pacing along the side of the pool. "What was he doing there?"

"We don't know that. I was hoping you could tell me a little more about his connection to your family."

Tate sighed. "He's a douche. I offered him a board seat when I was putting Diganda together, but he just screwed around until I got sick of him. He and my dad got along like gangbusters. I don't know what they did together. Maybe my dad took him fishing or something; he was like the son he never had."

"So it wouldn't be out of character for him to visit your father?"

Tate thought, *No, something doesn't feel right about it.* His instincts were signaling danger.

"But why now?" he said. "It's been more than a year. He never showed up before. No, something's going on. You need to find out what."

"There's been some discussion about it up here," said Kim. "We're prepared to look at Sulenski a little more closely. But we wanted to talk to you first. It will mean raising our profile slightly."

That was something that always worried Kim's people. They were all about discretion, running quiet, not giving off signals that someone might detect. He understood the need for it, but they took it all way too seriously.

"That's fine," he said after a moment. "I don't want to ignore this. One thing about Sulenski, you never know what he's going to do next. Him just popping up like that? No, it means something."

"As it happens, we concur," said Kim. "Opinion here is that the risk is minor. We'll take some steps."

"Yeah," said Tate, "take steps."

Soon after, he hung up, but the vibe was shot. He got the game show model out of the pool and took her to his bedroom, but part of him remained distracted. Things like this didn't just happen. Sulenski was up to something.

It was later that evening when a soft but insistent beeping woke Tate. He struggled back to consciousness. The girl lay still at his side, breathing softly. His head was still fuzzy from the ecstasy tabs.

It was the phone again, he realized. For a moment, he thought it might be Kim calling back with news about Sulenski. But the screen showed an IP address he recognized. It was the man known only as Lalo, the cartel boss, calling from Durango. This was unexpected. He rolled quietly out of bed, plucked the handset from his nightstand, and answered it as he walked across the room and out onto the balcony. The stars glittered brightly overhead, and a night breeze cooled his skin.

"What is it?" he said. Even with all the layers of security and scrambling, no names were used. It was just good practice.

"I'm afraid I have bad news," said Lalo. Then he explained how the *Gypsy* had been commandeered and run aground on the rocks at the south end of the bay. She'd caught fire and burned to the waterline as she sank. There was nothing to recover. The boat was a total loss.

Tate stood stunned. The boat wasn't the most expensive yacht in the world, but it wasn't as though he could carry insurance under the circumstances. Replacing it wouldn't be cheap. Nor would keeping his name off the paperwork. There would be bribes for licenses, forged documents, someone with their hand out at every step. And he'd put a lot of work into getting his cabin set up just the way he wanted it. He'd had some good times on that boat. Ah, damn! The videos he'd shot there had gone up with it.

Then the moment of shock passed, and he felt it like a kick in the crotch. Someone did this. It was an attack on him, meant to hurt. Someone was challenging him. Tate felt that on an entirely different level. He felt his anger boiling up inside him. He'd been hit, and he had to hit back, hard.

"Are you all right?" Lalo asked.

"Who did this?" said Tate. "Do we know who did it?" Even as he asked the question, he was pretty sure he knew the answer.

"An American named John Crane. I believe you've met. Is this a personal matter?"

"Oh, you better believe it's personal now!" Tate snapped. "Wait. *How* do you know it was him?"

"Our two friends were aboard when it happened. They gave a full report."

"Those two fuckups were *there*? Jesus! I sent them to get this guy out of my hair before, and they came back with some bullshit story. You need to get a better class of thug out there."

"We're doing what needs to be done."

"Well, I hope you do it better than you have up to now! I want this son of a bitch dead. No! No, strike that. I want him here. In front of me. I'll deal with him myself."

"We'll let you know. Have a nice day."

The line went dead, and Tate drew back his arm to hurl the phone out into the night, but stopped himself.

The cartel was pissed off. They blamed him for this guy Crane causing trouble and getting them involved. Well, let them be pissed off. They didn't help him because they were running a goddamn charity. They needed him, and it wouldn't hurt to remind them of that once in a while.

He stalked back into the bedroom. The girl was awake, looking up at him with concern.

"Is everything all right, baby?" she asked.

Tate snorted. "No, it's a long damn way from all right. The world is out of balance." He put the phone down on the nightstand, lowered himself to the bed, and reached for her.

"But it's going to be all right again."

Tate had read up on the history of this area. The local Indians, the Tepehuan, had revolted four hundred years ago against

Spanish and Jesuit rule. They slaughtered every Spaniard they could get their hands on and drenched the land in blood for four years before the Spanish managed to put them down. It was another century before the Jesuits came back to bother them again.

When he got his hands on this John Crane, he'd make those old bastards proud. And then, and only then, would things be all right again.

CHAPTER 16

Josh drained his coffee and tossed the wilting paper cup into a trash can as he walked by.

Just remember, you wanted this.

Not now.

More properly, he needed it. He'd been assigning some very strange tasks to Myria employees lately. Locating the right Amy Carpenter's family, out of all the Amy Carpenters in the country, based on a passport number. Watching hours of a stranger's bedroom sex tapes to see if he'd murdered someone. It wasn't what the regular workforce had signed on for.

What Josh needed was more of an irregular workforce, people with more specialized skills, people who wouldn't blink at the kind of unusual jobs he'd be throwing at them. So he'd gone through Maggie Nguyen's short list, interviewed the most promising candidates, and come up with what he hoped were the right people for his ... his what?

Scooby Gang? Impossible Missions Force?

Jesus, not now!

Josh walked into the war room and stood before the old climbing wall. He felt like a new teacher on the first day of school. His new students looked eagerly up at him from a long table.

There were four of them. Don Finney was a forensic accountant. That was pretty much all there was to him as far as Josh could tell. But that was what he needed, and Finney was apparently a very good one. He'd impressed Josh during the interview, so he was in.

Laura Berdoza was a Columbia law grad who, upon passing the bar, decided she had fulfilled her obligation to her parents and had no interest in working eighty-hour weeks at a white shoe law firm full of aging misogynists where she'd never make partner. She'd come to Silicon Valley to start over. She was smart as hell, and she could work with Finney to navigate the legal labyrinths people built to hide their skullduggery.

That's a great word, skullduggery. Use salacious next.

João Santos had grown up in a favela in Rio de Janeiro. It was an unlikely beginning for a brilliant hacker, but João was a prodigy. He'd learned to penetrate systems using a stolen laptop he'd gotten from a local gang, and he paid them back by cleaning up police records, disabling building security systems, and generally making their lives easier. All the while, he'd also been squirreling away money for the time when he would get a green card, come to America, and talk his way into CalPoly. He'd openly admitted all this to Josh in the interview because he wanted a chance to combine his more formal skills with those he'd taught himself back home.

Smart kid. Keep an eye on that one.

Finally, there was Perry Holland. Josh was still trying to figure him out. He'd gone to some oddball liberal arts school in Florida where there were no grades and students cobbled together their own degrees out of whatever interested them. Perry's was in something called Meta-Systems Analysis. His coursework appeared to bounce around from macroeconomics to anthropology to game theory. Perry had told Josh he'd gone after a job at Myria, and then this particular job, because he was intrigued by Josh's work and thought it could be expanded to fuzzier, more human applications than the mathematically intensive things Josh used it for. Josh had no idea if that was true, but he was interested in finding out. Perry's role on the team was still vague.

Generalist?

So there they were, looking up at him like ...

"Okay, seriously," he said. "You all need to stop that."

"Stop what, sir?" Finney asked.

"Looking at me like I'm some kind of demigod! I'm just a normal guy."

Yeah, I don't think they're buying it.

"Okay, no. But I used to be. I wasn't born rich. I was a little bit smart, but mostly I was really, really lucky. You know, I came this close to working with historical employment data instead of the stock market feed. It would have been easier, and right now, I'd be an underpaid adjunct professor somewhere with an interesting paper."

But you are, Blanche! You are in that chair!

"But I cracked the stock market, and now my life is very different. At the end of the day, you'll go home to your normal lives. Except maybe you, Perry. I'm not sure about you."

They laughed. *That's a good sign.*

"And I'll be driven home by a bodyguard and sealed into my security perimeter for the night. But behind all that is a normal person. I don't make the sun come up in the morning. And my point is ..."

You're sure you have one, right?

"My point is that we can be a lot more effective as a team if we can get past who I am and pretend I'm just one of you."

Well, the one in charge, obviously.

"Can we do that?"

They all nodded and murmured agreement. He was pretty sure Don Finney said, "Yes, sir," which kind of defeated the purpose.

But then João said, "Are you always this self-conscious?"

"Thank you!" he said. "That's perfect. Just like that. And no, I'm usually a lot more comfortable in my own skin. I'm nervous under the circumstances. Just like a real boy."

"So what have you brought us here to do?" Laura asked. Steering him back on point. That was a good sign too. This might work out.

"I do have a longer-term project in mind, but something pressing has come up. I want us to hit it from every angle we can think of."

He brought up one of the wall screens he'd had installed. "This man is Alexander Tate," he said, "in happier times."

Crane stood in the paved turnoff near the end of the airstrip, waiting for Malcolm Stoppard's charter to arrive. It was early afternoon, and the air was heavy and still. Chloe and Scott McCall waited in the shadow of the foundation pickup, and their bags were stacked in the bed. Chloe had her knee brace on over her jeans. She was still limping a little, but she'd gotten off easy. She and Scott had both been quiet and subdued on the ride out from town, and from their body language, Crane gathered there had been no reconciliation.

It hadn't been a pleasant day so far. That morning, Crane had been on the satellite phone with Amy Carpenter's parents. That wasn't an experience he was eager to repeat. They had been devastated, obviously. Grateful for his help in getting

Amy's body flown back home. Confused as to who exactly Crane was and how he was involved.

He'd ended up flipping the private detective story he'd used with the locals. He told them Amy had been in Bahia Tortugas catching up with a college friend. When she'd gone missing, that friend had gotten concerned and called him. He agreed to help because he owed the family some favors. It wasn't a bad story. It was Malcolm who'd taught him to keep his cover stories as close to the truth as necessity would allow.

But at least the situation with Amy was resolved. Now he would get Chloe and Scott settled. Once that was done, he would convince Captain Burch to take the *Emma* to Cabo San Lucas for a while. There were plenty of yachters there they could hector about proper sewage disposal, and getting them away from here would clear the field. He wouldn't have anyone else to worry about when Tate or his cartel buddies got around to hitting back.

Eventually the plane appeared out of the endless blue sky. It landed neatly, taxied into the turnoff, and came to a stop.

As Malcolm climbed out, Chloe hurried to him, wobbling a bit on her stiff leg, and they embraced.

"It's okay, Dad," she said. "I'm all right."

"I know," Malcolm said softly as he stroked her back. But his eyes met Crane's, and a look of gratitude passed between them.

Crane and Scott got the bags out of the truck, and Scott helped the pilot load them into the baggage compartment while Crane and Malcolm walked toward the edge of the tarmac.

"I don't know what to say," Malcolm said. "I can't thank you enough."

"You don't owe me anything."

"She's still my little girl, John." Crane could hear the emotion as his voice went tight. "If you hadn't been here ... The girl who didn't make it, did this Jason Tate kill her?"

Crane shrugged. "Autopsy shows she drowned. No other injuries, but she was seriously intoxicated. It looks like she just fell overboard from his yacht. But yeah, he was involved. With a lot of things."

"And he's untouchable?"

Crane gave a grim smile. "Oh, I wouldn't say that."

Malcolm nodded.

"I'm doing a lousy job of taking your advice, Malcolm," Crane said. "There's no vision at all here. This guy just needs to be taken down, and I'm going to do it."

"I'm not arguing. Long term, yeah, you need a plan. But when your house catches fire, you do what it takes to put it out. If there's anything you need, John, anything at all, you just have to call. Call anyway, and keep me posted."

"I will."

They shook hands before Malcolm headed back to the plane. Malcolm gripped Crane's hand in both of his for a moment. Neither of them spoke. It wasn't necessary.

CHAPTER 17

El Paso, Texas

If there was one thing you could count on from Jessie Diamond, it was the unexpected. The town car dropped Josh and Tim at the Santa Fe Street entrance to the El Paso Convention Center, and Josh got his bearings while Tim arranged for the car to pick them up when they were ready. He looked at the signage on the building. "Border Region Coordination Conference."

What the hell is she doing here?

When Tim returned, they walked through the huge glass doors and into the air conditioning. The cavernous lobby had all the trappings of a convention in full swing. Voices combined into a dull white noise. Men in suits and cowboy hats sat in clusters of barely comfortable chairs, talking business. People manned fabric-draped tables, offering literature and smiling like mad. A video crew shot b-roll under the big dome of blue glass in the ceiling. There was that same heavy traffic carpeting with the abstract patterns that Josh remembered from pretty much every convention center he'd ever been in, and the same dull light that seemed to come from nowhere.

They found the membership counter and bought a pair of day passes. Then they walked through the lobby while Josh flipped through his program. There were tracks of panels on cross-border public health, transportation and infrastructure, telecommunications, security, banking. *Well,* he thought, *Jessie did spend a lot of time crossing borders, usually without permission.*

He sent her a text message through his smart watch. "I'm here. Where are you?"

They followed the flow of the crowd, which seemed to be taking them to the booths in the main hall. Someone offered Josh a brightly colored tote bag with some kind of catalog inside. He politely declined.

Then his watch buzzed, and Josh checked the screen. "Where's Juarez Room B?"

Tim studied the map of the convention center they'd gotten at the counter. "Got it," he announced after a moment. "This way."

Tim led the way to a row of doors. It looked like a larger space had been divided up into several smaller rooms for panels. The door to Room B had a sign that read, "1067-A Cross-Border Spectrum Coordination in a Crowded Region."

Okay, sure. She has to be somewhere, I guess. Why not here?

Inside, perhaps fifty people sat in uncomfortable stacking chairs. They were the same chairs they had at all these places, like they came from a single storeroom that connected to every convention center on Earth. On the dais at the front of the room, someone was talking about increasing congestion in the ISM band, and there, in the back row, sat Jessie Diamond. Over a white blouse and a tan pencil skirt, she wore a fitted brown jacket that looked like some kind of cross between a business suit and a bomber jacket. Her blonde hair, usually worn up, cascaded down onto her shoulders.

Damn, she cleans up good. Now that's who you should ask out.

She's gorgeous. She's interesting. God knows she's not intimidated by your money.

For a moment, he entertained the idea. But no.

Too many passports. She's more Crane's speed.

She glanced over and took her large shoulder bag from the chair beside her to make room for him. Tim nodded and stood beside the door as Josh sat down beside her.

"How are you?" she asked softly.

"Good," he murmured. "It's good to see you. What in the world are you doing here?"

She gave him a quick look of disapproval. "What are you doing here?"

"I came to talk to you!"

"Well, okay, then."

In other words, stop asking me about my business.

Josh sighed. "All right, point taken."

And with that, his transgression was forgotten. "What do you need, and where do you need it?" she asked.

"I'm still working on the what," he said. "It won't all be legal."

"You wouldn't need me if it was, would you?"

"The where is Baja. Bahia Tortugas on the Pacific coast."

"Is this going to John Crane?" she guessed. "Are you two putting on another show?"

"It kind of looks that way."

"If you'll tell me the story, I might be able to help put your shopping list together."

"Sure," he said with a laugh. "I'll tell you about *my* dubious activities because *I* trust you."

She smiled and then reached out and briefly touched his shoulder. It was a strangely intimate moment.

"It's not that I don't trust you, Josh," she said. Then she was all business once more. "So what's going on?"

Josh quietly told her what Crane had found in Bahia Tortugas. He left out the backstory about Chloe Stoppard and decided it wasn't especially important at this point to go into whom "Brad Zahn" really was. But he hit the high points, covering Crane's raid on *Gypsy*, finding the missing radio engineer, the discovery that a Mexican cartel was apparently searching for and kidnapping people with advanced technical skills.

At some point, the panel concluded with a round of applause, and people began filing out. But Josh and Jessie kept their seats, and by the time Josh finished, she was looking at him with an odd expression. He could see her mind working furiously behind her dark eyes.

"I'm going to do something I never do," she said at last. "I'm going to introduce you to another client. Come on."

They stood up, and Jessie led him deeper into the room, past knots of people talking in the aisles. She approached a man seated near the stage, going through the messages that had come in on his phone during the panel.

"Sawyer Cottrell," she said. "Let me introduce Josh Sulenski. Sawyer owns a telecom company called Cochise Broadband and Wireless."

Sawyer stood up. "And Mr. Sulenski owns pretty much everything else," he said with a grin. They shook hands. Sawyer Cottrell was somewhere in his fifties, Josh guessed. He had the lean physique and bearing Josh associated with retired military. The haircut didn't change that assessment. He wore khakis and a white polo shirt with his company logo.

He's got a booth here that he's going to have to man later.

He seemed friendly enough. Josh grinned and said, "There's plenty of stuff I don't own yet."

"Well, you're still young."

"I think you should tell Sawyer what you told me," said Jessie.

Josh did, and he could see Sawyer react. Sawyer didn't speak until Josh had finished, but more than once, Josh noticed Sawyer and Jessie trading looks.

When Josh had told his story, Sawyer mulled it over for a moment, and then said. "We should talk somewhere more private. I've got a room in the Camino Real. Come on."

Josh introduced Tim as they crossed the street. "I don't really get to go places alone anymore," he explained.

Sawyer Cottrell was in a suite high in the hotel's main tower. He poured drinks from the wet bar, and they sat down in the suite's living room.

"I know the cartels are grabbing technical people," said Sawyer. "They've been doing it for years now. Dozens of them. And I know why. They're using them to build networks. What else would you do with a bunch of telecom engineers?"

He's angry. This is personal for him.

"I don't follow. What kind of networks?"

"Voice and data. Just like the one your watch there talks to," Sawyer said, pointing to Josh's wrist. "Just about as good coverage too."

"It protects them from eavesdropping," Jessie explained. "By the authorities, or just by their rivals. Find any cartel soldier on the street, they'll have a jailbroken smartphone or else a Nextel handset tweaked to work on the cartel's system."

Josh was astonished. "How is that even possible? Okay, I don't know that much about radio. But doesn't the government just find them and shut them down? I mean, they're broadcasting, right?"

"It's easier to hide a radio network than you might think," said Sawyer. "The backbone is low-power point-to-point links. Hard to spot. They hide the equipment in remote areas, power it with solar panels. It's totally off the grid. They need something like a cell tower for the last mile to the handsets, but even there you can trunk it across a bunch of different frequencies, hide your traffic in legitimate bands."

Damn! How cyberpunk is that? The street finds its own use for things.

"And yeah, they do find them from time to time," Sawyer said. "The army took down a three-hundred-foot antenna in Coahuila last year. But the equipment out in the field is cheap and easy to replace. They just find a new location to put in a new transmitter, rejigger the network topology a little. They're back up in days."

"To be clear," said Jessie, "this is very sophisticated stuff. Military grade. And cartel members tend not to be the guys who did real good in math in school."

"So they're hunting down people with the technical skills they need, and just taking them," said Josh. It made sense once you accepted that the cartels could really blanket all of Mexico in their own private, illicit telecom systems.

"It's been going on for at least seven years now," said Sawyer. "An engineer here, an antenna construction crew there. Dozens of them. No ransom demand, no communication. They're just gone. Not a one has ever been seen again."

"And you're involved because ..."

Because they took one of his.

He saw Sawyer's fist clench. "Because eight months ago, they took my son."

Oh. Worse than you thought.

Jessie filled the sudden silence. "Sawyer's son, Martin, was an RF engineer for the company. He went missing on vacation in Cabo San Lucas. There's been no contact, no ransom demand, nothing."

"I'm sorry," said Josh. "What have you done?"

"Started with a private detective," said Sawyer. "He managed to trace Martin around Cabo for most of a week. His last day there, he rented an ATV and rode out into the desert. He never came back. A few days later, they found the ATV abandoned. Trail went cold at that point."

"That's when Sawyer came to me," said Jessie. "I put him in touch with some other resources. We've learned a lot about the networks and how they're run. But not how they identified Martin as someone they wanted, or where he's being held."

"Got people down there right now taking the whole damn country apart a brick at a time," said Sawyer. "I've got a team ready to move in, if we can just tell them where to go."

"I can't tell you where he is," said Josh, "but I think it's clear now how they found him."

"This fellow your man rescued," said Sawyer as he rose to refill his whiskey glass, "you say he actually interviewed for this?"

"He needed a job," said Josh. "The man doing the headhunting told him he was recruiting for Telcel."

"And he's American. White guy? That was what was odd about them taking Martin. Victims are usually Mexican nationals. Didn't think they'd want the attention of grabbing an American."

"He's someone who could move in the right circles to find Americans to target."

"Sure would like to talk to him," said Sawyer. "Just for a few minutes."

There's an undercurrent to this guy. Try not to get on his bad side.

"You're not the only one. But we've lost him, for now at least. And what you really want is to find the other end of the chain."

"You've got an idea how to do that?"

They need engineers because they don't have the skills themselves. Which means they don't understand what those engineers are actually doing.

"If something goes wrong with a piece of hardware," Josh

mused, "they'd take it back to wherever they're keeping their captive engineers, right? That's what they're for. And once they'd fixed that piece of hardware, it would go back out into the field again. Something goes in, something comes back out. That's a communications channel."

Yeah, this could work.

"I think we can help each other, Mr. Cottrell."

Sawyer thought for a moment and then glanced over at Jessie.

She nodded. "I'll vouch for his man—Crane. He's good."

Josh could see Sawyer's mind was made up. "Yeah," he said. "Yeah. If you can help us locate them, Jessie can fly my people in. They'll bust Martin out, and anyone else they find. Jessie flies them all back out across the border."

Sawyer stood and offered Josh his hand. Josh stood as well, and they shook.

"Welcome to the team, Mr. Sulenski," Sawyer said. "Glad to have you aboard."

"I thought you two would get along," said Jessie. "Now let's hear a little more about this idea of yours."

CHAPTER 18

It was a rare cloudy afternoon in Bahia Tortugas. The sky was a leaden gray, and the breeze off the bay was choppy and relatively cool. It looked like the kind of sky that should produce a thunderstorm, but so far it hadn't. Crane sat on the patio at the La Playa with his bag at his feet, watching the *Emma* under sail, heading out toward the open sea. Crane had gotten Captain Burch alone and told him just enough about what was going on to convince him that it was wise to take his boat and his crew down to Cabo San Lucas for a while for a change of scenery.

Crane couldn't be certain that they'd be in danger if they stayed, but he was expecting some kind of response from Tate and the cartel, and he had been staying with the foundation on their boat. It was best if they were out of the way.

Hector the bartender brought Crane his fish tacos and a Pacifico. "Hey," he said. "You're staying with those kids on the catamaran, right? They're leaving without you, man!"

"Looks that way," said Crane. "Guess I'll have to move ashore. Where's a good place to stay around here?"

"Straight up the road from the pier," said Hector. "Motel

Maria. My cousin will set you up. Tell him I said to take care of you."

Crane thanked him and turned to his lunch. The fish was fresh from the bay that morning, and the tacos were excellent, with lime, jalapeño, a bit of ancho chili powder. Crane decided he'd found his hangout in Bahia Tortugas.

After lunch, Crane walked up Calle Independencia from the pier until he found Motel Maria. It was a square compound of pale green walls and white trim at the doors and windows. A low cinder-block wall closed off most of the street frontage to create a central courtyard surrounded by a dozen or so rooms.

Hector's cousin showed him around. The rooms were small, not air conditioned, and sparsely furnished. But they were clean. Crane paid for a week in advance, dropped his bags, and grabbed a quick shower.

Then he decided it was time to get to work.

That morning, Crane had walked over to the former bar where Chloe had ambushed Tate. He'd let himself in and explored in hopes of finding something useful, but it looked as though Tate had abandoned the place. The ground floor was nothing but dusty old scaffolding to begin with. It looked like nobody had done anything there for years but walk through to get to the stairs. The two upstairs rooms were clean but empty. Crane guessed Tate had told Arturo and Juan Manuel to clean the place out in a hurry. There was no sign of the Escalade around back.

So it had been a fairly unproductive morning. If he wanted better results from the afternoon, Crane decided, what he needed was some local expertise. He locked his room and walked back down to the pier. As expected, he found Luis hanging around in his Versa, waiting for customers. Luis saw him coming and popped his seat back up to driving position.

"*Buenas tardes*, Mr. Crane!" he said. "Going somewhere today?"

Crane squatted down beside the driver's door and slipped Luis a fifty. "Could be, Luis. You don't miss much around here."

Luis accepted the compliment with a smile and a tilt of his head. The fifty vanished into his shirt pocket.

"Boz has a big black Escalade he likes to roll around town in when he's here. You know it?"

"Sure. Everyone knows it. He makes sure of that, the jackass."

"You know where he keeps it these days? I checked his place, but it's not there."

Luis laughed. "You up to no good, eh?" He cocked his head toward the passenger seat. "Get in."

Crane walked around and got in, and Luis drove off with a grinding shift of the Versa's overworked gearbox. They drove around the western edge of town to a street that had only a few scattered houses, and those only on the right side.

A few hundred yards up, Crane spotted a structure on the left side of the street. Beyond it was nothing but scrub and the occasional cactus.

"That's it up there," said Luis. "What do you want to do?"

"Drive by slow."

As they rolled by, Crane checked the backyards across the street. He didn't see anybody outside. Closed blinds covered the windows. If he didn't raise too much of a disturbance, he doubted anyone would realize he was there.

The garage itself was a low-slung cinder-block building. It had three rusting metal bay doors, the last one hanging open. Crane noted there were no power lines or other cables running to it. That meant no lights, and also no alarms unless they were battery powered. He didn't see any problems.

Crane let Luis get a hundred yards or so past the garage, and then said, "Okay, pull over."

Luis did, and Crane got out. "I'll be back," he said. "Five minutes tops."

Then he walked calmly back toward the garage. Nobody else was on the street. He passed the fenced backyards on his left now. To his right were only the garage and sandy hills dotted with Joshua trees and scrub brush.

When he reached the garage, he circled it. There was nothing behind the building but a cache of empty beer bottles and cigarette butts. There were no doors, but each bay had a window to let in some light. The third window was barred.

When he had circled the building, he checked the open bay. The metal door hung half off its hinges, and there was nothing inside but a skinny stray dog that lay on the cool cement floor, watching Crane warily.

The middle bay was locked with an ancient, rusted padlock and chain. But the third bay had a long metal bar, hammered flat at both ends and locked with two new heavy-duty disc locks. It wasn't hard to guess which bay held Tate's Cadillac.

He glanced around again and confirmed that no one was watching. He noted a backyard tool shed across the street that would be the perfect place to set up a remote surveillance camera if he had one. He mentally added it to the list of things to request from Josh. Then he examined the door one last time for signs of alarms or other security.

When he was satisfied, he took out his picks and opened the two locks. He lowered the heavy metal bar to the ground and opened the doors just enough to slip through.

The Escalade was inside. The windshield still showed the cracks and spider-webbing from the two rounds he'd put into it, and Chloe's clip-worth of bullet impacts was still visible on the passenger side. Ballistic glass replacement windows would have to be shipped in, probably with a technician qualified to actually replace them. He made another mental note to keep his eyes open for that.

Apart from the Escalade itself, the garage was empty except for a couple empty oil cans in one corner and a plastic funnel. Crane turned his attention to the SUV itself. He jotted down the license number and VIN, and then tested the driver's door and found it unlocked. He climbed in and gave the SUV a methodical search. There was no registration or insurance information in the glove compartment—just the Cadillac-issued owner's manual. Given that an apparently powerful cartel was involved, one with the ability to make Chief Moreno stay well clear of Tate, he found himself wondering if the vehicle was registered at all.

He climbed into the back and felt under the seats. There, at last, he found something. A business card with something written on the back in a thick pencil. *"Carne asada torta, elote, dos Tecates. FRIO!"*

The front said the card belonged to a William Kim of a law firm called Cancio, Hopkins, and Metcalfe in Los Angeles. "High net worth estate planning." Crane pocketed it and felt around for something else, but the card appeared to be all he was going to get.

He got out, closed the door, and shook his head. The card was probably nothing. After all, Tate had jotted down his lunch order on it—a steak sandwich, spiced corn, and two cold beers—and then lost it under the seat of his SUV. But Josh would look into it and make sure. Otherwise, this had been a waste of time. If he had the right gear, he could have at least put a tracer on the Escalade. But that would have to wait. He closed the garage door, replaced the metal bar, and walked back to Luis.

Luis drove him back to the motel. On the way, they passed the police station, and Crane noted a black Chevy Suburban parked outside. It was obviously not local. It was new and gleaming. It had to have driven in from Vizcaino and then had the dust of the long, mostly unpaved road washed off once it got here.

"Know who that is?" Crane asked.

"No," said Luis. "Nobody local. I seen it around a couple times today, but not before."

"Drop me back at the pier," said Crane.

"I can take you to the motel, no problem."

"No, the pier."

Crane wandered the beach after Luis dropped him off. He checked the MHS pistol he'd taken from Orly Wilde and made sure it was ready at the small of his back. Before too long, he spotted the black Suburban driving slowly up the waterfront toward him.

Crane walked calmly toward a large rock formation above the high tide line and leaned against it. The Suburban parked, and a man got out and walked toward him. He was short but slim and taut, with dark hair slicked back. He wore black pants over cowboy boots of some kind of exotic leather, an intricate piteado belt, and a white silk shirt. Crane noted that he kept his hands away from his sides as he walked.

"Excuse me," he said, "are you Mr. Crane? Mr. John Crane?"

"That's right."

"I'm Enrique Salinas," the man said, stopping perhaps twenty feet away. "I'm an insurance investigator. Do you have a moment to talk?"

"Why not?" said Crane. He was under no illusions that Salinas was an insurance investigator.

"Mr. Bradley Zahn is a customer of my company. We provided full value hull coverage for his yacht, the *Gypsy*."

"I see," said Crane. "Guess that wasn't your best deal in retrospect."

The man shrugged. "That's what insurance is for. We just

want to know what happened. Do you know what happened to the *Gypsy*?"

"Just what I hear around town," said Crane. "And of course, I saw the fire. Everyone saw that."

"I've been asking people what they saw all day. Some say you were aboard the *Gypsy*."

"They haven't said anything to the police," said Crane.

The man who called himself Salinas smiled. It was cold and mirthless. "People in Mexico don't like to talk to the police. Nothing good ever comes of it. You do know the owner, Mr. Zahn. I hear you and he had some difficulties."

"He's not the easiest man to get along with," said Crane. "I don't imagine that's news to your company."

"But do you have some specific quarrel with him?"

Crane smiled. It sounded as though the cartel was earnestly trying to understand what kind of trouble Tate had gotten them into.

"As I said, he's a man who makes enemies easily. I'm sure his business is worth something to your company. But a man who lives the way he does is going to keep having incidents and filing claims. I guess you have to be the ones to decide when the risks outweigh the premiums he pays. You're the insurance experts."

The man was silent for a long moment. Something in his eyes reminded Crane of a snake's.

"The people in town say you are a detective," he said at last. "You came here looking for the missing girl who, sadly, was found dead."

Crane didn't say anything.

"If that's true, then your case is closed, Mr. Crane. Why are you still here?"

Crane shrugged. "It's a nice town."

The man glanced up at the dusty, unpaved streets and ramshackle buildings. He laughed.

"*Buenas noches*, Mr. Crane," he said. Then he turned and walked back toward his Suburban.

Crane watched him go, watched the Suburban do a three-point turn and head away. *Still your move*, he thought. Whatever the cartel was going to do, though, he gathered they would be getting around to it soon.

CHAPTER 19

Marin County, California

Josh and Tim rented a car at SFO, on the grounds that it would be harder to trace an airport rental, and Josh drove them north on the Pacific Coast Highway. It was foggy along the coast, the marine layer pushing in from the sea. Josh found it frustrating that he could look out to his right and see the thick cloud layer abruptly stop a half mile or so inland and give way to pure blue sky.

It's a beautiful day over on the 101.

Yeah, but you're going to be glad that fog's there when you get where you're going.

They were headed back to the hospital at Fallon Landing, though their approach would be quite different this time. In the trunk of the car was a police model automatic license plate reader with a high-resolution camera and a cellular radio, all powered by a high-endurance battery originally developed for Navy sonobuoys. It was the sort of thing Crane would have asked for in one of his ridiculous shopping lists. Josh felt like James Bond just having it in the trunk.

Possession of the license plate reader by civilians was already legally iffy. But there was no doubt about the plan to infiltrate the Fallon Landing grounds and install the system in a tree overlooking the approach road so it could log traffic coming and going from the hospital.

No, that's just illegal as hell. Crane never gets arrested because he's Crane. That doesn't apply to you.

It had been Perry Holland's idea. While Finney and Berdoza immersed themselves in a swamp of holding companies and blind partnerships, Josh and the rest of the team had been trying to learn more about Alexander Tate's medical status. They'd been stonewalled at every turn. Between HIPAA regulations and simple obscurity, they'd wasted a couple days now asking questions and getting no answers. They didn't even know who Alexander's doctor was.

"Whoever's in charge of his treatment has to be at the hospital, right?" Perry had said finally. "I mean, once in a while, anyway. They have to check on him, right? And there's only one road into the hospital. Whoever we're looking for, sooner or later, they're going to drive down that road."

Josh had considered the idea and decided he liked it. The next question was, who was going to plant the camera? Josh had decided he couldn't ask anyone else to do it, so he'd go himself. When he announced that, Tim had first tried to talk him out of it, and then insisted on coming along. Josh had let himself be convinced. He was glad of the company, if nothing else.

"Next left," said Tim, navigating with his iPhone. "About a quarter mile up."

Josh slowed and spotted the turnoff. He turned onto a gravel road and followed it for a hundred yards or so until it ended in a small parking area and a trailhead. The only other car was a Subaru with Oregon plates. Josh pulled in beside it.

"All right, let's do this," he said.

Yeah, that didn't sound at all lame.

The camera was in a backpack. Tim offered to carry it, but he would already be using a handheld GPS unit to guide them to the spot they'd chosen for the camera. Josh shrugged on the pack, and they set off.

The trail led down to the cliffs overlooking Point Reyes, and then along them for a couple miles. But it also ran along the edge of the Fallon Landing property for more than half a mile.

Josh and Tim made their way down the trail. The fog grew thicker as they went lower and closer to the sea. They walked in silence, seeing no sign of any other hikers. Tim carried his GPS unit in one hand, checking the screen from time to time. Back in Palo Alto, they had worked out a course that would get them to their destination quickly while keeping them under cover of woods as much as possible. Every yard of their trip was preplanned and loaded into the GPS.

They rounded a gentle curve in the trail, walked another few yards, and the GPS beeped as they reached the first waypoint. They stopped, looked back up the trail once more to make sure they were unobserved, and then cut off the trail and into the brush. About twenty yards from the trail, they came to a woven wire fence covered in vines. Josh cleared the foliage away, and Tim cut through the fence with a pair of wire cutters. They carefully slipped through and bent the fence back.

Okay, you're definitely breaking the law now. You personally.

Beyond the fence, they moved through a stand of trees that wound along a ridgeline and gave them cover for a while.

"Thanks for coming, by the way," Josh said to Tim as they walked. "You didn't have to. I appreciate it."

"My job's keeping you out of trouble," Tim answered.

"Within limits. I mean, if I said I was going to rob a bank, would you come with me?"

"I'd stop you."

"Right. But for this, you came along. So thank you."

The GPS beeped again. They'd reached their next waypoint. Josh turned and peered out of the trees, across a slope covered in tan grass. In the distance, he could see another mass of trees looming out of the mist.

"That way, straight line," said Tim. "Walk fast, but don't run. We're hikers who got lost. We wouldn't be running."

Josh took a deep breath. He knew the hospital had security patrols. He'd seen them driving around in their electric carts on their last visit. Those would be quiet. There was nothing to do but risk it and hope they weren't seen.

"Let's go," he said, and they strode out into the open.

They moved quickly across the open ground, and Josh was surprised to find himself enjoying this. He'd been nervous in the car, thinking about it. But now that he was committed, it was actually exciting. He wondered if this was how John Crane felt in the field.

Then they reached the trees and were hidden again. Josh laughed.

Yeah, tell Crane how you're just like him now because you walked across a field.

They made good time down a slope, crossed another open patch without incident, and soon found themselves nearing the road. So far, he had to admit, this had been easy.

"Fifty yards this way," Tim said softly, following his GPS toward the final waypoint.

They'd chosen a spot where the road curved around a wooded hillside. They would find a tree to conceal the camera and radio. It would be up where someone would be less likely to notice it, and it would have a clear angle onto the road so it could pick up license numbers easily.

They spent about ten minutes walking the slope above the

road, studying trees, until Josh found one he thought would work. There was a branch positioned just right to take the camera in a spot where it would be hard to see, but would still have a clear shot of the road. If a car passed doing normal speed for this road, its plate would be readable for several seconds.

Josh shrugged off the backpack, and Tim hauled himself up into the tree until he was seated astride the branch facing the trunk.

Yep, that's why you brought him along. He was probably playing football in high school, while you were—

"Yeah, this'll work," Tim announced. "Drill, please?"

Josh sorted through the pack and passed up the small battery-operated drill. Tim started drilling holes for the camera's swivel bracket.

When Tim was ready, Josh handed up the bracket and then sat down at the base of the trunk as Tim worked. It was peaceful, the mist in the trees giving the birds' cries a distant, mournful quality.

Peaceful, but lonely.

What are those birds doing?

They're looking for someone to be with.

"I'm ready," said Tim.

Josh stood up and handed the camera up into the tree. "Okay, give me a reference point."

They'd taped a five-milliwatt green laser onto the housing to aim the camera. Tim fitted the camera into the mount and switched it on. A green dot appeared on the asphalt.

Josh walked down to the road and considered the dot's placement. "Higher, I think. Little to the left."

The dot slid up the road.

"Better. How're things with Emily, by the way?"

"Huh? Oh. Okay, I guess. Her mother's in town. They're going totally over the top with wedding planning."

"You should bring her out to the house sometime," said Josh. "I'd like to meet her. We can grill some steaks or something. Bring her mother, if you want."

Great. You sound pathetic. I'm a poor lonely rich boy. Won't you be my friend?

He could hear the awkwardness in Tim's voice. "Uh, okay. I'll speak to her about it." Then he hissed, "Down, down. Get off the road!"

As Tim was speaking, Josh heard the soft whirr of electric motors and snatches of a voice. He sprinted across the road and dove into the underbrush. He rolled onto his side in the fetal position and tried to keep as still as possible. He could see Tim in the tree across the road and above him. Tim's body was pressed against the trunk. Unless they were looking in the trees …

Jesus Christ, the laser!

But no, Tim had had the presence of mind to switch it off. The electric cart rolled past the point where the laser would have been right in the driver's eyes, and then slid by him. Two hospital security men in their black pants and white polo shirts rode inside. One was saying something, but Josh only caught a stray word as they passed. A few moments later, it disappeared around the curve, headed for the hospital.

Josh let out a breath.

As he was standing up, Tim dropped down from the branch with the tools and the laser, and packed them back into the backpack. Josh took out his phone and checked the app João had written to receive data from the camera. It was online. Everything was working. Now all they needed was some cars to drive by so the camera could scan the license numbers and send them back to the war room.

"We good?" Tim whispered.

Josh nodded. "Let's go."

They headed back the way they had come, following Tim's GPS through the woods. Josh was breathing more heavily now. It didn't seem like fun anymore.

"I am definitely going to need a drink after this," he said.

"Yeah," Tim agreed. "Maybe a couple."

CHAPTER 20

The next day, Crane and Luis sat in the Versa at the airstrip, listening to Luis' tape deck. Luis' tastes were too sugary for Crane's liking, but it was his car, his music. Bahia Tortugas was back to its usual sun and cloudless skies, and the breeze came through the open window hot and dry. Crane felt a bead of sweat run down the back of his neck.

The song ended, and a new one began. "Ah!" said Luis. "This is Belinda. Listen, listen!"

Luis had apparently decided it was his responsibility to bring Crane up to speed on Mexican pop. "She's fantastic! The video for this, with the leopard on the beach! Unh! Super hot!" He pounded the steering wheel a couple times for emphasis.

Crane noticed the faint drone of airplane engines rising through the music. He checked his watch. It was almost three. Whoever Jessie Diamond was, she was right on time.

Crane had checked in from the landline in the motel's office the night before, but the connection was terrible, and Josh was in a rush about something. Crane gathered that the cartels were running their own illicit telecom networks, which explained why they were kidnapping technical people like Scott. Josh had run across some Texan businessman who knew all about it. And someone named Jessie Diamond was coming down. The rest they would figure out once she got here.

Crane got out of the car and stretched. The approaching plane was a boxy cargo hauler with twin engines and a braced overhead wing. As it descended, Crane recognized it as a Short 330. The fuselage was square, with a loading ramp that dropped down in the rear. The wing, the diagonal bracing struts, and the twin vertical rudders were just as flat. Apart from the nose, there was hardly a curved line to be found on it. It was cheap, bulky, and slow, but it worked well enough for short-distance cargo runs. The military version was the C-23 Sherpa, and Crane had spent a fair amount of time jumping out of one during his training. Pilots affectionately called it "the shed."

This one was white with blue trim and didn't carry any company identifiers. It looked like the cargo hold had been modified too. Crane wondered what she was carrying. Then the plane touched down, twin propellers kicking up dust, and taxied in.

Crane walked toward it as it pulled off the runway into the service area and killed its engines. A few moments later, the side door opened and the pilot stepped out. Jessie Diamond wore black cargo pants tucked into her boots, a sand-colored tank top, and mirrored aviator shades. Her blonde hair was pulled back into a French braid, and topped off with a beaten olive-colored baseball cap.

"Good afternoon, Mr. Crane," she said, as if she knew him.

"Welcome to Bahia Tortugas," Crane replied. She was about his height, somewhere in her late twenties, fit and toned. Her eyes were gray and alert. An old, fading scar ran down her left bicep. There was something familiar about her, actually, but Crane couldn't place her.

"Glad to be here," she said.

"Need help with anything?"

"Nope," she said. "Got it. Give me a second. Got some toys for you in there."

She climbed back into the plane. Crane knew he'd seen her before. He was still trying to figure out where when the plane's rear ramp lowered, and Jessie drove out in a Ford Raptor pickup. As the ramp closed, she got out of the truck with a pair of Baja California Sur license plates and a screwdriver.

"That's your stuff in back," she said, kneeling in front of the truck. "I don't know how much Josh has told you." She started screwing one of the plates onto the front bumper.

"Not a lot, actually."

"Okay. Is there a decent bar in this town? We should spend some time sorting out what we're going to do."

"As it happens," said Crane, "there is a pretty good bar that looks out over the water and makes damn fine fish tacos."

"Works for me."

Crane walked over to Luis and sent him back to town. As he returned, Jessie was loading a Heckler and Koch VP9. She slipped the pistol into a holster built into a cargo pocket on her thigh, and then practiced quick drawing it a couple times. When she was satisfied, she slid the gun back into place and smiled sweetly at him.

"Ready to go?"

On the way back into town, Crane looked over the interior of the truck. It was armored as well, though not as seriously as Tate's Escalade. He was starting to wonder if everyone drove armored vehicles around here. The engine had been upgraded to handle the additional weight. That was definitely the older V8 under the hood.

And where the hell did he know Jessie Diamond from?

He was positive now that he'd seen her somewhere before,

but he couldn't place her. Finally, he gave up and just asked her. "I'm sorry, this is cheesy, but have we met before?"

She smiled. "Smooth line."

"No, I'm serious. I know I've seen you somewhere before, and I can't figure it out."

"Prague," she said. "I brought you your Audi. The one you wrecked. And then set on fire."

That was it, he realized. She'd been dressed as a chauffeur and her hair had been short, but she was the woman who'd met him at the airport.

"Wait, you work for Josh? I thought you worked for some guy in Texas."

"Sawyer Cottrell. He's a client. So's Josh. But I run my own outfit. Diamond Transport."

She pulled a business card from the visor and handed it to Crane. It had her name, the company name, and a series of e-mail addresses and telephone numbers. Beneath her name was the slogan "When it absolutely has to be there. Or anywhere *but* there."

"So how much do you know about what I do?" Crane asked.

"Eh, I know where you go and what kind of stuff you need. Beyond that, not a lot. I know Josh was excited as hell when he found you. Which way up here?"

"Uh, right."

Crane pocketed the business card. So that was how Josh got weapons and various other illicit gadgets wherever Crane happened to need them. He glanced back up at Jessie and decided he was impressed.

They drove to La Playa and sat on the patio. Crane had Hector bring a bottle of tequila along with some salt and limes, and they started trading life stories.

Jessie Diamond turned out to be the child of sovereign citizen survivalists who had raised her pretty much off the grid in the Pacific Northwest. They made their money smuggling pot from British Columbia, and they hung around with gunrunners, cypherpunks, militia types, and a whole range of characters from whom Jessie had learned all kinds of useful skills.

She'd clearly inherited her parents' disdain for authority, but she also didn't seem to have much use for the anarchic counter-culture she'd been raised in. Crane sensed a distance about her as she talked about the people in her past and her experiences. He got the sense that she felt like a kind of outside observer in the world.

At the same time, she was friendly, outgoing, interested in him. As it grew dark and the bar started to fill, she did a good job of drawing out details about his life. Sometime during the second bottle of tequila, while the locals were dancing to the juke box, he realized he was telling her about his mother and the accident when he was eight.

"So how do you and your father get along?" she asked, licking her hand between her fingers and thumb and sprinkling salt over it.

"It's always been kind of complicated," he said.

She licked the salt from her hand and knocked back a shot of tequila. "I'll bet," she said finally. "He had to raise you on his own, and you were always there to remind him of her. And she hurt him so badly. He had to keep it all bottled up inside because it's not like he could dump it on an innocent little boy."

She grabbed a lime wedge and sucked on it. Crane was still unpacking what she'd said.

"I knew people like that," she said, in a voice weighted with hard memories. "Broken people. Real life beat them up until they retreated into fantasy, playing make-believe revolutionary. You should call your father, John. I bet you two don't talk much."

"Not much," Crane admitted, and reached for the tequila.

By the time the bar began to empty out, they were both

pleasantly drunk, and Crane realized he still didn't know exactly what Jessie was here to do.

"So what's the plan?" he asked as they left the bar and walked into the breezy night air.

"Well, we're not driving," she replied. "We're drunk."

"We're reasonably drunk," he said. "It's a reasonable amount. No problem. The motel's just up the street."

They stopped at the truck so Crane could retrieve the bag Josh had sent down. Then they headed up the hill toward Motel Maria.

"I mean the plan," said Crane. "What are we going to do?"

"Ah. In the morning, we go hunting. We're going to find a cartel transceiver and bring back extremely detailed information about it."

"And then?"

"Then Josh and his people rig up a trick circuit board. We go back out and install it in the unit, and it starts to intermittently fail. What are they going to do when that happens? They're going to take it back to the engineers to fix it. They'll take it right where we want to go."

"With a bug on it?"

She shook her head. "Josh says too risky. With a message coded into the ROM. Something only the techs will be able to read. It'll tell them how to transmit their location to us."

"They've been kidnapped. Are we sure they know where they're being held?"

"Josh says they'd have to," she said. "No way they could design all those point-to-point links without really good maps. They just code that into the board and it sends the location back to us. We go get them."

Crane thought about it. That could work, he decided. His plan had been to harass the cartel until they decided what Jason Tate did for them wasn't worth the price of protecting him. This would raise Tate's price considerably. And even disregarding Tate, if they could find the other kidnapped engineers and rescue them, that was worth doing by itself.

As they approached the motel, Jessie suddenly said, "And I'm going to need my own room. Because we're not sleeping together."

Crane was still running the scenario back and forth in his head, looking for angles, and was taken by surprise.

"What? No! I know!" he stammered. "I didn't mean to—"

"I just want to be clear about that up front. Because you've got kind of a reputation. Josh told me about you."

Crane didn't know what to say. Jessie was certainly attractive, but ... "I ... yeah, of course, separate rooms. I never thought ..."

They stopped at the office and got Jessie the room beside Crane's.

"You don't have a bag?" Crane asked.

"Grew up traveling light," she answered. "Good night, Crane."

Then they went into their separate rooms and closed their doors.

"For Christ's sake, Josh," Crane muttered as soon as he was inside. Why the hell would Josh tell her something like that? He pulled off his shirt and tossed it on the flimsy chair in the corner of the room. "How would you even know about ... ?"

He stopped short and let out a sigh. Then he stepped outside and knocked on Jessie's door.

"Josh didn't really tell you that, did he?" he said when she opened the door.

"No," she admitted. "Of course he didn't."

"You were trolling me." Crane rolled his eyes. "All right, point for you, then."

He was turning back toward his own door when she said, "Crane?" He stopped, and she nodded at his shirtless torso and raised an eyebrow. "Looking good," she said. "You been working out?"

Crane grinned. "Shut up."

As he closed his door behind him, he heard her knock on the wall between their rooms, and then her muffled voice. "Get to sleep. Early day tomorrow."

"Good night, Diamond."

"Good night, Crane."

He stripped and got into bed. It occurred to him that she'd done a very deft job of quickly establishing where they stood while warning him that she could outmaneuver him if she wanted to. She had laid the ground rules for their partnership quickly and with a hint of misdirection.

He liked her, he decided, and he was comfortable with things as she seemed to want them. There was some kind of natural chemistry between them, but it wasn't really a sexual thing. Something else.

Too bad, really, he told himself as he drifted off to sleep.

CHAPTER 21

The next morning, Crane and Jessie met in the motel courtyard as the sun was still rising. She was wearing the same clothes since she hadn't brought any bags from her plane. She thrust her H&K into the holster in her cargo pants, closed the door to her room, and said, "Morning."

"Morning," said Crane.

Then they walked down to the waterfront to retrieve Jessie's truck. Jessie had Crane open the glove compartment, where he found a bag full of granola bars. They each had one for breakfast while Jessie drove through town.

The truck kicked up a plume of dust as Jessie drove a bit faster than she should have down the access road to the airstrip. Her Short sat waiting at the corner of the tarmac. Jessie parked in its shadow and keyed a remote. The plane's rear cargo ramp pivoted smoothly down.

"Give me a hand, will you?" she said as she strode around the back of the plane and jumped up onto the descending ramp.

Crane followed. At the rear of the boxy cargo hold was a small curved shape with rudders, tricycle landing gear, a shaft with braced rotor blades ...

"An autogyro?"

"Aerotrek ELA G8," she said proudly.

"We're flying in that?"

"Yeah, that's what it's for," said Jessie as she swung the autogyro around until its nose faced the ramp. "What did you think we were doing?"

Crane had assumed they'd be flying the Short to search for radio sources, and then marking what they found and going back over land to investigate. Apparently not. Crane hoped the thing was airworthy. The fuselage reminded him of a kayak, one with a propeller and stabilizers in the back and rotor blades above. But she meant to fly it, and he had no intention of letting her get the upper hand again.

"All right," he said. "I'm game."

Behind the autogyro's nose cone were two tiny open cockpit seats, each with its own windscreen. Crane went around to one side as Jessie went to the other. They grabbed the fairing beneath the forward windscreen, threw their weight into it, and rolled the machine down the ramp and onto the tarmac.

"Josh sent down some radio detection gear," Jessie explained. "It mounts on the left side of the rear cockpit where you'll be, so you'll have to get in on the other side." Crane helped her get the frame installed and tested the gear while Jessie removed the braces holding the carbon fiber blades in place and double-checked the engine.

It took about half an hour to get the autogyro ready to fly and confirm that the radio gear was properly installed. Then they found a chart of the surrounding area and spread it out on the hood of the truck. The map showed the desert as an unbroken stretch of brown for hundreds of miles in every direction but west. Crane looked for something that suggested any particular spot in that sea of brown was a better place to put a radio transceiver than any other spot.

"How big is this thing we're looking for?" he asked at last.

"Hard to say," Jessie answered. "I've seen pictures of some that the army found, and they vary. Depends on what parts the person making it has access to. And how good they are, I guess. Average? Maybe so by so." She used her hands to indicate something perhaps the size of a high-end stereo receiver.

"But then there's the antenna itself," she added, "which has to be dug in and guyed. Plus the solar panels and mounts. The tools to get it all built. It's a pretty good load."

Crane saw where she was going. "So you wouldn't want to haul it any farther through this kind of terrain than you had to, would you?"

"Not if you could help it," she said. She traced the long highway that ran from Bahia Tortugas back to Vizcaino. "I'm thinking we fly east, more or less following this. I'm betting we'll find something within a couple miles of the highway. Just far back enough that it's not obvious from the road."

Crane thought that sounded reasonable. "Let's do it."

Jessie had a pair of helmets with built-in intercoms. They put them on, Jessie did one more walk-around of the autogyro, and then they climbed aboard and plugged their helmets into cockpit jacks.

"You hear me?" Jessie said in Crane's headphones.

"Got you." He powered up the radio gear beside his seat and heard a series of beeps and tones, and then signal indicators as he swept through the major bands. "And I'm getting radio noise. We're good to go."

He dialed back the detectors as Jessie powered up the engine. They were looking for a small source close at hand. He didn't want to be picking up the main radio tower in town.

The engine sprang to life with a snarl, and the autogyro started forward. The blades overhead picked up the headwind and began to whirl. Crane thought Jessie was taxiing out to the runway to take off, but the autogyro seemed hardly to have covered a hundred feet before Jessie pulled back hard on the stick and they were airborne. The autogyro climbed sharply, the nose pointing up and the acceleration pushing Crane back into his seat.

She took them up to about five hundred feet and then banked sharply, rolling the aircraft nearly onto its side and pointing the nose northeast, toward Vizcaino. The aerobatics seemed uncalled for, Crane thought.

"You're just doing this to mess with me, aren't you?" Crane said.

"Tweaked the engine a little bit," Jessie replied, and he could hear the laugh in her voice.

Once she was at altitude, Jessie pulled back the throttle, and the engine settled down into a more comfortable drone. They flew over a pale tan desert landscape with the dark line of the highway just visible off to their right. The wind was hot and dry as it whipped around the windscreen. The outboard radio gear in particular seemed to be deflecting wind into his face.

Crane turned his attention to the radio panel, scanning through frequencies, listening for signals that shouldn't be there. Below, he saw long, angular ridges and arroyos, rocky slopes studded with cactus, and occasional patches of sparse green where the drainage brought together enough water to support plants.

Once he got used to the cramped space in the autogyro, and Jessie's penchant for dangerous piloting, it was a pleasant way to fly, he decided. The thing was steady, and it could maneuver like a startled cat—something Jessie seemed to delight in demonstrating at random moments for no obvious reason.

They'd flown for nearly half an hour, and Jessie said they were about forty miles from Bahia Tortugas, when Crane picked up the first traces. The board began to light up, and a warning tone went off in his headphones. He hit a key that started recording data for Josh's people to analyze later.

The tone grew stronger, and the readouts on the panel suggested they were getting closer. Whatever it was, it was faint. He asked Jessie to veer off and fly a straight north-south course for a few miles while he turned the antennas and focused them to the east.

The tone was faint for the first minute, and then suddenly it was anything but. The needles buried themselves in the meters, and the tone was an angry snarl in his headphones. Then, no more than thirty seconds later, it dropped off again. Crane was convinced now that he'd found what they were looking for. A high-gain antenna was transmitting a narrow radio beam—the open desert was the perfect environment for it as long as you didn't find a ridge in the way—and they'd just flown right through the beam. That gave him a heading. He passed the info to Jessie, and she wheeled the autogyro around and flew in the direction Crane had identified.

Another ten minutes of flying with the signal growing stronger, and they found it. Jessie spotted the antenna near the end of a narrow track that left the main road and twisted through a line of low hills before it simply stopped. As she came in lower, Crane spotted the remains of an abandoned shack, long since fallen in on itself and reclaimed by the desert. Someone had tried to live out here once. Crane had no idea why.

Jessie came in low and slow and circled the site while Crane took photos with a Canon point and shoot. Then she brought the autogyro down on the packed earth at the end of the road. They dropped down to the ground and simply stopped.

"You just love to show off in this thing, don't you?" Crane said as they climbed out.

"I thought you liked a little thrill!" she said as they took off their helmets. "They got a Denny's back in town? We get done here, I can drop you off in time for the early-bird special."

Crane was unloading a tool bag and a pair of cameras from the autogyro. He stopped and turned back to look at her in annoyance.

"Grandpa," she added with a grin.

"No, I get it."

He tossed her the tool bag, and she caught it with a heavy clatter of the tools inside. She slung it over her shoulder, and then they both set off for the antenna.

Crane was struck by the quiet here. There was the faint rustle of the hot breeze through the patchy grass, but nothing else. He listened but couldn't even hear a bird cry. A snake startled as they approached, and took off across the sandy ground, and Crane could actually hear it moving.

"Peaceful at least," said Jessie.

Crane nodded toward the ruins of the house off to their left. The roof had fallen in, and sand had collected against one side and drifted around the corners. Wind-blasted boards stuck up like the ribs of a wrecked ship.

"That's because nobody can live out here," he said. "It's like being on the moon."

The transceiver was in a scarred metal box bolted to the base of the antenna mast. A transformer took power from a small bank of solar panels positioned low against the ground a few yards away.

Jessie was already logging their map coordinates. She'd brought a lengthy checklist of information they needed to collect to give Josh's team everything they needed to understand how the system worked and then convincingly sabotage it. He and Jessie were to record radio signal graphs, map the surrounding area, and take extensive pictures of the unit's components, including any part numbers or other identification. It was going to take a while.

One of the cameras was a small action camera to record video of the entire operation. Crane clipped it to his shirt.

"Ready to record," he said. "Can you try not to troll me on camera? I have to work with these people."

"I'll do my best," she said. "But it is a lot of fun. And you make it so easy."

Crane rolled his eyes and hit record.

The box was sealed against water and windblown sand by a black rubber gasket, and locked with what Crane assumed was a three-point lock. He took his picks from his pocket. "You want to do the honors?"

Jessie took the picks and quickly opened the lock. She opened the door to reveal a stack of circuit boards, power supplies, cooling fans, and a nest of cabling.

They got to work.

CHAPTER 22

Palo Alto, California

The architects who designed what was now the Myria Group building had, at some point, painted themselves into an architectural corner. Caught between their clients' demands for special features and the requirements of the California Building Standards Code, they had finally thrown their hands in the air and left a large, irregularly shaped chunk of dead space in the center of the building's sixth floor. It had no windows and only one door at the end of a narrow hallway that went nowhere else. It was spectacularly unsuited for any normal purpose—until Georges Benly Akema had stumbled across it one day and claimed it as his workshop.

Georges was a computing and electronics prodigy from Cameroon whom Josh had discovered working as a busboy in an Indian restaurant down the street. When he learned that Georges had used discarded PCs and hand-coded software to make his own smaller version of the supercomputing architecture he'd used to predict stock fluctuations, he'd snapped him up immediately. He took it as just one more example of the kinds of talent that tended to wash up in Silicon Valley in one way or another.

Georges had a desk in the war room like the rest of the team, but he spent most of his time in his private playground, tinkering with gadgetry and working on odd ideas. All too often, he became so engaged in his work that he didn't notice his phone ringing, and so Josh would have to go downstairs and find him, as he was doing now. It was worth it, Josh thought, given the number of Georges' creations that ended up going out into the field with John Crane.

Josh traded greetings with someone from the marketing department as they passed in a gallery with tall windows looking out over the lake. Then he turned down the long, empty hallway that led back into the center of the building. The hallway ran for more than a hundred feet, passing nothing at all. Josh hummed the theme from *Get Smart* as he walked. Finally, it ended at a heavy, olive-colored metal door with no markings. There was nothing here but a badge reader beside the door-frame. Josh swiped his badge and let himself in.

Georges' lair was an overstuffed labyrinth of old computers, machine parts, server racks, a 3D printer, and other things even Josh didn't recognize. Between the odd shape of the room and the placement of shelves and storage bins, Josh had to navigate by ear. Tinny music came from somewhere, a man rapping in French over brassy reggae.

Josh followed the sound and finally found Georges standing in front of a rolling whiteboard taped up with the photos of the cartel transceiver that Crane and Jessie had sent back. The music came from a huge vintage boom box that looked like it had been through a war. He could see Georges rapping along under his breath.

"Who's this?" he said, and Georges started in surprise.

"Ah, good afternoon, sir," he said in his lilting accent. Then he smiled. "Didier Awadi, from Senegal. Good stuff, yeah?"

There was a moment of distortion as one of the boom box's speakers briefly fritzed. "You know, we can get you a decent sound system in here," said Josh.

Georges smiled. "I tried that. Very nice Bluetooth speakers. They sounded too good. It wasn't right. I had to send them back and dig this thing up on eBay." He leaned over and turned down the volume. "So how's the plate reader working?"

"Working fine," Josh replied. "Downloaded a new batch of numbers this morning, and João's running them through DMV." He gestured toward the whiteboard. "You got anything on this?"

"Yeah," Georges said, "yeah. It's odd." He pointed out photos of circuit boards that Crane had taken and block diagrams he'd drawn himself to figure out how the transceiver worked. "You can buy a unit off the shelf to do this, you know. Tested and design optimized, burned in, and ready to install," he explained. "But they didn't do that. They cobbled it together out of parts that don't really want to work together. Right here, these two boards don't even agree on clock speed. They would have had to hand code some custom middleware just to get them to talk to each other."

Georges was impressed. Josh could hear it in his voice.

It's the kind of stuff he used to build himself back in Cameroon, when he had to scrounge whatever parts he could find and improvise. But he did that because he didn't have any money. That's no problem for these guys. Why didn't they just buy a box?

"There any technical reason to do it this way?"

Georges shrugged. "Not that I can think of. It must have been a real pain to debug."

"There's got to be some reason that makes sense to a cartel," said Josh. "Maybe the market for equipment like this is small enough that people watch it. Maybe if you buy a bunch of them off the shelf and you're not a telephone company, somebody takes notice. Is there a believable way to break it?"

"Oh sure," said Georges, as if that was a foregone conclusion and the only interesting question was how he'd done it. "Breaking it's no problem, believe me. But getting a signal back out to us is going to be tricky." He pointed out elements on his block diagram.

"There's a software-defined radio, controlled from an embedded processor, here, so that's no problem. But look at this radiation plot."

Josh wasn't especially well versed in radio electronics, but he could see that the transceiver's antenna was extremely directional. It was a point-to-point link, after all. By focusing all its energy in one narrow beam, it was able to transmit more effectively at lower power, and was also harder to detect and intercept. But that also made it more difficult for them to hijack the system and send their own signals out.

"I've got an idea," Georges said after letting it sink in for a moment. "But it's going to mean putting our own hardware out in the field to pick up low-power transmissions and relay them back. It'll mean more work for Crane and Ms. Diamond."

"Eh, they're used to that. When can you have it ready?"

Georges considered this for a moment, and then said, "Tomorrow morning?"

Josh nodded. "Good, let's get it done."

He left Georges happily noodling around with circuit models, and headed back upstairs. When he reached the war room, he discovered Perry Holland busily rebuilding the climbing wall. As Josh entered, he was ten feet up, limbs splayed across the wall, screwing a chunk of blue rubber into a hole with his free hand.

"Is that really necessary, Perry?" he asked.

"I have to move to think," Perry called back. "It's meditative, opens up the imagination and the intuitive faculties. You should try it!"

"Yeah, I'm not going to do that."

Across the room, he noticed João in a huddle with Don Finney and Laura Berdoza. Berdoza glanced over at him, and then they pulled closer together and argued in hushed whispers. Josh decided they looked like people who had something to tell him. He walked over to their table.

"Good news?"

They all stood, traded looks, and turned to face him. "Yes ... some of that," João said after a moment's hesitation, "and some bad news too."

Josh sighed. "Give me that first."

"The business card Crane sent up is another dead end," said Berdoza. "So far, at least. The company exists, but it's like all the others. You try to figure out who owns it, and you're in quicksand again. Trusts, holding companies, trusts holding holding companies. These guys are really good at hiding."

Josh could hear the frustration in her voice. "What about the phone number?"

"Goes to an automated conference bridge," said João. "They're using it like a proxy server. You dial in, and it completes a call to them and hooks you together, but you don't know where you're really calling. They could be in Siberia. And that's only if the bridge likes you. It didn't like us."

"What do you mean?" asked Josh.

"I assume the bridge checks your number against a whitelist before it connects. Call from an unapproved phone, and you just get kicked out."

"That's what happened when we tried calling them," Berdoza interjected.

"Now I can try hacking the bridge," said João. "I'm not ready to give up. But I haven't had time yet. I've been focusing on the good news."

"Well, don't be shy," said Josh. "What have you got?"

"Numbers from the plate reader at the hospital," João explained. As they'd expected, most of the plates traced to local addresses, usually apartments. They belonged to hospital staffers, and Marin County wasn't cheap. A couple belonged to doctors, but there was nothing suspicious about any of them.

"But there was one this morning that isn't registered to a person at all," João said. "It's a Cadillac CTS registered to a Rockridge Medical Group. I figured it's some guy with an incorporated practice, and he has it buy his car for the taxes. But I tried to figure out who it was, and this Rockridge has no website, no listed phone number, no public presence at all. That's when I brought it to Don and Laura."

"We tracked down their articles of organization with the Secretary of State's office," said Berdoza. "They have the same registered agent and official address as another company called Firesta. Firesta is a limited partnership that funds medical and pharmaceutical research. Among its partners of record is an investment trust called KMAC Strategies."

Josh had brought the team in precisely so he wouldn't have to figure out things like this. "Where is this chain taking us?" he asked.

Finney stepped in. "Alexander Tate's trustees have sold significant assets to KMAC in the last two years. Three months ago, KMAC loaned Tate twenty-five million dollars with other Tate assets listed as collateral. The people we're trying to track down, whomever they may be, are connected to a very shadowy medical research group that appears to be providing medical care to Alexander Tate at Fallon Landing."

"We still can't identify them," said Berdoza, "but we can identify the doctor."

"How?" Josh asked.

João grinned. He picked up an iPad and opened a window. "Five months ago, the Cadillac got pulled over in San Rafael for failure to stop. Ticket was issued to a Vincent Dabrowski."

He flipped to another tab. "Doctor Vincent Dabrowski, age forty-two, graduate Duke Medical School." And another tab. "Address in Bel Marin Keys."

Josh let it sink in. It all added up. It was too much of a coincidence that a doctor at Fallon Landing would be connected to the same shadowy circle of holding companies and blind partnerships that had ensnared Alex's financial empire. This Dabrowski had to be Alex's doctor. Even if he could tell them nothing about the legal and financial labyrinth they were trying to untangle, at least he could provide information about Alex's medical condition.

"Good," he said quietly. "Very good, all of you. That's excellent work."

I just want to tell you both good luck. We're all counting on you.

He turned and started walking slowly over to his own desk.

"So we'll keep chasing it down?" Berdoza said, uncertainty in her voice.

"Absolutely," Josh answered. But his mind was already racing ahead to grapple with the equally thorny question of what to do with the knowledge now that he had it.

CHAPTER 23

"I don't think this airstrip's seen this much traffic in years," said Crane.

Jessie made a vague sound of acknowledgement. "You should set up a B&B."

They were sitting in her Raptor with the engine on and the AC running, parked beside Jessie's Short 330. Ahead of them, a small plane descended. It touched down and taxied to a stop on the parking area.

Georges Benly Akema climbed out and slung a canvas satchel over his shoulder. He shielded his eyes against the glaring sun as Crane and Jessie came to meet him.

"Georges! It's good to see you again," said Crane. "Have you met Jessie Diamond?"

"I've not," said Georges, and offered her his hand. "A pleasure, Ms. Diamond."

While they made polite small talk, the pilot removed a wheeled road case from the cargo compartment and rolled it over. Crane had been expecting something smaller.

"Okay, here's the job," Georges said. He opened his satchel and showed them a photo Crane had taken of the interior of the transceiver. It showed several circuit boards stacked like dominos beside a row of status lights. One of the boards was circled in red marker.

"This is the board you're looking for," he said. "It's socketed into the bus. No problem. Just pull it out." He pointed out one of the status lights. "This light will go out."

Then he took another circuit board wrapped in anti-static cloth from his bag and handed it to Crane. "Then you just plug this one in. When it's seated properly, the light will come back on. That's it."

"Then what happens?" Jessie asked.

"The transceiver will start to randomly fail," said Georges. "We're hoping the cartel will come get it and take it to their kidnapped engineers to be fixed. Any decent technician will trace the problem right away to this board and this chip. When they dump the ROM, they'll find a message from us. It tells them to reprogram the radio to send their location on a particular frequency every night at midnight."

"You make it sound simple," said Crane. "There's a lot that can go wrong there."

Georges acknowledged the point. "If it doesn't work, we try something else."

Jessie nodded toward the case. "I'm thinking there's more to this."

"I'm afraid so," said Georges. "That antenna's very directional. To send the location, it's going to have to transmit omnidirectional at pretty low power. So we'll need our own receiver pretty close by to pick up their signal and relay it back."

Georges opened the case. Nestled in the foam were a box and a small dish antenna. Inside the top was a topographic map of the area with marked points and notes in thick red ink.

"We need you to install it here," Georges said, pointing out a spot on the map. "A little over half a mile away. Close enough to pick up the signal, far enough so they won't spot it."

"No solar panels?" said Jessie.

Georges shook his head. "Internal power cell. It will wake up each night at midnight, listen for a signal, and then go back to sleep. It'll last for weeks, if it has to. Let me walk you through the setup process."

After Georges' plane was airborne and headed north again, Crane and Jessie sat in her truck with the replacement circuit board in the center console and the black case with the relay in the bed.

"Was really hoping we could just fly back out and get this done," said Jessie.

But they clearly couldn't carry the relay in the autogyro. They were going to have to drive it out to the site. They stopped in town to top off the gas and pick up some bottled water. Then they headed back out of town on the main highway. The first ten miles or so were paved. But then the pavement gave way to packed dirt that followed the contours of the landscape with no fills. The truck rattled and bounced over the washboarded surface until Crane began to reconsider the autogyro.

They rode through a landscape of rocky hillsides, scrub trees and cacti, and salt flats. Occasionally they passed a windblown house or a dirt road leading back to some remote farm. They passed the time trading bad jokes and recommending decent restaurants in various foreign cities. Crane was telling Jessie about his favorite barbecue place in Peshawar when her GPS pinged, and she veered off the road into the desert. The Raptor bounced through a dry stream bed and climbed the slope on the far side, throwing up dirt. Jessie powered up the hillside and stopped at the top of the low ridge.

According to Georges' map, this was where they were meant to set up their relay. They got out, and Jessie swept the hills with a pair of binoculars. "There's the other one," she announced. She handed Crane the binoculars, and he found the cartel transceiver on the next ridge about a half mile away.

Crane hefted the case out of the back of the truck, and they placed the relay and its antenna amid some clumps of dried brown grass. Packed beneath it in the case was a square of netting with what looked like tufts of grass and brown foliage woven into it. It looked like a tiny ghillie suit. They draped it over the relay, and from twenty feet away, it was practically invisible. Crane decided it would do.

Now all that remained was to install the board in the cartel's transceiver. Crane and Jessie both looked across the ridge at the antenna. "We shouldn't drive over," said Jessie. "We don't want to leave tracks."

Crane agreed, so they set off on foot across the narrow basin and up the far slope. When they reached the transceiver, Crane picked the cabinet lock. They found the right board and pulled it out of its socket. Then Jessie installed the new board, and the status light came back on. They locked the cabinet and cleaned the site.

"Well, that really was simple," said Jessie as they walked back to the truck.

"Now we see if it works," Crane answered. "Let's get back to town, and I'll buy us a couple Pacificos."

As they drove back to Bahia Tortugas, Crane sat back in his seat and glanced over at Jessie from time to time. She was beautiful—there was no denying that. He was especially taken by the way a loose tendril of hair curled around her ear and the way she bit her lip when she was thinking. But even so, he knew things weren't going to go beyond the odd bit of flirting they'd been doing. Even that wasn't with intent. It was as if they flirted with each other precisely to tell each other that they both got that that was all it meant.

Crane had had platonic friendships with women before; it wasn't as though he couldn't grasp the concept. But this was different somehow. He wasn't quite sure what to make of it.

He was still thinking about it when he spotted a black open-topped Jeep parked beside the road on top of the next rise. A figure was standing up in the back, leaning on the rollbar, and scanning the road with binoculars.

"Birdwatchers?" said Jessie.

"Yeah, that's probably it," Crane said. He took the MHS pistol from his belt and set it in his lap.

They flew past the Jeep, and Crane saw two more men in the front seats, and the driver starting up the engine. The Jeep kicked up dust as it wheeled around onto the road and came up fast behind them.

"Okay, not birdwatchers," said Jessie. She floored it, and the Raptor jumped as if kicked.

But the Jeep was still closing. It came up behind them and rammed the Raptor's rear bumper. Jessie swore and pushed the truck faster. Then Crane heard the crack of gunfire, and bullets ricocheted off the bed and tailgate. One hit the rear window with a loud whack that left a white impact scar on the bullet-resistant glass.

The Raptor's rear window couldn't be opened, and Crane couldn't get a shot at the Jeep out his door window. The only way he could return fire was to pull himself up and out of the window to sit on the doorframe and fire over the roof. And he had no intention of trying that at ninety miles an hour the way the truck was bouncing around on this terrible road.

He looked out the back again and saw nothing but the cloud

of dust they were kicking up. Then the Jeep materialized out of it, right on their bumper, and slammed them forward again. Jessie fought to keep control of the Raptor. They pulled ahead, and the Jeep was lost in the dust cloud again.

It can't be very pleasant driving through that, Crane thought. *Especially in an open vehicle.* Then the Jeep appeared out of the dust on Jessie's side. Crane saw a figure in the passenger seat, hanging on to the windshield frame. The one standing in the rear had the gun, some kind of automatic rifle. He wore goggles and a bandanna around his mouth and nose.

Jessie lowered her window as the Jeep came up on her side. "Give me that!" she shouted over the wind and engine noise, and she grabbed Crane's pistol.

"I thought you had a gun!" Crane shouted back.

"Can't really get to it and drive the truck!" Jessie answered. "Here. Use this." She hit a switch under the dash, and a drawer slid out from beneath his seat. He looked down and saw a Tavor CTAR-21 rifle nestled in gray foam.

"You drive around with an Israeli military assault rifle under the seat?" Crane said.

"In situations like this, I find some of my passengers like to actually shoot back!" she snapped.

"Okay, okay." Crane grabbed the bullpup weapon and turned around in his seat just as the gunner in the Jeep opened up and the rear window splintered and cracked. Jessie held the wheel in one hand and fired the MHS out the window with the other.

Crane punched out the shattered safety glass with the muzzle, and as the Jeep reappeared through the dust, he opened up with a long burst. His shots went wild as the truck bounced, but he put a couple rounds into the hood and a couple more into the windshield. The Jeep veered off and fell back.

"Where are they?" Jessie said as she steered back and forth across the road to keep them from pulling alongside.

All Crane could see behind them was the roiling dust. "I don't have them!"

She turned to take quick glances over her shoulder as Crane peered through the dust, looking for the Jeep's boxy outline.

Then he heard Jessie shout, "Shit!" and whirled around. Directly ahead of them was the afternoon bus to Vizcaino. It filled the windshield as they bore down on it at nearly a hundred miles an hour. Jessie was crossing directly into its path; there was no going back. Instead she hit the gas and sped off the side of the road.

"Brace, brace, brace!" she shouted as they soared off the edge of a small, rock-strewn arroyo. The Raptor's nose hit the dirt, and the skid plate slammed against a rock with a jarring impact. Crane was thrown forward, and then the seatbelt locked and he stopped hard. Somehow Jessie more or less kept control of the truck as they bounced over the arroyo's far bank into sandy ground. She spun the wheel and brought the Raptor around as she braked to a stop.

Now Crane pulled himself up through the window and sat on the doorframe. Just as he got into position, he saw the Jeep come off the road after them and sail off the edge of the arroyo. It hit hard and bounced on its large tires. The man standing in back was thrown clear. Crane saw him tumble away and disappear into the Jeep's dust plume. Crane steadied himself on the roof and drew a bead on the Jeep's windshield.

The Jeep was up on two wheels as Crane opened up with the Tavor and blew the windshield into a million fragments of safety glass. Steam erupted from the engine. The Jeep careened in an arc and rolled, tumbling toward them. It rolled over twice, finally coming to rest on its side next to a large cardon cactus. Crane watched the Jeep for movement, but saw none. He scanned the ground near where the third man had been thrown free and saw a dark pant leg and boot lying among the rocks. It wasn't moving, either.

Crane slid back down, and they got out of the truck. Crane checked the Jeep while Jessie drew her own pistol and went to check on the third man. Both men in the Jeep were dead. Crane checked their wallets and found cash but no identification. There was no registration in the Jeep's glove compartment. The license plate was probably fake. These were cartel soldiers.

Jessie returned and shook her head. "Friends of yours?" she asked.

"Friends of the guy whose boat I blew up, I expect."

They stood there for a moment, the silence overwhelming after the chaos and noise. The bus was long gone; the driver and passengers wanted nothing to do with whatever was happening behind them.

He'd wanted a reaction, and he'd gotten one.

"I guess we'd better sleep with one eye open," said Jessie.

CHAPTER 24

Among the many changes his exile had brought to Jason Tate's life was a change in hobbies. Here, in the middle of nowhere, he had discovered a strong interest in off-road racing. He'd even put a significant amount of money into building a rally truck and hoped to drive it in the Baja 1000. It was a surprisingly effective way of dealing with stress when he was bored, frustrated, or angry.

Today it was frustration that had put him behind the wheel. There was still no news on John Crane, the man who had sunk his yacht. The cartel had promised action, but so far had delivered nothing. They weren't the brightest people, the cartel's thugs. They earned their fearsome reputations through ruthless brutality, not by their cunning or wit. But what had happened to the *Gypsy* was a humiliation, to him and, by extension, to the cartel itself. He'd expected them to at least understand that and take the matter more seriously.

So today he had taken the truck out and torn his way across the desert for much of the afternoon. Now, strapped into a four-point racing harness, he drifted the truck around a tight curve in the road back to his hacienda. He checked the digital stopwatch clamped to the dash and smiled. He was almost three seconds ahead of his best time up the road. Now he just had to keep it up.

Tate didn't like his line through the last turn, but he floored it and sped through the open gate. The photocells tripped, his stopwatch beeped, and the Tag Heuer display showed he'd set a new personal best by just under two seconds.

He slapped the steering wheel in triumph and sped past the engineering compound in a cloud of dust. He pulled up at the garage, left the truck in the hands of his mechanic, and headed into the main house.

As he entered the main foyer, one of the servants was waiting with a phone handset on a silver tray. Tate took it. So he'd kept them waiting. Good. Let them wait a little longer. They'd kept him waiting long enough.

He carried the phone through the house to his game room and shut the heavy studded oak doors behind him. The room was the color of sand, with exposed dark wooden beams. Tate's gun case was near the doors, and hunting trophies lined the walls. Per his standing order, there was a glass of tequila waiting on the pool table. Tate knocked it back with his free hand and set the empty glass down on the red felt. He picked up a ball and rolled it the length of the table until it bounced off the far bumper. Then, and only then, he tapped a button on the handset.

"I'm here," he said. "What can you tell me?"

"Nothing good," said the voice. It wasn't Lalo, but one of his underlings. A bad sign. "There was a fight on the highway in Baja. Three of our men are dead."

Tate sighed. They did nothing for days, and then they screwed it up.

"What do you know about this man?" the voice asked. "Who is he?"

"A private detective. He's nothing. What is the damn problem here? Get some guys who aren't idiots—you do have some of those, right? And bring the son of a bitch to me."

"There's been a change of plan," said the voice. "Orders from the top. This vendetta is not doing anybody any good. Whatever your problem with this man is, you need to let it go and move on."

Tate's intake of breath was sudden and sharp. "Move on? Move on? What the hell? I'll move on when the son of a bitch is dead. Just because you can't deliver."

"This is a personal thing between the two of you. It has nothing to do with us. Unless there's something you're not telling us. Is this perhaps a matter your other friends could take care of?"

Tate fumed and swore, but the man at the other end said nothing. He simply listened, and Tate realized he wasn't going to change their minds on this. All he was doing was humiliating himself.

After he hung up, he saw the glass on the pool table, snatched it up, and flung it across the room. It shattered against the wall, and Tate followed it with a hurled cue ball. Then he turned away, breathing hard and pacing about the room with nervous bursts of energy.

Who the hell was John Crane?

The man had gone through Arturo and Juan Manuel to sink the *Gypsy*. Then there had been the motorcycle chase through Bahia Tortugas. And now this. Tate didn't like it. This didn't sound like some bottom-feeding private detective eking out a living tracking down straying husbands and runaway rich kids. Not after all that.

Maybe it was a matter for his other friends after all. Whomever Crane really was, he was no match for Turnstone.

He waved off the servant who hurried in in response to the noise. She went back out and closed the door behind her, and Tate retrieved a fresh glass from the bar and poured himself another tequila. He didn't like calling them, especially with his hat in his hand like this. He knew instinctually that it was a bad idea to show them weakness. If they did something for him, it should be as payment, not a favor.

But there were things they wanted from him. He could let them have something. He'd been ignoring a call from his contact there for some time now. But now, perhaps it was worth doing.

Tate took his phone from his pocket and called up a photo of John Crane that Arturo and Juan Manuel had taken in Bahia Tortugas. He was coming out of La Playa, taking his sunglasses from the placket of his shirt and raising them to his face. It was a clear shot.

He downed the tequila he'd poured and then called up the keypad and dialed a number before he could change his mind. It was a long number with prefixes that didn't conform to the Mexican numbering system, the North American Numbering Plan, or standard international formats. It was a number that should have gone to an intercept telling him to hang up and try his call again. But it didn't. It rang exactly twice, and then was picked up.

"May I help you?" said a pleasant female voice.

"This is Jason Tate," he said. "I'm returning a call from Mr. Keating."

"Of course, sir. Please hold."

He heard faint signaling tones for a few seconds, and then, "Good evening, Jason. It's good to hear from you. Is everything all right? I was worried."

"Of course, of course. I'm fine. All's well here. I'm sorry I didn't get your message earlier. I've been unreachable for some days. My staff alerted me as soon as I returned."

"Well, I'm glad it was nothing more serious."

Tate laughed politely. "No, no. Your message mentioned you were interested in a meeting with Lalo. Of course I can arrange that for you. Is this a meeting Turnstone will be attending personally?"

The man he knew only as Keating was silent for a long moment, and Tate worried he'd misstepped. But then Keating said, "Someone will need to take that meeting for him. But I know he will appreciate your introduction. Your contacts with the cartel are proving valuable. Shall I make the usual payment to your account?"

"What? Oh, no, no. This is nothing. It's really no trouble for me at all." He paused for a moment and then added, as if it were an afterthought, "I suppose there is one thing you could do for me, if you've a moment."

"Of course," said Keating. "And what is that?"

"I'm going to send you some pictures of a man I ran across in Bahia Tortugas. I was wondering if he's known to you, and what you can tell me about him. He claims he's a private detective named John Crane."

Josh had been at Myria late last night. It had been nearly two in the morning by the time he'd gotten home to grab some sleep. But Josh was used to being up all night in a blaze of creative energy on one project or another. This was like being back in college.

Except for the money, of course. That changes pretty much everything.

He arrived back at Myria before nine. He had meetings for most of the morning, but his first stop was Georges' hidden lab. There was no music, he noticed when he let himself in this time. The place was quiet. Most of the lights were off.

Josh made his way through the racks of equipment, following the lights, and found himself in a back corner where Georges sat on a metal stool with a tall cup of coffee. A heavily modified espresso machine sat nearby, and his ThinkPad X1 Carbon was open on the table beside it as he studied his RSS feeds.

"Morning," Josh said as it became clear Georges hadn't heard him approach. Georges turned rather sluggishly and nearly spilled his coffee.

"Oh, hi, Josh. Good morning."

"I've got people waiting," Josh said, "but I wanted to check in and see if we got anything last night."

Georges' face lit up as he put the coffee down and his fingers flew across the ThinkPad's keys. "You're going to love this."

The speakers played a few seconds of static, and then the distant tones of a modulated signal. It was a lonely, mournful sound, the digital age equivalent of a train whistle in the night.

"Came on at 11:58 last night. Repeated this signal for four minutes, and then went dark again."

Josh's heart raced. This was it. They had them!

"Does it parse? Can we read it?"

"Oh yes," said Georges. "It decodes just fine."

Holy hell, it actually worked.

Josh let out a breath, and then he held out his palm for a high five.

"What does that make us?"

"Big damn heroes, sir," Georges said, and they slapped palms.

He finally got that right. This is a day of many great achievements.

Josh tapped his watch and called his office. "Cancel my meetings," he said. "I didn't want to sit through them, anyway. And I need you to call some people. Get them here as soon as they can make it."

CHAPTER 25

Josh waited in the war room, in a far corner where he had left the lights off. He sat back in a swivel desk chair with his feet up on an empty bookcase. On the far side of the room, there was light and a bustle of activity. He could hear Laura Berdoza on the phone, trying to social engineer her way past receptionists and records clerks. She'd been at it for a while, and Josh could tell that she was good. But it wasn't getting her much. Apparently what they were looking for was just too sensitive. Whoever had their hooks in the Tate finances was covering their tracks very well.

If you're bogged down on the eastern front, attack from the west.

Josh tapped his watch. "Tim, I'm in the war room. Can you join me, please?"

By unspoken agreement, Tim tended to give Josh a little more space at Myria on the grounds that he was safer on his own turf. But Tim's badge would get him into the war room, and he'd been here before.

He arrived within a couple minutes, nodded to the rest of the team, and joined Josh in his dim corner.

"I have to ask you a favor," Josh began, "and I feel a little awkward about it."

"Not at all," said Tim. "What do you need?"

"The meetings I cancelled today, some of them were real, most of them weren't. I intended to do something with that time, and I was going to take you with me because, based on past experience, I didn't think you'd let me go without you."

Tim looked taken aback, but only for a moment. "This is about the doctor? In Bel Marin Keys?"

"Yeah," Josh admitted. "Dabrowski." The casualness of his position suddenly struck him as disrespectful under the circumstances. He took his feet down from the bookshelf and turned to face Tim. "I was going to go out to Bel Marin Keys and see what I could find out. But something important's come up. I have to be here."

"So you want me to go," said Tim. He paused for a moment.

Well, this is a test of your budding friendship, isn't it? Hey, you want to go risk jail for me while I stay here and have a meeting?

"Yeah, I can do that," said Tim.

Josh sighed. "Before you answer, I'm not asking you to drive by and see if the lights are on. Some of this will be illegal."

Tim smiled. "If I do this right, it sounds like there's going to be at least some breaking and entering."

"Thank you, Tim. I mean it." He gestured to the team working across the room. "We need to know all there is to know about this guy. We're spinning our wheels here, and I feel like time's slipping away from us."

"What's the plan?"

"Take the Mercedes up there. It's a gated community, but you're on the visitor's list for today."

Tim huffed in surprise. "How'd you handle that?"

"João did it. The plate's on their list, under the name Noah Spenser."

Josh bent down and retrieved a leather satchel from the bottom shelf of the bookcase. "Georges pulled together some gear for me. It's the same stuff we give Crane. GPS tracer, goes on the underside of the Cadillac, if you can find it. Lockpick gun. Camera—leave your phone here, by the way. If you find a computer, just power it up. You don't need a login. Just plug this into a USB port to download a drive image and leave some malware behind."

Tim let out a low whistle. "The rich really are different."

"Most important thing, don't get arrested. I already feel bad about sending you."

"Piece of cake," said Tim.

They sorted a few final details. As Josh watched Tim walk away across the war room, he hoped he wasn't making a mistake someone else would have to pay for.

Among the toys Josh had sent down with Jessie Diamond was a radio bug that listened to the relay they'd planted in the desert. The previous night, just before midnight, it had started to blink. That meant it had picked up a transmission from the relay. Crane had switched on the audio and listened to its plaintive wail through the static. Then he'd knocked on Jessie's door and let her hear it. An hour later, they were flying north in Jessie's Short. After some sleep, and a shower and breakfast, Crane arrived at Myria just before eleven.

Entering the war room, Crane saw Josh had been busy since the last time he'd been here. There were more desks, with more computers, and several large flat-screen monitors on the wall. On one side were four people Crane took to be Josh's new support team. Josh was at the far end of the room, talking to Georges. Then the door opened behind him, and Jessie entered with a middle-aged man in a suit with cowboy boots and a bolo tie. Jessie introduced him as Sawyer Cottrell. When they joined Josh and Georges, there was another round of introductions.

"You found them?" Cottrell asked. Crane thought he looked like he hadn't slept well.

"We have," said Josh. "Georges has pulled the data. I wanted all of you to hear it so we can decide what to do next."

"It says there are six of them," said Georges.

"Is my son there?" Cottrell asked.

"I'm sorry, it doesn't give any names," Josh answered, and Crane watched Cottrell's face fall. "It just says six men."

Georges typed a command, and a wall screen flickered to life with a map of Mexico. A pulsing dot appeared on the mainland, near what looked like the middle of the country.

"There are the coordinates," said Josh. "It's in the state of Durango, in the Sierra Madre Occidental mountains. It's remote. Nearest town is Santa Catarina de Tepehuanes, over here."

The satellite view zoomed in, and Crane made out the town to the southeast of the marker. It kept zooming in on what looked like empty wooded mountains until it framed a compound on a mountain ridge. Crane saw walls and several detached structures. There were two gravel roads out of the compound. One twisted its way down through the mountains for several miles until it reached a paved highway. The other ran across the ridge for what looked like about three miles to an airstrip with several low buildings clustered at one end. They might be hangars or warehouses. *Either way*, Crane thought, *there are more than one would expect at a remote dirt airstrip in the middle of nowhere.* It looked like a cartel shipping depot.

"That's the place," said Josh. He grabbed a laser pointer and picked out a building in a far corner, surrounded by a wall of its own. "The message says they're being held here. It's a workshop with a basement where they live. Other than that, you've got the main hacienda here. What looks like a big garage, a couple outbuildings."

"Closest airport in the States looks like El Paso," said Jessie.

Georges' fingers flew across the keys, and another marker appeared at El Paso. The compound was almost dead south of it.

"How far please, Georges?" Jessie added.

He traced a line connecting the dots. "Just shy of four hundred and fifty miles."

"Good," she said. "Good. We'll fly out of there. The Short can make that and back on full tanks with a couple hundred miles of reserve."

When they started talking details, Crane tuned them out and studied the imagery. They'd have to land at the airstrip, obviously. If he was right, and some of those buildings were drug warehouses, he had to assume they'd be guarded. That would mean they'd be hitting cartel resistance as soon as they landed. There would be no surprise. Once they had secured the airstrip, they'd have to move overland some three miles to the hacienda and free the hostages. That part actually looked pretty straightforward. But then they'd have to get half a dozen civilians back across three miles of rough country to the airstrip. If they were lucky, there would be a vehicle they could commandeer to get them to the plane quickly and keep them contained.

It would be better if we could take the airstrip last, he thought. Parachute the team in somewhere along those slopes to the east, extract the hostages, and then secure the airstrip and call in Jessie to pick them up. He might recommend that, but right now he didn't know how long Jessie would be able to remain in the air, or whether Cottrell's team of mercenaries was trained to parachute into mountainous terrain.

It could be done, he decided, but there were challenges. And he'd want considerably better intelligence about the place than Google Earth.

The others' voices were rising, and Crane realized there was an argument going on.

" ... know why you're making all the damn decisions all of a sudden!" Cottrell snapped at Josh. Josh's body language was defensive. He and Cottrell were in each other's space, and Cottrell was clearly angry.

"I've been working on this for eight months! It's my son in there!" He turned to Crane. "It's nothing personal, but I don't know you, Mr. Crane. I'm not going to send some stranger in, guns blazing, and hope you can pull him out. I'm going with people I know."

"Come off it!" Josh shouted back. "You've been on this for eight months, and you didn't get jack. We're on board less than a week and boom! If it wasn't for me, you'd still be sniffing around Cabo!"

"Shut up!" Jessie snapped. "Both of you. This is no time for a pissing contest."

They both stopped short and looked at her in surprise. Crane smiled to himself.

"Josh, a little compassion, please," Jessie went on. Crane noted that Josh had the good grace to look a little ashamed of himself. "Sawyer, we know what's at stake, all right? Nobody's questioning that. But that doesn't mean you're qualified to plan a rescue mission. I am. And it's my plane, so John's coming with us, or else your team can walk in."

Sawyer stepped back and sighed. "Okay, yeah. I know. It's just ... that message. There's no way he would have let it go out without something, just to tell me he was there and he was okay, and he was waiting for me to bring him home."

Sawyer was about to break down, Crane realized.

"If he's there, we'll get him out," said Jessie. "We need better intel and some time to plan a mission. How long will it take to get your team together?"

"A few days," said Cottrell. "I'll have to call them. They've been waiting around a long time now." *Now he sounds defeated*, Crane thought. *Going through the motions because he's decided that his son isn't there.* Crane had no idea what the truth was. He'd been taught to prepare for contingencies, but also to assume everything was going according to plan until he knew it wasn't.

"Start making calls," said Crane. "We'll put together a mission brief."

Cottrell closed his eyes and nodded. "Sure. Yeah. I'll do that."

Crane saw Jessie give Josh a look, and Josh put a hand on Cottrell's arm. "Come on," he said, "let's go to my office. We can start pulling your team together, and you look like you could use a drink."

He guided Cottrell toward the doors. Then Georges zoomed the satellite image in to the closest view of the compound the resolution would support, and they got to work.

CHAPTER 26

Palo Alto Airport

A helicopter brought Josh back across the bay from Hayward, where he kept his Gulfstream. It was annoying, but Hayward was a former army airfield and had a runway long enough for the jet to take off, whereas Palo Alto did not. He was returning from Hayward because he'd taken Sawyer Cottrell there and had his standby pilots take Sawyer back to El Paso. Sawyer needed to assemble the team of mercenaries who would be conducting the rescue mission, and El Paso was to be the staging area. Sawyer was on his way now, and Josh could return his attention to other things.

The helicopter brought him in and landed near a hangar in the general aviation area. Josh's Mercedes was waiting for him as he thanked the pilot and climbed out.

As he hurried over to the waiting car, he realized Tim was there, back from his mission to Bel Marin Keys. That was unexpected. He'd assumed Tim wouldn't be back until well after dark.

Tim opened the door for him and then got in front.

He looks like his doctor just gave him a week to live. Something went wrong.

"Everything okay, Tim? What happened?"

"Nothing," said Tim. "It was a dead end." He started the car and headed out of the airport.

"How so? What happened?"

"It was weird," said Tim. "I got through the gate just like you said. But after that, it went south real fast. The Cadillac wasn't there. That didn't surprise me. I figured he'd be at work. I was going to check the house, and then wait for him to get home, and tag the car."

Josh nodded. "Right."

"But when I got there, there were a couple white vans out front. Unmarked. And the front door was open. I thought, okay, if there's work crews, maybe I can get inside, talk to them, see what's going on."

Unmarked? Why aren't the vans marked? Plumbers, electricians, remodelers, all of them, the vans have names, logos, phone numbers, slogans. Who doesn't want to advertise that your neighbors hired them to work on their house?

"So I went in the front door, and there's nothing there. I mean no furniture, nothing. Turns out the workers are—"

"Crime scene cleaners," said Josh.

Tim stopped, startled. "Huh?"

"That's who shows up in a plain van."

"Okay," said Tim. "Well, you're right. They were washing the whole place down with solvents and bleach."

Good God, they're worried about leaving DNA behind? What are we up against here?

"I talked to the foreman," said Tim. "He said he'd been out to Bel Marin Keys twice before. Once for a messy suicide. The other time was an old lady who had a stroke and died on her kitchen floor and nobody found her for a couple weeks. This time, there was nothing. Everything had already been cleaned out. The place was ready to show. He had no idea what they were doing there."

Movers. Clean up. How long would it take to get that done? Track it back, when did they figure out we were on to their doctor?

"Did he say when they got the call?" Josh asked.

Tim shook his head. "Sorry, I didn't think to ask."

"That's all right," Josh muttered, sinking back into his seat in thought.

"They knew we were coming," said Tim.

"Yes, they did."

When isn't what matters. The real question is how did they know?

He spent the rest of the trip trying to come up with ways the people he was trying to unmask could have figured out that he had identified Dr. Dabrowski. But no matter how many angles he approached it from, there was only one answer that made any sense.

Someone told them. There's a leak in your team.

The next morning, Josh met with Don Finney and Laura Berdoza in his office. He didn't want to do it in the war room because Perry Holland was climbing the wall again, and he was in no mood for it. Josh hadn't slept well.

Of course not. You've got half a dozen people running this show and one of them's betraying you.

That's ... not confirmed.

Yeah, keep telling yourself that.

Josh was late because he kept finding ways to distract himself from his morning routine. He didn't want to do this. Especially after Tim's report last evening, he worried that he wasn't going to like what Finney and Berdoza had to say.

You're running out of cards to play, Ace.

Shut up. I liked it better when you were doing Mambo Number Five over and over again.

They were waiting in the outer office when he arrived. His secretary had gotten them coffee—tea in Berdoza's case—and they were reading the morning news on tablets. They stood as he came in.

"Good morning," he muttered. They replied in kind, overlapping one another.

Is one of them selling you out? How would you know?

"Come on back," he said.

Josh's office was a sprawling expanse of white marble, black leather, and frosted glass. Some very expensive interior designer had put it together for him. He used it to impress visitors, but otherwise spent little time here. He led them out to the balcony. He'd hauled some of the very expensive original Knoll Barcelona chairs out there and spent most of his time looking out over the grounds and the pond.

He sat down now and gestured to them to take the other chairs. Then he sat back and looked out across the pond and the trees. He said nothing. They said nothing. A duck took off from the surface of the pond with a splashing sound.

"It's a beautiful morning," Berdoza said at last.

Josh checked his watch. It had taken her a minute and twenty-three seconds to break the silence.

So what does that tell you? Is she the spy? Come on.

"The doctor was a dead end," he said. "We lost him. Out of leads to follow on the medical side. I'm really hoping for better news on the legal front, and I don't think I'm going to get it, am I?"

Finney stammered a bit, but Berdoza took the bait. "No," she said. "You're not."

Josh sighed. "All right, fill me in. What's the problem?"

"They've been at this for a while now," said Finney, apparently deciding to just charge ahead now that Berdoza had opened the way. "And from the looks of it, they've got a dozen different law firms working full time, filing registrations for s-corporations and real estate investment trusts and anything else they can think of."

"As soon as one exists, it starts trading assets, making negative amortization loans, and so on," Berdoza added. "When one's run its course, it folds up, or sells itself to another company that takes on their liabilities and transfers collateral to a creditor trust. It just keeps going."

"We can trace most of this," said Finney, "but it's hard, and it's time consuming."

"It's a structural problem," she said. "It's just easier and faster for them to build up layers of the onion than it is for us to peel them away. They've got a head start, and they can run faster. We're not going to catch them this way."

One of them couldn't sabotage the operation without tipping off the other one. They're not both in on it, are they? No. No.

"We can tease these things apart," said Finney. "Eventually we'll find the answers, but not in a useful time frame."

That was what Josh had been afraid of.

"What do you suggest?" he asked, a note of defeat slipping into his voice.

Berdoza and Finney glanced at each other. Berdoza gestured for Finney to speak.

"We have to slow them down if we're going to catch up," he said. "I don't know how to do that. We need to disrupt them somehow."

Josh shook his head.

This is worse than you thought.

"It's possible they could make a mistake," Berdoza offered tentatively. "Do something that connects a new company to one of the ones we've already investigated. That would let us skip ahead."

"But they haven't done that yet," said Finney.

Another silence fell over them. Josh was looking for ways to disrupt ... whomever and give his team a chance. But he wasn't coming up with anything that sounded plausible.

"Okay," he said finally. "Thank you for that. Please keep it up, and I'll see if I can find a way to take the pressure off you."

After they'd left, Josh stood up and leaned on the balcony's aluminum and wire railing. He needed something big and unexpected. He needed to toss a grenade into this mess and blow it up.

Heh. What do you do when you need something blown up?
You talk to Crane.
Bingo.

CHAPTER 27

Coronado Hills, El Paso, Texas

Sawyer Cottrell had found a wet bar in Josh Sulenski's Gulfstream as it flew him back from California. Under the circumstances, he thought it was appropriate to help himself, and he was already about two thirds drunk by the time the plane touched down at El Paso International.

Now, back home, Sawyer had locked himself in his study and continued drinking. His wife Ellen wanted to know what the surprise trip had been about, what he'd found out about their son. He had to convince her it was nothing, a dead end. How could he tell her the truth? But they'd been married for thirty-one years now, and Ellen was no fool to begin with. She knew he was keeping something from her, and he wouldn't keep good news to himself. She was upstairs in bed right now, crying into her pillow, and that was one more thing for Sawyer Cottrell to carry, one more reason for him to drink.

He drained the last of the Macallan and went looking for another bottle. He was pretty sure there was an unopened bottle of Bowmore. He lurched up out of his deep leather chair and stumbled across to the bar.

Of course, the problem with that was that the wall behind the bar was covered in pictures of Martin. Martin in his football uniform from high school. Martin with the two of them at college graduation. Martin proudly beaming from the bicycle he'd gotten for his eighth birthday. That was Sawyer's favorite of all of them. He still remembered that day. It had been a day so perfect that it should have terrified him. How could any day ever reach that high ever again? What could life be from that point onward but loss?

Sawyer's knees buckled beneath him, and he sank to the floor. He felt his world contracting down to a point. Nothing he had done mattered anymore. Nothing he had was worth anything. The company, the Chamber of Commerce awards, the big house in Coronado Hills. None of that mattered. None of it.

That's what Sulenski couldn't understand. He didn't seem like a bad person, but he didn't know Martin at all. He had his own agenda, and it had occurred to Sawyer that he couldn't trust Sulenski to put Martin first. If Martin was still alive in that compound, he didn't doubt that the mercenaries he'd assembled would get him out. And if he wasn't ... well, if he wasn't, nothing really mattered. Sawyer wasn't interested in spending the money he was spending, breaking the laws he was breaking, just to rescue a handful of strangers.

No, if Martin was ... if Martin wasn't coming home, then he had less than zero interest in helping Josh Sulenski do whatever it was he was trying to get done down there. If Martin was dead ... If Martin was dead, what he wanted, what he owed his son and his grieving wife, was revenge.

Sawyer controlled his breathing, pulled himself back to his feet, and found himself once again looking at that old photo of a beautiful, innocent little boy so proud of his new bike, so full of energy and potential, his future spooling out before him. Sawyer walked slowly and carefully to his desk, picked up a cordless handset, and dialed a number from memory.

After several rings, the call connected and a tired-sounding voice said, "Stratton."

For eight months now, Sawyer had been pouring money into nearly every private detective he could find. Chris Stratton was the one who still impressed him as a man who knew what he was doing.

"Sawyer Cottrell," he said. "I've got something. I know where my son is."

Is, he thought. *Not was. Not until you really know. And this man doesn't need to be wondering.*

"That's great news," said Stratton. "How did you get this information?"

"It's trustworthy," said Sawyer. "Let's leave it at that. It's a place in Durango. Nearest town is called Santa Catarina de Tepehuanes."

"Hold on." Stratton's voice sounded tired. Sawyer checked his watch and realized what time it was. He'd probably awakened Stratton.

"Okay," Stratton said a few moments later. "Got it."

"It's a hacienda in the mountains a few miles northwest of the town, off Highway 23. I can get you latitude and longitude, if you need it, but it's kind of hard to miss. It's the only place out there for miles."

"I can be there by noon tomorrow," said Stratton. "What do you already know, and what do you need me to find out?"

"I don't know much," said Sawyer. "I'll need a general briefing. The town, local police, and so on. See if anybody's seen Martin. But mainly, what can you find out about that compound? Especially who owns it and what they do there. How are they protected? How are they vulnerable?"

"All right," said Stratton. "Like I said, I can be there sometime tomorrow. I'll start asking around. I'll let you know as soon as I find anything. There'll be some expenses."

"I understand," said Sawyer. "I'll transfer funds to the holding account. You spread it around, do what you have to do." He grabbed the glass from his desk and drained out the last drops of the Macallan. "Let's be clear," he said quietly. "When I find out who owns that place, who lives there, does whatever the hell they're doing there, that guy's got a target on his back. And it never goes away. Never. You hear me?"

"I hear you."

"Do you know people down there? People who can handle something like that?"

"I know some people down here," said Stratton. "If they can't handle it, I'll find someone who can. There's always someone down here."

"All right," said Sawyer. "Find out what you can. The money will be there. This ... this means a lot to me. Keep that in mind."

"I know what it means to you," said Stratton. "You'll know as soon as I find anything."

"Thank you," said Sawyer, his eyes closed, the cool pressure of the glass against his forehead. "Thank you."

After he hung up, Sawyer staggered back to the bar and cracked the seal on the Bowmore. He was unsteadily pouring a couple fingers into his glass when he suddenly realized where the bottle came from. Martin had given it to him for Father's Day last year.

He stopped short, sloshed a bit of the whiskey onto the bar. Then he set the bottle down and looked back across the photos of his son. Josh Sulenski could get screwed. If the bastards had killed his son, he wouldn't be playing around with secret messages and planning surgical rescues. He would take every dollar he had, every favor he could call in, every resource he had, and he would soak them all in napalm and burn the whole fucking country to the ground.

CHAPTER 28

Crane met Josh for lunch at the Myria building's rooftop restaurant. He wore a navy Brunello Cucinelli sweater over a white V-neck, and gray cotton trousers. After so many days in cargo pants and boots, eating dust in Bahia Tortugas, he found he was ready for something more refined.

"You trying to impress me, John?" Josh asked as Crane joined him at his table. Josh was at least not wearing the cargo shorts and graphic tees he favored away from the office. But looking around at the crowd of young Silicon Valley tech workers, Crane decided he was actually slightly overdressed.

"Just want you to think you're getting your money's worth," he said.

Josh laughed and passed Crane a menu.

"Well, that's one good thing, anyway. I'm having a lousy day —week, really."

A waiter came to the table, and Crane ordered a grilled avocado, followed by reginetti with savoy cabbage and pancetta —the food at La Playa had been good but, here too, Crane was ready for something a little more sophisticated.

"So what's the problem?" Crane asked over drinks while they waited.

Josh told him how both his avenues of investigation into whoever had taken over Alexander Tate's life and businesses had run aground.

"We're at a dead end," Josh said as their food arrived. "We need to change the rules somehow. And I think I know how."

Crane began to recognize the shape of the conversation. This was how mission briefings began. Josh's idea for shaking his investigation loose would involve him doing something. Probably something dangerous.

"Do you remember I told you that Jason disappeared a couple steps ahead of some nasty rumors about a sexual assault indictment?"

Crane nodded. "Date that ended badly? Powerful family?"

"That's right. I've been on the phone with them. Turns out there was a grand jury investigation, and Jason was supposed to be subpoenaed to testify. But by then, he was gone, and he was never served. The investigation went nowhere. But if we can bring him back here ..."

"They arrest him as a material witness, and an indictment soon follows," said Crane. "But how does that solve your problem?"

"Jason's a beneficiary of several of his father's trusts. My legal and financial people say it would be very hard to do what they've done without his involvement."

"You think he did that to his own father?" Crane was horrified. He knew some of the things Jason Tate was capable of, but this was a whole new dimension. More than ever, he was convinced Tate needed to be taken down hard.

"If he is involved, then some legal pressure might get him talking. If nothing else, seeing him handed over to the district attorney's office should scare the hell out of his accomplices."

"So you want to add a new mission objective. While we're in there, you want me to extract him."

"Can you do it?"

"Probably," said Crane. "Jessie and I are still working out details. I'll see what we can come up with."

"I wouldn't mention this to Jessie," Josh said. Crane raised an eyebrow, and he went on. "I don't want it getting back to Cottrell. He's already on edge, worried we're taking over his operation. He'll see this as putting his son at risk."

"We're all on the same side here," said Crane.

Josh nodded. "I spent some time with Sawyer. He's a good guy. He's just been at this for a long time now. He's getting nowhere, and every day makes it a little less likely he ever gets his son back alive. It's taken a toll. Let's just handle him gently."

Crane nodded. "Okay, that's your legal front. As it happens, I may have something for you on the medical front."

Josh looked surprised. "Really?"

Crane slid a small cardboard box from his pocket and handed it to Josh.

"I told you I had a friend who used to do very unusual medical work for Hurricane? I asked her if it was possible to artificially induce the kind of symptoms you were talking about. When I got back last night, this was waiting for me."

Josh opened the box and slid out a gray plastic cylinder, like a thick, stubby ballpoint pen. The cap flipped open with a thumbnail. It was a medical autoinjector.

"If you wanted to do to someone what you described, you'd want something similar to a barbiturate coma," Crane said. "Though my friend said there are some highly modified special purpose benzodiazepines that could more precisely target the areas of the brain you'd need to impair."

"But you mean it's really possible?" Josh asked. "That's ... scary as hell. What's this?"

"Receptor antagonist," said Crane. "Apparently it started out as something called flumazenil, which is used to treat benzo overdoses. It targets the receptors in the brain and inhibits uptake of the drug. But this is now a long way from stock flumazenil."

"You got this from someone who works for the government?" Josh asked.

"Well, not anymore."

"Who does she work for now?"

"I don't ask," said Crane. "And she doesn't ask me. It works better that way."

"Okay," said Josh, "point taken. So if I can get in to see Alexander again, I should inject him with this?"

"Thigh muscle would be the best place," said Crane. "If—let me emphasize if—someone is dosing Tate the elder with something to reduce his level of consciousness, this should start to bring him out of it. For a while, at least."

"What if he's not drugged? What if it's really organic brain damage?"

"Well, then you're not going to do him any favors," said Crane. "Severe agitation, hypersensitivity, seizures. You better be pretty sure before you use that."

Josh nodded thoughtfully and slipped the autoinjector into his pocket.

"I guess we've both got our work cut out for us," he said.

Sveti Stefan, Montenegro

In the middle ages, the hotel had been a fortress built on a tiny island just off the beach on the Adriatic coast. It was a warren of hand-laid stone and red tile roofs, buildings tumbled together from one end of the island to the other. History had washed over it in waves, one after another, bringing warlords, pirates, royalty, Communist Party officials, and Hollywood stars, each in their turn.

Finally, now connected to the mainland by a narrow causeway, it had become a modern five-star luxury resort overlooking the hilly coast and the gleaming blue sea.

In one of its very expensive suites, the sun shot rays through open French doors and gauzy curtains that billowed in the morning breeze. The light bounced off five hundred-year-old plastered walls and caressed discarded lingerie on the floor. Then a telephone chirped somewhere in the room.

In the bed, a pile of rumpled covers moved. It slid to the side, and a naked woman emerged. She stood with a languorous stretch and made her way around the foot of the king-size bed. She was young, with a taut body and short-cropped hair dyed bright blue. The phone kept up its digital whistling as she stood beside the table where it sat and looked out the open French doors at the suite's patio and private pool, and the sea beyond.

She stretched once more, her hands clasping over her head and her legs flexing. Then she picked up the phone at last.

"Yes?"

"It's Mauro Rossi calling."

She stifled a yawn and ran her free hand through her hair. "Of course, Mauro, how are you?"

"I'm well," he said. "I'm calling about an incoming request that's crossed my desk."

Mauro hadn't called her in quite some time. He was a minor functionary she'd planted in Turnstone's organization to keep an eye on him and warn her if he made any moves against her. But she soon discovered that his position was too peripheral. By the time Turnstone's schemes made it down the chain to Mauro, they had been broken up into a dozen innocuous components that looked like normal business. She'd realized her mistake and placed someone much closer to Turnstone himself. But Mauro was still there, patiently waiting for his chance to earn the rewards she'd promised for useful information. So why was he calling now?

"It came from Jason Tate," Mauro was saying.

"Do I know him?"

"Doubtful. He's an informal liaison to the Obregon narco cartel. More trouble than he's worth from our point of view. But he's the cartel's problem to deal with. Suddenly he's requested any information we have on a man named John Crane."

Oh, she thought. *Oh. How delicious.* This was just what she needed.

"You'd mentioned wanting to be notified if that name came up."

"Indeed," she said. "You were right to call. Do you know why he's interested?"

"Not yet. I can make inquiries, but we have few resources there. That's why we humor Tate."

She stepped onto the patio and let the sun warm her skin.

"Does Turnstone know about this request?" she asked.

"I can't be certain," Mauro replied. "But the request came from Keating. He's a mid-level deputy, and he's delegated it with low priority. I doubt this went upstairs."

Even if Turnstone knew about this, she could guess how he'd handle it. He would assume it was unimportant, so he'd kick the whole matter to the curb. If nothing happened in a day or two to bring it back to his attention, he'd take that as confirmation that he was right and forget about it. Getting Turnstone's attention usually meant doing something twice, though he'd lately begun to make exceptions in her case.

"Make sure it doesn't," she said. "Bury it somewhere, and make sure nothing comes back."

"Understood."

"And send me whatever you have on Jason Tate."

"Already done," he said. "It's in your secure folder."

"Thank you, Mauro," she said as she walked out onto the grass and luxuriated in the feel of it against her bare feet. "You've done well. Do keep me informed."

"Of course," he said as she was hanging up.

John Crane, she thought as she walked slowly across the grass, past the pool, and toward the stone and mortar wall overlooking the sea. The man did have a way of turning up at odd times. They'd never properly met, but she'd been putting out feelers since the thing in Buenos Aires, seeking more information about him—who he was, whom he worked for, what he was trying to accomplish. He was a new player, not tied to any of the existing factions, as far as she could tell. And he'd managed to turn up in the middle of her assignment to deal with Branislav Skala, providing a very convenient scapegoat for his death among those few people who were unhappy to see Skala dead. It was as if the two of them were dancing with each other blindfolded, moving in unison by sheer instinct.

She heard a distant voice calling, "Madame, madame!" and turned to see an elderly man in hotel uniform hurrying toward her across the lawn with a white hotel bathrobe held out in front of him as if to hide her.

"Madame, you are in a public area of the hotel!"

"Yes, of course," she said, and then looked down and pretended to just discover her nudity.

"My word," she said, "whatever could have happened to my clothes?"

He thrust the robe at her while trying to simultaneously avert his eyes.

"Oh, I don't think it's mine," she said. "I'd definitely remember wearing that." Then she sidestepped him and headed back across the grass as the man hurried after her, holding the bathrobe like a screen.

John Crane. What was he doing in Mexico?

CHAPTER 29

Sierra Madre Occidental Mountains, Mexico

The steady sound of the engines was almost calming after a while, Crane thought. The Short had flown steadily south through the night, down the backbone of the continent. This was very remote country, and there were no lights below. There was only deep darkness and the blazing stars overhead, untouched by the light pollution farther north.

Crane stood in the dark in the boxy cargo hold. Pale red lights let him maneuver without ruining his night vision.

"Almost on point," Jessie's voice said in his headphones. "You ready?"

"Ready when you are," he replied. Then he clipped the safety line on his belt to the rail that ran along one side of the cargo hold.

A few moments later, the cargo ramp began to swing down and let in the chill night air. At the forward end of the hold, a small aircraft sat on tricycle landing gear. The drone's wingspan very nearly touched both sides of the fuselage—it would barely fit out the cargo door, but they'd gotten it aboard, so Crane knew it would go back out again. He knelt down to unsnap the clamps that held it in place on the deck.

"Say the word," he said.

"Stand by."

He had to hold the drone in place as the plane began a gentle climb. Then Jessie said, "Let her go!"

Crane pushed off and ran the drone down the deck. He released it and watched it sail out into the night and vanish into the darkness.

The drone plummeted through the night toward the mountains below in a steep, silent dive. Then its electric pusher propeller came to life and its ailerons twitched back and forth as it stabilized itself. A few moments later, it pulled out of the dive, oriented itself, rechecked its GPS position, and headed off to the southeast.

Aboard the plane, Crane heard the cargo ramp close behind him as he headed back to the cockpit. He let himself in and settled back into the co-pilot's seat beside Jessie.

"Welcome back," she said. "Drone's looking happy."

Crane checked the displays on his console, which were devoted to the drone instead of the plane itself. Its batteries were fully charged. The night vision and thermal imagers were working. All was well. The drone would maintain course and speed to a waypoint near Jason Tate's hacienda. There, it would do a flyover of the compound before Crane took manual control and went in for a closer look at anything interesting from that initial pass.

When they had everything they needed, the drone would depart, flying deeper into the mountains until it self-destructed over inhospitable terrain many miles from Tate's compound. *It's a shame, really*, Crane thought. But they had no way to recover it.

"We're good," said Crane. "Few minutes."

"Beautiful tonight, isn't it?" said Jessie, leaning forward to look up into the starry night. "Stuff like this is why I wanted to fly," she said. "What about you?"

Crane shrugged. "I never really thought about being a pilot," he said. "Hurricane taught me a lot of things, and that was one of them."

"Been meaning to ask you," she said. "How did you end up working for some super covert spy agency in the first place? Josh said you were a philosophy major?"

Crane laughed. "Well, you don't need to sound so dubious. It's an honest profession! Philosophizing, I mean. Steady work wherever there's ... okay, I've got nothing there."

She laughed. "So come on, connect the dots for me. How'd you get from that to being a spy?"

"I was an *agent*," Crane said. "No, I went into the Coast Guard after college. Figured I needed to balance all that thinking with some practical experience. Hurricane recruited me out of there. I fit their psych profile, until they got shut down. Then Josh found me, and here we are, aboard this fine airplane, sneaking through Mexican airspace in the dead of night. Which segues nicely into how you got here from a life of anti-government radicalism in the Pacific Northwest."

"Oh, that's easy," she laughed. "Gunrunning, pot smuggling, hiding fugitives, dodging the feds—I grew up doing this job. I just never bought into the ideology, so now I do it for money. In fact, I know someone who works for a Fortune 100 multinational. Her title is Senior Mobility Manager, and she gets people where they need to go. Everything from charter flights to visas and customs clearance. When you have one guy who can troubleshoot a forty-thousand-ton tunnel-boring machine somewhere in Central Asia, and you're losing a few hundred grand in performance penalties every day it's down, you need that guy onsite fast. She gets him there. That's what I do. Just less legal. One way or another, I can go pretty much anywhere in the world, and bring pretty much anything or anyone in or out, depending on what you need. Turns out, that's a very marketable skill."

Crane could see that. When he was with Hurricane, he had all the resources and clout of the US Government to insert him wherever he needed to go. Now he didn't, and Jessie had apparently already proven a pretty good substitute.

"Drone's on station," she said.

Crane checked the panel and saw that she was right. It had reached its waypoint, and was now orbiting a point half a mile away from the hacienda at an altitude of five hundred feet. Crane told it to power up the sensors and proceed with an overflight.

New windows began to light up with imagery as the drone swooped in over the hacienda. Near-infrared lidar built a precise physical model of the compound, down to individual trees. Thermal cameras scanned for body heat, and ground-penetrating radar probed the insides of structures.

"That's where we think they're being held, right?" Jessie said, pointing to a walled building in a far rear corner of the compound. As they watched, traces of body heat began to pop up.

"And there they are," said Crane. "That's six hostages, two, maybe three guards." He fiddled with an adjustment on the radar and said, "They're in a basement beneath the main level. Ah. It's looking through a metal roof. That's why it's having some trouble resolving them."

He studied the screens, watching the blurry human figures move. "Four rooms, two on either side, with a central hallway. I'm thinking maybe a larger room at this end. Probably where the stairs will be."

"Where are you getting that?" Jessie asked. "I don't see any internal structure."

"No," Crane admitted, "but look how they're grouped in pairs. They're bunked two to a room. Walls are probably just two by fours and drywall, not showing up through that roof."

"Okay, I'll buy that," she said. "Look over here. Is that a loading dock?"

Crane followed her finger across the screen. "I think you're right," he said at last. "That's how we'll take them out, then. Find a couple trucks. There must be something in this garage over here, or maybe at the airstrip."

"There's the opposition," said Jessie, pointing to another building across the compound, bright with human figures. "Guard barracks, right? I count maybe a dozen."

So their team would be outnumbered when they arrived, but not badly, especially if they managed to maintain surprise. Crane had noticed that, apart from a couple men on patrol, it seemed as though the entire detachment was inside and asleep. If they hit at the right time, they could overcome a small disadvantage in numbers easily.

"Put a sniper on this hillside over here," he said, pointing to the screen. "He can cover the ground between the barracks and the prison. Keep them pinned down and out of our hair."

"Agreed," said Jessie.

They were beginning to lose coverage as the drone swept past the hacienda and headed out again into the empty night.

"We have what we need?" Jessie asked.

Crane put the drone into a slow banking turn. "I'd like to do another pass while we're here."

He brought the drone back in again, low and slow, and focused the sensors on the sprawling main house with its courtyards and swimming pool. The lidar had already scanned the exterior structure. Now the radar probed the house's interior, and the thermal camera looked for people. Crane made out corridors and sweeping staircases. He identified the kitchen and storage rooms, and the warren of small occupied chambers tucked in behind them. Servants' quarters.

And there, at the end of a long gallery, was a large room with one—no, two people in what Crane took to be a king-size bed. One of those figures was his target.

"Why are you searching the big house?" Jessie asked.

"Just don't want any surprises," said Crane.

"So you're going after Tate."

Crane turned toward Jessie. "Why do you think that?"

"It's what I'd do."

Crane smiled. He hadn't expected this to work, anyway. "I'm not supposed to tell you that," he said. "Josh thinks Cottrell won't like it."

"Sawyer's very focused on getting his son back," said Jessie. "He won't want anything to distract from that, and he's especially upset that the reply didn't come from Martin or make any mention of him."

"We don't know what that means," Crane reminded her.

"No, but we can make a pretty good guess, and so can Sawyer. But just the same, this is about more than Sawyer's son. Jason Tate needs to face justice. We can't just snatch away his engineers and say we're done. He'll go out and get more. So we shut him down, haul him back to the States, and let the criminal justice system have him. It's better than he deserves."

The drone pulled away from the hacienda once more. "Got what you need now?" Jessie asked.

"I think so," said Crane. "Initiating extraction."

He sent a command to the drone that activated its exfiltration and self-destruct program. It pulled up into the night sky, leaving the hacienda behind. It steadily made its way west, toward its final waypoint. When it reached it, small charges would destroy the cameras and electronics, and the remains of the drone would tumble out of the sky. Most likely, no one would ever find it. If they did, they wouldn't know what it was, and they certainly wouldn't connect it to a remote hacienda in the mountains many miles away.

"All right, let's get out of here," Jessie said. She banked the Short around and flew north. She glanced over at Crane, studying the data replaying across the screens. "We've got work to do."

CHAPTER 30

The Santa Clara County District Attorney's office maintained a branch office in Palo Alto. Josh spent much of the morning there, accompanied by his own lawyer, discussing Jason Tate's case. It was the sort of meeting designed to put Josh's teeth on edge, full of ambiguous language and contingent statements from his attorney carefully crafted to not actually admit that they knew where Jason was. It was more than two hours of phrases like, "If, hypothetically speaking, Mr. Tate could be induced to return to the United States," and, "my client is simply a concerned citizen eager to see justice done."

But by the meeting's end, both sides had accomplished what they set out to accomplish. Josh had made it clear to a bright young assistant district attorney that he knew where Jason was hiding, and was prepared to effectively kidnap him and bring him back to the United States. And his lawyer managed to do it without actually admitting to anything beyond Josh's name. At the same time, without committing her boss to anything, the ADA made it clear that any questions regarding Jason Tate's departure from Mexican territory were the domain of the Mexican government. Her office was not concerned with how

Tate came to be on American soil, but would be prepared to take him into custody as a material witness the moment he landed. Overall, he thought, it was a success.

It was two hours you could have spent playing Grand Theft Auto.

Tim was on his phone in a waiting area as Josh and his attorney came out. Josh was talking with his lawyer, but quickly realized that Tim wasn't happy.

"I told you, I don't know," Tim said in a hushed tone that still carried because of his intensity. "I'm not there. Yeah, I understand."

When he looked up and saw Josh approaching, he turned away and cupped the phone in his free hand. "I can't talk now. Yes, yes, I said I'd do it." Then he hung up and hurriedly jammed the phone into his jacket pocket. He fell in beside Josh as they walked out toward the lobby.

"That didn't sound good," said Josh. "What's going on?"

Tim shook his head. "Nothing, nothing. Don't worry about it. Just ... wedding stuff with Emily's mother."

He's lying. Something's wrong.

"Do you need to deal with it? I can drive myself around."

"No! No, it's okay. It'll be fine."

In the lobby, Josh and his lawyer went separate ways after setting up a conference call for the following week. If all went well, Jason would be back in the States by then, and things would start to shake loose. Josh watched his lawyer walk off across the lobby. Then he and Tim went outside and headed for the parking garage.

Tim is really freaked out about something.

In the parking garage elevator, Josh couldn't help noticing it. Tim was agitated and on edge, and that was making Josh nervous.

"I've got a foundation board meeting in ninety minutes," said Josh as they walked down a lonely row of parked cars. Josh could hear street noises below and the sound of a revving engine echoing through the garage.

"I know your schedule," said Tim.

"What I mean is, I'm going to be there for like three hours, with lunch and so on. There's plenty of time for you to take off and deal with whatever's got you so worked up."

He stopped as they reached the Mercedes.

He always moves around and opens the door. Why isn't he opening the door?

"I mean, you're obviously—"

Josh turned back to Tim and saw the gun. Tim held it low and close to side, the muzzle pointed at Josh's midsection. He stood motionless and silent for a long moment.

Oh? No witty remark? No obscure reference?

"Get in," said Tim. "You'll have to drive."

"I don't know what ..."

"I said get in!" Tim pulled the key fob from his pocket with his free hand and unlocked the car. Josh walked slowly around the Mercedes as Tim followed him with the gun, raising it to aim over the roof. Tim kept his eyes on Josh as he opened the front passenger door. Josh opened his door, and they both carefully got into the car.

Tim sat with the gun in his right hand, held across his torso and pointed at Josh as Josh started the car and drove out into morning traffic.

They headed north up El Camino Real, and then Tim told him to take a left onto Sand Hill.

They turned him! They got to your bodyguard! You are so screwed! How much closer can they get than that? Where the hell is he taking you?

"I have to say, I thought there was more of a mutual respect between us," Josh said. "I thought you were a friend, Tim."

Tim said nothing for a moment, and when he did answer, his

voice quavered at first until he got it under control. "I don't know where you got that. You seem like a decent guy. Kind of lonely."

Tim's voice trailed off.

They can put that on your gravestone. He was a decent guy who was kind of lonely. Great.

"I wish I could afford to not give a damn about your money," Tim said. "But it's always there, isn't it? You can try to shrug it off, and I can try to ignore it. But it's always there. Just the sheer weight of it. Stack anything else up against that and ... well, you know. Keep going here."

They were driving into Rancho Corral de Tierra, Josh realized. It was a nearly four-thousand-acre patch of undeveloped parkland with mountains, farms, and hiking trails. It would be a very easy place to lose a body in. Was Tim taking him to someone, or was he expected to do the job himself? Josh felt a bead of sweat edging down the back of his neck. He was going to die today.

"Whatever they're paying you—"

Tim let out a short, humorless laugh. "See? There's always the money." He sighed and shook his head. "I thought about that. But there's more to it. They've got a carrot; you've got a carrot. But you don't have a stick. I knew you might pay me off. But you'd never hurt Emily."

"Oh, God! Did they ... ?"

"No. But they could. At the end of the day, I knew they would, and I knew you wouldn't. So here we are."

The road twisted and switched back on itself as it climbed the grassy hills. Near the top, there would be parking areas and trailheads. Josh imagined a black car full of dangerous men who would take him off Tim's hands. He pictured them sending Tim away in the Mercedes and then walking him down a trail to some isolated spot overlooking a drainage gully choked with foliage ...

Tim's fingers drummed nervously on the armrest, and one leg trembled.

He doesn't want to do this, but he's going to do it. You can't let him hand you over. Pop quiz, hotshot. What do you do? What do you do?

All comes down to the gun. You have to control the gun.

Yeah, this guy's a trained fighter. You're ... you. You're going to beat him up?

Have to try. Seatbelt. Can't move.

Josh dropped his right hand into his lap and pressed the release button on his seatbelt. He held it in place, and Tim didn't seem to notice.

"Last chance," Josh said. "We turn around now, and we go to the police, tell them what happened, and they protect you and Emily. What do you say, Tim?"

Tim waved the gun at him. "Just shut up! Don't make this any harder."

Josh steered through a tight turn onto a relatively straight, climbing stretch of road. He took a deep breath. Then he took his other hand off the wheel, held it against his chest, and released the seatbelt.

The belt retracted across his torso and hurled the latch against the window with a loud crack. Josh grabbed for the gun with his right hand and slammed it against the dashboard. The car veered toward the edge of the road, and a harsh warning tone came through the sound system. The evasive steering assist feature turned the Mercedes sharply back to the right, and the momentum helped carry Josh over the center console as he pushed off with both legs. He grabbed Tim's wrist with both hands and tried to force the gun away.

The seatbelt restrained Tim, but he had the training that Josh lacked. He hit Josh hard on the shoulder with the blade of his hand, and Josh felt the shock run through his body. The car let out its warning tone again and veered back to the left as it tried to maintain the center of the lane.

Josh slammed Tim's hand against the dash again, and this time the gun flew free. It hit the windshield and bounced back across the car to tumble into the steering wheel and vanish into the driver's side footwell.

Tim was pressed back against the door, Josh trying to crush him against it, pushing against his own door's kick panel with both legs as he lay across the center console. Tim hit him again, and then his hands closed around Josh's throat, and he pulled him even farther out of his seat. Josh fought to breathe, but he couldn't draw air. He felt his heart pounding, heard blood rushing in his ears. He was no match for Tim to begin with, and he was already growing weaker. He clawed at Tim's hands, but he couldn't dislodge them. He looked into Tim's eyes, and it was like Tim was the one who was dead. He'd switched part of himself off to do this. There was no empathy there, no mercy.

Josh thrashed, and the car veered right again, and something fell from his jacket pocket into Tim's lap. The autoinjector Crane had given him. In desperation, Josh grabbed it. He flipped open the cap and stabbed down into Tim's thigh. The autoinjector hissed.

Tim looked down in surprise for a couple seconds. Then he began to scream.

Josh ripped Tim's hands away from his throat and gulped in air. Tim's shrieks grew more intense. He tried to push Josh away, but he was twitching and uncoordinated. Then his eyes rolled back in his head, and he began to seize. His body shook, and he began to grunt, short sounds in a rhythm with the convulsions.

The car finally braked itself to a stop, and Josh reached back and grabbed the wheel to pull himself up. He threw the door open. As he got out, he kicked Tim's pistol, and it flew out onto the pavement. Josh scooped it up. He looked around wildly, as if the people Tim was delivering him to were watching.

But he saw nothing. Clutching the gun, he ran around to the passenger side and opened the door. Tim lurched over, falling against the seatbelt with a groan. He tried to reach up for Josh with one hand, but his arm fell limp and twitched awkwardly.

Josh leaned over him to pop the seatbelt. Then he hauled Tim out of the car and lay him down on the pavement.

What the hell do I do?

You don't know who's here. Who's coming. You go. Get out of here!

Josh bent down, grabbed the still-shaking Tim beneath his armpits, and dragged him off the side of the road onto the dirt shoulder. He looked down at Tim once more, still twitching and making high-pitched keening sounds. Then he hurried back to the car.

He slammed the passenger-side door, ran around the car, and got in. Then he peeled out. A few yards ahead was a gravel turnout. Josh steered into it and slewed the car around, fishtailing and throwing back gravel. He got the car turned around and headed back down the hill. He glanced over at Tim as he passed, still lying on the ground in his dusty suit. Then he was gone.

Josh drove and tried very hard not to think.

CHAPTER 31

The Indian Ocean, off Réunion

She flew from Tivat to Athens, and then on to Ramgoolam airport in Mauritius where the seaplane was waiting for her. Now the endless expanse of the Indian Ocean glittered below her in the bright afternoon sun.

"How long?" she asked the pilot.

"Another twenty minutes, miss."

She wasn't looking forward to this. Dealing with Redpoll was challenging enough when it was over e-mail or by phone from thousands of miles away. She didn't want to do it in person, especially on his home turf. But, of course, he almost never left his absurd yacht anymore. She wasn't sure how long it had been since he'd set foot on land. More than a year, anyway. He was even wary of straying into national jurisdiction these days, and mostly stuck to international waters. That made it easy to stay away, but now he wanted her home, and she had things to tell him.

It's not home, she reminded herself. *He's not your father, and that's not your home.*

The pilot was challenged by radio and gave a series of code

words that changed every day. Then she saw it. The *Orion* was huge, twice the length of a 747, her gleaming hull formed from white metal and glass. She could make out the outdoor pool—as opposed to the indoor one—the retractable balconies that extended out over the water, and the eight-meter satellite dish built into the superstructure. As they came in to land, she thought the figure standing alone on the upper promenade might be Redpoll. There was something about the way he carried himself. Then the plane touched down and slashed through the water until it settled to a stop near a waiting boat.

The boat took her to the stern landing dock where the security team waited to check her aboard. She was familiar with the procedures. She'd left most of her things in a hotel room in Mauritius. She carried no handbag. All she had was what she wore: a pair of chunky black Manolo Blahnik boots and a skimpy floral print cocktail dress by Giambattista Valli. Her shopper at Harrod's had described the dress as "frothy and feminine." It signaled innocent sexuality, but her short-cropped blue hair and the boots gave her a contrasting dash of punk attitude. Together, it presented her as a rebellious little girl, which she knew was just how he saw her. She'd learned long ago that the best way to handle him was to show him what he expected to see.

She held her arms up while the millimeter wave scanner spun around her. Then a crew member gave her a perfunctory sweep with a metal detector wand, which beeped softly at the buckles on her boots, and welcomed her aboard.

"You're expected in the third deck gallery, miss," he told her.

She thanked him and headed forward.

It had been some time since she'd been aboard the *Orion*, but she remembered the layout. The yacht was an odd mix of cruise liner and battleship. She walked up the sweeping staircase that encircled the outdoor pool, passed by a spa and gymnasium and through a lavish entertainment space that was all white marble floors, glass, and rich brown leather. Forward of that was the signals intelligence bay, where a dozen crew members busily worked satellite connections. They listened to tapped phone calls, intercepted diplomatic cables, and fed an unending stream of data into a complicated computer model. She thought of it as a weather map for the end of the world.

Going up another grand staircase, she found herself on deck three. The gallery was an enormous space, the width of the ship. There was a huge circular opening in the center that looked down several decks onto the indoor pool. Hanging over the opening were two enormous sculptures, airy cylinders of brass made of huge numbers of small, individually engraved plates. Brass art deco statues overlooked the gallery, stylized swords held in front of them.

It was a space designed for intimidating billionaire industrialists and heads of state. *Why did he bring me here?* she wondered. *Am I to be scolded?*

Redpoll stood at the railing overlooking the central opening, beneath the glittering brass mobiles, looking down to the swirling water below. He wore white linen and leather sandals, and she noticed that his once jet-black hair was finally beginning to go gray. She knew he was considerably older than he looked. The olive skin at his temples was beginning to sag and wrinkle.

He turned, rather theatrically she thought, as she entered, and smiled. His piercing blue eyes had lost none of their impact. He was still ruthless, cunning, dangerous, as anyone who overestimated his decline would soon find out.

"Here you are!" he said, stretching out his arms to her. "How wonderful to see you. Come here and kiss me."

She let him embrace her and kissed his cheek. Then he held her at arms' length and studied her, smiling warmly.

"Too long," he said, "too long."

He released her with a mischievous smile. "But no bags? I'd hoped you'd stay awhile."

"Well, you know how it is. The schedule is very demanding."

He nodded. She was always struck by the difference between the doting father she visited here and the stern commander who ran her field missions. She honestly wasn't sure anymore which she preferred.

"You know you've upset poor Turnstone again," he was saying.

She made a dismissive face. Not everything is worth worrying about, it said.

"That may not have been wise, coming so soon on the heels of Buenos Aires. He wasn't pleased that you took it upon yourself to kill Tamarind."

Again, she said nothing. She knew that killing Tamarind had been risky, but he'd taken her side in the end. She suspected that had upset Turnstone more than the loss of Tamarind itself.

They strolled to one of the panoramic windows that looked out over the sea.

"You're very quiet," he observed.

"I'm letting you speak," she said. "The sound of your voice comforts me."

He threw back his head and laughed. "Well, it's a sweet thing to say anyway." Then he added, "Turnstone is a dangerous enemy. If you were crossing him in service of some goal, that would be one thing. But it seems you just enjoy tweaking his nose."

She shrugged. In fact, she had a very good reason for playing Turnstone the way she was, but she wasn't about to discuss that here.

"He demanded a full trace on your movements and communications," Redpoll said.

"Which you turned down, I assume."

"I wouldn't be so confident of that, my dear," he said. "You know we have several other sector heads, and you don't have these issues with them."

She smiled sweetly. "I respect them."

He sighed and looked out at the sea.

"I won't always be here to protect you," he said. "When I'm gone, if it hasn't already happened by then, there's going to be a power struggle. I installed each of them. They're all of equal status in their eyes, each with a valid claim to the leadership."

One way to handle that would be to announce his chosen successor and then step down, but she didn't think he'd ever do that. He could never bring himself to walk away.

She put a hand on his. "You don't have to worry about me."

"But I do!" he said. "I do. This tiff with Turnstone is obvious. But all of them have reason to distrust or fear you because of who you are."

"That's not the only option," she said. "Vanga actually wants to marry me."

He said nothing for nearly a minute, and she began to worry that she'd said too much. He always played half a dozen moves ahead.

"My point is, you should be making friends," he said at last. "You should be building alliances. Instead you're making powerful enemies of those who could support you."

He strolled out onto a wing overlooking the sea, and she followed. He always took for granted that she would tag along wherever he led. But then she always had, she admitted. When it counted, at least.

"I have plenty of friends," she said. "I'm making more all the time. I'm going to Mexico from here to meet someone. He might be a friend. I'm not sure yet. I told you about him. He was following Tamarind."

He sighed. "And why do you think he's important?"

"He keeps turning up. I want to know why. Whether he's a threat or a usable asset. Just like you taught me!"

She leaned over, grabbed his head in her hands, and kissed his cheek.

"Don't try to butter me up," he said, but he was smiling as he said it. "And it's just coincidence that you're doing this in Turnstone's backyard after he's made it clear you're to stay out?"

"The man's in Mexico," she said. "If I want a closer look at him, I have to go where he goes. Besides, you didn't seriously think I'd comply with that absurd demand, did you? You'd never respect me if I did."

He expected a degree of rebelliousness from her, she'd learned. The trick was to give him the kind he expected to see, the kind he was prepared to tolerate, while concealing the kind that would bring swift and brutal punishment. It was a delicate game, but a game he'd forced her to learn to play well.

"I don't need drama with Turnstone right now," he said after a pause. "Slip in and out, and try not to draw his attention."

"Of course. He'll never know I was there."

That, of course, was a lie. If Turnstone didn't notice her incursion on his own, she'd have to do something more obvious to get his attention. Drama with Turnstone was exactly what her plans required. When she'd started to cause trouble, it was Turnstone who'd taken the bait and come after her. Since then, nothing had gone quite right for him. Worse, Turnstone was becoming less discreet all the time, increasingly committed to a course of action that let her draw him out and humiliate him. Indiscretion was unforgivable to the sector heads. Soon, if they hadn't already, the others should begin to notice that the universe tended to take a vague but potentially crippling dislike to her enemies.

"All right," Redpoll said at last with a chuckle. "All right, go to Mexico and see what you can learn about this fellow. I'll await your report with great anticipation."

He drew her close, patted her back, and then shooed her away. "In the meantime, there are clothes in your cabin. Get changed and have a swim before dinner. I've told the chef to make your favorites. Keep me company, and you can go to Mexico in the morning."

It was a reasonable compromise, she thought as she headed up yet another grand sweeping staircase to another sumptuous, showy deck of guest cabins. John Crane could wait another day. *But then I'm coming for you,* she thought, *and we'll see what you're made of.*

CHAPTER 32

Crane pulled into the parking lot of a motel in San Mateo. It offered weekly rates and appeared to cater primarily to construction crews. Josh had called him from here an hour ago in a panic. It was hard to make out what had happened, but he gathered Josh's bodyguard had made an attempt on his life. That was very bad, indeed.

Though he supposed they should have expected something, Crane thought as he walked up the concrete stairs to the second level. If they kept annoying powerful bad guys, sooner or later, one was bound to hit back. He assumed this was connected to the Tate empire. He knew Jason wouldn't think twice about murdering someone who got in his way. He imagined Tate's accomplices probably thought the same way.

He knocked at the door of Room 17, and after a moment, the curtain moved aside an inch. Then the door opened, and Crane cautiously entered. Josh had moved back from the door and now stood by a flimsy table with local shopping guides, a cheap pad of paper, and a standup room service menu. He was holding a pistol.

"Close the door!" Josh stammered.

Crane did, and then said, "If we're going to do this, you're going to have to give me the gun."

Josh said nothing, but he also didn't resist as Crane moved to him and gently took the pistol from his hand.

Josh stood, looking bereft. The bass thump of Chicano hip-hop leaked through the walls from another room.

"Sit down, and start from the beginning," Crane said. "What happened?"

Josh sat down on the foot of the bed and told him the story. Once he'd gotten started, there was no shutting him up. Crane was used to seeing Josh confident and eager, the guy in charge, giving out mission briefings from thirty thousand feet in his private jet.

But this was a man who'd been shaken to his core. It became clear to Crane that it wasn't even the danger itself that had unnerved him so much as the loss of certainty that it implied.

"It's not safe," Josh stammered. "Nowhere is safe. Tim drove me everywhere. He was in my house! I trusted him. I thought we were friends! How can I feel safe again?"

"Focus," Crane said. "Breathe. Here's what you do first. Step back. Focus on the details. You left him there? By the side of the road in Rancho Corral de Tierra?"

Josh shuddered. "I don't even know if he's alive or dead! That stuff you gave me, that does not mess around."

"It won't kill him," Crane said. He checked his watch. "It should have worn off by now. Either he took off on foot, or maybe the people who sent him after you came looking when you didn't show up, and they found him. Either way, he's probably not there anymore. I don't know what he'll do next. My guess is we'll never see him again. Either way, we'll change all his access codes, revoke his badge, put security on alert to watch for him."

"Yeah, yeah, I know all that," said Josh. "That's not the problem."

"Okay, what's the problem?"

"They turned him! They threw money at him and threatened his fiancée until he ... what's to keep them from doing the same thing to the next one? How do I trust anyone? They can have my secretary put a knife in my back, or have my chef poison me. How can I keep fighting them?"

He looked up at Crane with despair. "How do I just go on with my life now?"

Crane nodded. He unloaded the gun and set it on the desk, and then sat down beside Josh.

"When I was a kid," he said, "we used to go to the beach. One time, my mom was still alive, so I was young, but I was old enough to swim by myself. And I swam out past the breakers. I was having a great time. Then suddenly I couldn't stop thinking about what was down there. I don't know—the water was probably ten feet deep where I was, but I thought it went down for a mile. And there were sharks down there. Giant, man-eating squid. Dinosaurs. Monsters. And I was terrified. I wasn't afraid of drowning. I was afraid of those unspeakable horrors down there in the dark. And I almost did drown, I was so full of panic and terror. I barely made it back to shore. And after that, I wouldn't go in the water for a long time. Suddenly I hated even to go to the beach."

"How did you get over it?"

"I took up diving. I found out what was down there."

"There's still a lot more 'down there' than you can dive, John."

Crane conceded the point with a gesture. "There's always danger," he said. "You do what you can to prepare, and then you try not to worry about the rest of it."

"That's the part I'm not good at," said Josh.

Even so, Crane noted, his voice seemed calmer. They sat in silence for a minute or more. Finally Josh said, "I can always back off. Stop investigating. I can stop pushing them and hope they figure I got the message."

"Does that feel right?"

"No, of course not."

Crane nodded. "Because what that tells them is they can push you around. And if they can, so can somebody else."

Josh stood up and walked to the window. He pulled back the curtains and looked out across the parking lot at the traffic rolling by on the highway.

"This is where I ran? This place sucks."

"You can afford better," Crane said with a smile.

Josh turned suddenly. "Tim didn't want to do it," he said. "This wasn't his idea. He was minding his own business, trying to get married ... They didn't just come after me. They used him to do it. They ruined his life because of me!"

"Good," said Crane. "That's good. 'Who else will they hurt?' is better than 'Who can I trust?' That's something you can use."

"And that poor girl he wanted to marry. Son of a ... I want to hit them, John. I want to hit them back. Hard."

Crane grinned. "Okay. I have news on that front. Jessie called this morning. Sawyer's mercs are assembled in El Paso. They're ready. We can go in tonight."

"And if you can bring in Jason, that should blow a hole in their plans," said Josh. "Good. Good."

"You ready to get out of here?"

Josh nodded. He took the room key from his pocket—an actual metal key on a bright plastic tab, Crane noticed with mild surprise—and tossed it on the bed.

As they were walking down the poured concrete stairs, a thought occurred to Crane.

"Why me?" he asked.

"Why you what?"

"Why did you call me when you didn't trust anybody to not kill you?"

"Huh." Josh took a few more steps, thinking. Then he said, "I guess none of that applied to you."

"All right, then," said Crane, "let's go mess up Jason's shit."

Josh grinned back. "Yeah. Let's get up in his areas."

They headed down the stairs to the parking lot.

CHAPTER 33

Jason Tate was swimming laps in his pool when two men from the household staff brought him the wallet. They stood respectfully while he climbed out and someone brought him a towel.

"Two local men brought him, sir," they said. "They say he was asking questions in Santa Catarina. About this place, and who lives here. They're looking for the reward."

Tate looked through the wallet. The ID belonged to a Christopher Stratton. Texas driver's license, couple of credit cards. And a Texas private investigator's license. He looked at that one for a long minute.

Another private detective from the States. It wasn't John Crane under some other alias. The man in the license photo was older, with sandy blond hair and a different look in the eyes. But he was here. Crane had come because of the girl in Bahia Tortugas, and that one wasn't even his fault. The last time he saw her, she'd been fine, if blasted out of her mind. It wasn't his fault she'd wandered up on deck and fallen overboard. He'd been asleep.

But another one, and here in Tepehuanes, was worrying. Maybe he was here because of the other girl, the one in LA. Or maybe it was something else entirely. Whatever the reason, he had to find out. And he was in the mood for some adrenaline, if he was being honest. Not being able to put his hands on Crane had him on edge, twitchy. Until he had Crane, Christopher Stratton would have to do.

"Yeah, pay them," he said at last. "And take him down to the pump room."

Simply because of where it was, the hacienda had to be almost entirely self-sufficient. Part of that was providing water. There were two different well shafts on the property, sunk deep into the mountainside. Down in the hacienda's sub-basement, electric pumps drew water from both wells, put it through ceramic filters, dripped it through tanks full of special resin beads that softened it somehow, and stored it in huge cisterns.

Tate found the pump room calming and peaceful. It was cool and dark there, with the whirr of the pumps, the sound of dripping water. And the walls were heavy cement, so sound didn't carry up to the house.

By the time he dried his hair, got dressed, and made his way down to the pump room, the detective from Texas was zip-tied to the metal chair in the middle of the room. They'd laid down the plastic sheets around the chair, and a couple of men were watching him. He looked up as Tate came in, trying to keep cool, trying not to look afraid. Tate liked that. The local boys had roughed him up a little bit; he hadn't gone down without a fight. There was a cut over his eye already, bit of blood. But not too bad, really. Plenty left for him.

"So you're a detective," he said. "Interesting job, I bet. Go places, meet new people."

He opened a metal locker and took out a white Tyvek coverall. He caught a bit of a tremble from Stratton as he stepped into it.

"Ever want to do anything else?" he asked as he zipped up

the suit and pulled on the little elastic booties over his shoes. "Was there a moment when you might have ended up selling insurance, say, or being assistant manager of a plant that makes those little French toast sticks they serve at IHOP? Something like that? Is there a moment you can think of when you turned onto this particular path? Because that was a really lousy day, and you didn't even know it."

"Look, man, I don't know what's going on here," Stratton said, trying to control his voice. "My client's a Hollywood guy. Big producer. He's looking for a place to buy in Mexico, right? Out in the country, but he wants all the luxuries. So I'm looking for him. He just heard this place was out here, and he wanted to find out who owns it to maybe make an offer. That's it!"

Tate wheeled his tool cart over. It rattled across the cement floor.

"See, I am going to ask you some questions," he said, "but this is why we don't start there. You still think you can talk your way out of this. We've got to level set first so we're all on the same page, know where we stand."

He opened a drawer, rifled through the tools inside, and finally came out with an eight-inch half-round hand rasp. Yeah, that was the place to start. Hurt like hell, lot of visible damage, but it was all surface. Nothing that would put Stratton down before he had what he wanted from him. After that, the pliers, the awl, and the tin snips for when he got a little more serious.

He flipped the rasp and caught it, and Stratton blanched. "Jesus, man," he said. "Jesus."

He walked over and checked Stratton's hands. The men who tied him to the chair did it right. His fingers were wrapped around the ends of the arms and had nowhere to go. Of course, hands weren't the best place to start. People were accustomed to hurting their hands; they said they were "getting their hands dirty." Now, snipping off fingers, that would have an effect. But that was later. The scalp was a good place to start with the rasp. Lot of blood, but he wouldn't be able to see just how bad it was, so he would picture it. And, of course, you got down to bone a lot faster there.

"Come on, come on, we don't have to do this," said Stratton, and the fear was cracking through his voice now. "I'll tell you what you want to know."

Tate smiled at him. "Like I said, I don't want to know anything yet. When I do, you'll know."

Then he got to work and felt the rush as the blood spattered his white coverall and the screams echoed off the cisterns.

When he was done, he stripped off the bloodstained coverall and put his watch back on. It had been a little over an hour. The wreckage of Detective Stratton slumped in the chair, his breath a wet gurgle.

"Get rid of him," he told the men who had quietly watched him work for the last hour. He added a waving gesture to take in the plastic sheet, the coverall, the bloody booties. "And burn all this."

He headed upstairs and found Esteban waiting for him in the game room. Esteban was the cartel's ranking man here, the one in charge of the soldiers, the one who reported back to Lalo when there was a problem—a problem like this one.

Esteban was a tall, lean man in his late thirties, with jet-black hair he wore oiled back and a nasty scar next to one eye. He twirled an unlit cigarillo around his fingers because Tate didn't want smoking in the house. As Tate came in, he crossed his legs with a flash of the silver trim on his boots, and said, "So?"

"So Martin, the guy who tried to escape. You remember how he kept claiming his father was a big-deal businessman back in

Texas? Turns out he wasn't bullshitting us. This guy works for the father. He's had him and a couple other detectives running around Mexico, looking for his son ever since he went missing."

"Including this man who sunk your boat?"

Tate poured himself a shot glass of tequila. He was still coming down from it, and the liquor mixed nicely with the last of the adrenaline rush.

"No, strangely enough. He knew a couple others. I got names and descriptions. But he didn't know John Crane. It's not the first time someone's sent a PI looking for a lost loved one."

"But it's the first time they've come here," said Esteban. "How did he find this place?"

"He doesn't know. The father sent him, but he just gave him the location. But he did know that they're putting together a rescue mission with a bunch of hired guns."

Esteban leaned forward, concerned. "How many hired guns?"

"He thought maybe half a dozen. Not much."

Esteban stood up and stuck his unlit cigarillo back in his shirt pocket. He shook his head. "That's not good," he said. "A half-dozen mercenaries we can handle, but Lalo won't like that this location leaked. He's going to want to know how."

"They don't know anything," Tate said. "They don't know the kid's dead. They don't know my name. The guy was fishing. That's all. For all we know, they could be sending people to look at every big hacienda in Durango. Let them send their mercenaries. We'll bury them out back with the detective, and that will be the end of it. All they'll know is they don't want to mess with us."

"We need a show of force," Esteban agreed. "I'll talk to the boss. See about getting some more guys up here, some heavy weapons."

Tate heard a muffled gunshot from outside, and that was the end of Mr. Stratton. Tate smiled. When his friends came on their useless rescue mission, they'd get the same welcome.

CHAPTER 34

There were eight of them, plus Crane himself, sitting on bench seats in the cargo bay of Jessie's Short. Crane had met them at El Paso just before they took off. They were ex-military, and not impressed that Crane wasn't. He didn't talk about himself, and certainly didn't mention the Hurricane Group. But apparently Sawyer had let slip that Crane came from some kind of civilian intelligence background, and word had gotten around. They weren't thrilled to have Crane along, and especially unhappy with the idea that he was in charge. But they needed a command structure, and Jessie had made it clear up front that Crane had the knowledge and the plan, and they were to follow his lead.

Now they were high over the Mexican mountains, the Short droning through the night toward Tate's compound. The men were cracking bad jokes and bragging about past exploits, the sort of thing Crane had seen soldiers do to build rapport when they hadn't fought together before. Everything was last names—Hicks, Buskirk, Alvarez—except for one named Fralin who everyone called "Major." Crane gathered he was the leader of the group.

Crane sat in the back, talking with Finney, the sniper who

was recently back from Afghanistan. He cradled a Barrett MRAD with a long scope and night-vision optics and discussed with Crane where he should set up. Crane showed him video from the drone overflight and pointed out the location he'd noticed.

"Yes, sir," said Finney. "That'll work just fine."

"Any concerns about the range?"

"No, sir. This weapon will punch through level-three body armor at nine hundred meters. Unless they're driving tanks, I can put them down."

"All right, leave securing the airstrip to us," Crane said. He traced a route across the hills with a fingertip. "As soon as we're on the ground, move out. Notify us when you're in position. From there, you'll know what to do."

"I'm sure I'll find some way to occupy my time," Finney said with a grin.

The others were armed with suppressed M4 carbines, probably because they'd trained on them in the military. It wasn't Crane's favorite weapon, but it would do here, where combat was likely to be at short range. For himself, Crane had chosen an F2000, a compact NATO bullpup rifle that would be usable in the tight quarters he expected in the building where the hostages were kept. For backup, he had the Sig Sauer MHS pistol he'd taken from Orly Wilde.

The plan they'd worked out was simple. They'd be landing in the dark a couple hours before dawn. Even so, they couldn't assume surprise under the circumstances. They'd eliminate any resistance at the airstrip and leave Jessie there to hold their beachhead. Then they'd move as quickly as possible to the compound. Ideally that would be in trucks they'd take at the airstrip. They could move on foot if they had to, but that would slow them down going in, and especially going out when they'd have to herd a group of frightened civilians a couple miles back to the airstrip.

But there was a building across the runway from the warehouses that looked like a multi-vehicle garage to Crane. He was confident they'd find something there that they could use.

Either way, as they approached the compound, they'd split into two groups. "Major" Fralin would lead five of them in a feint toward the main house and the barracks Crane had identified. Crane hoped the defenders would take the attack for an assault by a rival cartel. Meanwhile, Crane and the other two men would go into the walled-off building in the far corner of the compound and free the hostages. They'd get them out and onto a truck, and then both teams would withdraw and meet up on the dirt road back to the airstrip.

What Crane hadn't mentioned yet was that he'd be diverting at that point for his side mission to retrieve Jason Tate.

From the cockpit, Jessie's voice crackled over the speakers. "Beginning descent," she announced. "We're on the dirt in ten. If you have a reason we can't go as planned, say so now."

Nobody did. "All right, then," she said. "Get ready to move."

The landing was dark. The airstrip wasn't lit, and Jessie had turned off the Short's lights and was flying with night-vision goggles. Crane and the others put on their own goggles, shrugged their packs on, gave their weapons one last check, and got ready to move.

The Short came in hot. It hit the ground and kicked up dust, rolling in fast with the cargo ramp already lowering. The moment it stopped, Crane leaped out the back, followed quickly by the other mercenaries. Finney immediately set off into the scrub brush, heading for his sniping position. Crane scanned the buildings, familiarizing himself with the layout he'd seen from above in the drone footage. Here were the warehouses, probably stacked with cocaine, heroin, or meth. There was the garage. The five bay doors were all closed, but Crane was still hopeful there would be a truck behind at least one of them. At the far end of the garage was a smaller building scaled for people.

Just as Crane looked toward the building, a door flew open and three men charged out, bent over low as they ran. Crane caught a white shirt, a submachine gun held in one hand. Then the gun opened up, and muzzle flashes flared bright in his goggles.

The mercenaries had already been moving in on the building. The one in the white shirt was cut down immediately, and then the one behind him. The third man quickly stopped, dropped his gun, and threw his hands in the air.

They'd been on the ground less than two minutes, and they were in command of the airstrip. Two men questioned the prisoner while the others fanned out to check the rest of the facility. Crane slipped into the garage by an access door at the end of the building. He saw no movement inside, but he did find a pair of heavy pickup trucks and a GMC medium-duty flatbed with wooden fencing on the bed. It would be perfect.

He got the bay door open and the lights on. The keys were on hooks on a pegboard. Crane was working out which keys went with the flatbed when one of the men, Buskirk, hurried in.

"Prisoner says they're expecting some kind of VIP," he said. "That's why we didn't get more of a reception. They thought we were her at first."

"Her?"

"What he said. Doesn't sound like he's too clear on who she is. He says they were just supposed to keep an eye on the warehouses, and when this mystery woman landed, call up to the hacienda and then stay out of her way."

"And she's supposed to be getting here now?"

Buskirk shrugged. "That's kind of vague too. Sometime in

the next twenty-four to forty-eight. He says he thought we were early, but they didn't really know what to expect, and none of their own planes were scheduled in, so they figured we must be her."

Crane checked his watch. It was not quite five in the morning. He had a hard time imagining Tate's mystery visitor showing up this early. If all went well, they'd be back in the air and gone inside of an hour.

"Tell Jessie," he said, and tossed Buskirk the keys. "Then get this thing moving and let's mount up."

Within a few minutes, they were underway, standing in the back of the truck and holding on to the battered wooden fencing as they bounced over the packed dirt road. Finney was in position now. His voice crackled in Crane's earpiece.

"Activity on the ground," he said. "They definitely know something's going on, but they look confused. They're setting up a fire team at the rear gate. Looks like six men. I've got targets. Standing by."

When they were a few hundred yards from the gate, flood lights clicked on and bathed the road. The gate was open. It was set in a large stone and wood arch with the lights mounted on the top. Crane saw figures hurrying to swing the barred iron gates shut. Gunfire erupted from behind the stone wings on either side of the road.

Crane thumbed his mic. "Finney, keep those gates open!"

The mercenaries returned fire over the roof of the cab as Buskirk floored it and the truck lurched forward. Crane saw one of the men on the gates go down, and then the other a moment later.

"Two down," Finney said in his ear. A moment later, he added, "Three."

The muzzle flashes coming from the gate slowed and then stopped. The truck shot through the gate, and Crane got his first look at the grounds. He mapped the layout to the aerial and satellite images he'd seen. There was the garden with its fountains and hedges. There the garage. There the western wing of the main house and the building that apparently served as barracks for the cartel soldiers. He saw figures running near the barracks. As he watched, one was cut down. Finney again, proving very useful, indeed. Crane thumbed his mic again.

"Finney, any activity at the target building?"

"No, sir," Finney answered. "Lights went on a minute ago, but no activity outside. Looks like they think you're going for the main house."

Good, Crane thought. That was the plan. Now they'd reinforce that idea.

As they pulled through the compound, Buskirk slowed the truck, and most of the mercenaries leaped down and scattered into the night. The gunfire was a steady crackle now, and Crane could hear shouting in Spanish. As soon as the men were clear, Buskirk hit the gas again, and they lurched forward. Crane readied his F2000 and glanced over at the man who would be going in with him. His name was Stokes, and apparently he'd been a marine. That was all Crane knew about him. Stokes nodded back at him.

The truck rounded a corner of the house and sped toward the smaller building where the hostages were kept. Crane heard the others calmly giving tactical orders and reports over their radio channel.

"Get ready," Buskirk said, his voice tight. Then, "Go!"

Crane sprang down from the truck bed and hit the ground running. Stokes was right behind him. They were a few yards from one end of the building. To Crane's right was a walled yard that he guessed the prisoners used for outside exercise. Around the side of the building to his left was a loading dock. Buskirk was taking the truck there. He would secure the area and get the rollup door open. Crane and Stokes were approaching a door on the end of the building. They would enter that way, free the hostages, and lead them out to the dock.

Two lights on the corners of the building flooded the area around the door. Stokes put them both out with quick shots from his suppressed carbine. Crane fell into a crouch beside the door. He pulled a pick gun from a leg pouch and quickly snapped the tumblers and twisted the lock open.

He and Stokes crouched on opposite sides of the door, backs against the wall. Crane reached over to turn the knob and push the door open.

There was no reaction, no spray of bullets. The inside was dark and quiet. Through his goggles, Crane saw bright green lines—workbenches, equipment racks. Nothing that looked alive, nothing that moved. He signaled to Stokes and then spun and quickly moved through the door, leading with the F2000's muzzle. Behind him, Stokes moved through the door and took up a new position.

They were in.

CHAPTER 35

The workshop was still and silent as Crane and Stokes moved through it. They heard gunfire from the main building and quick, snapped commands through their earpieces. But here they moved slowly, quietly, looking for anything that might present a threat or give away their position.

Crane passed down a row of storage racks lined with plastic bins labeled in black marker on masking tape. Power supplies, handset batteries, cooling fans, antenna assemblies. He reached the end of the row and glanced over to see Stokes at the end of the next row over. They nodded to each other and moved on to the next section.

At the far end was a drywall partition, and behind that, a carpeted room with a desk, cheap chairs, and a closed door that had to be the stairway to the basement. That was where the hostages would be. Either they were locked in their rooms, or the guards would have collected them in the common area at the bottom of the stairs. Crane saw light beneath the door.

He and Stokes crouched at opposite sides of the door and considered how to breach the lower floor. It wasn't a great tactical situation. The stairs were the only way in or out—obviously the builders hadn't worried about fire codes. It was a choke point, but worse, it was one that would let the guards downstairs cover the door while making it very hard for them to get through without exposing themselves to fire. The drone hadn't provided enough detail to tell Crane how the stairs were built, but he was guessing they were of open plank construction, meaning someone might even be able to fire on them from behind.

Tactical doctrine counseled against pushing the fight under these circumstances. They were supposed to secure the perimeter and bring in the hostage negotiators. But there was no time for that. They needed to get in and out in the window the others were creating for them.

"Flashbang and pie?" Stokes whispered.

"Flashbang, anyway," Crane answered. Slicing the pie meant traversing a corner in stages to sweep successive sections of the area beyond it. But the stairway would limit the area of the room below that they could see until they moved down the steps, and that would put them at risk.

"Boss won't like it if we shoot his boy," said Stokes.

Crane nodded back. "Let's try not to do that."

Crane thumbed his mic. "Buskirk, what's your status?"

"Loading dock's secure," came the reply. "Truck's in position. I can open the door anytime."

"There should be an electrical panel on that side of the building. Do you see it? Can you kill the lights on my word?"

There was a pause, and then, "Here we go. Master cut-off right here. No problem."

"Okay, stand by." To Stokes, he murmured, "Lights, door, flashbangs, me, you. I'll go right at the bottom; you take left."

Stokes nodded back. He reached over and gingerly turned the doorknob to release the latch, but held it in place while Crane pulled two flash grenades from his pack.

"I'm thinking they'll cut loose up the stairs when the door opens," said Stokes. "Keep low."

Crane agreed. The guards would be on edge. They could hear the shooting outside. No reinforcements were coming. Their instinct would be to aggressively defend the one doorway into their basement fortress.

He readied the two grenades and then knelt down as low as he could get and gave Stokes a look. Stokes nodded back, indicating he was ready.

Crane thumbed his mic. "Give me a three count and then kill the lights."

"Roger that," Buskirk answered. "Three, two, one, go!"

The strip of light beneath the door vanished. Crane heard someone shout.

Stokes whipped the door open, and just as he'd predicted, a hail of gunfire erupted up the stairwell. Bullets hissed by overhead, scarred the drywall, slammed into the ceiling. Crane could see the muzzle flashes from the darkness. Some part of his brain instinctively told him there were two shooters firing pistols. With all the flashes and noise in that confined space, the grenades seemed almost superfluous. But he tossed them down the stairwell, the first one away to the right, and then the second back to the left. They clattered down the stairs and went off, one a second before the other, with two shattering bangs and bright flashes of light.

The shooting stopped, and Crane whipped around the corner, leading with the muzzle of his F2000. His goggles picked out two figures standing near the bottom of the stairs. They were blinded and deafened, holding pistols. Crane cut them both down with quick bursts of the rifle. He kept moving, sweeping the room for any other shooters. He spun as he neared the bottom of the stairs and checked behind him. But there was no one there. All he saw were other figures on the floor, scrambling in the darkness for a safe corner.

Crane veered right at the bottom of the stairs. Behind him, Stokes was coming down fast, and headed left. Crane scooped up the pistols the guards had dropped while Stokes swept the room.

"Clear," he said.

"Nobody move!" Crane shouted in Spanish. "We're here to rescue you. Everyone sit up. Keep your hands where we can see them."

He thumbed his mic again. "Buskirk, lights."

The lights gave a dim flicker and then came back on. The room was a dingy living area, furnished with cheap, mismatched couches and chairs and a scarred coffee table. At the far side of the room, a hallway stretched the length of the building. Back there were the bedrooms. Here there were six men. They wore boxer shorts or pajamas, and they looked up at him with an odd mix of fear and hope.

"Point out any guards," said Crane. It was doubtful, but he wanted to make sure no enemy was trying to hide himself among the hostages. But nobody moved or spoke.

"Martin Cottrell," Stokes shouted. "Martin Cottrell, are you here?"

The men were all Mexican. They looked back and forth at each other, and then one timidly raised his hand.

"I knew Martin," he said. "I roomed with him. He's not here. He tried to escape ... he didn't make it."

Sawyer is going to be devastated, Crane thought. He'd poured all his hope into this raid. Crane was glad he wasn't the one who would have to tell him they were too late.

Crane watched the men while Stokes swept the hallway and the bedrooms and found nothing else. Then he switched his radio to a new channel.

"This is Crane," he said. "We've got six civilians. What's your status out there?"

Fralin's voice came back. "Getting hot up here. This is definitely more than half a dozen men. We've got them contained for now, but don't waste time."

"Roger that," he said. "Moving the hostages out now."

The hard part would be getting out, Crane knew. When they withdrew, the cartel defenders wouldn't be bottled up any longer. They'd pour out of the hacienda like angry wasps and go on the offensive. They would need to get the men onto the truck and get out of the compound without taking any casualties. Then it would be a race to the airstrip.

"When I point you out, give me your name!" Crane said to the hostages. He got the names and relayed them to Jessie. Then he beckoned Stokes over.

"Give them two minutes to get dressed and then get them upstairs and on the truck," he said. "Tell Buskirk to rendezvous with the Major and withdraw."

"Wait, where are you going to be?"

"I've got something else to take care of," said Crane.

"What? Nobody told me about anything else!"

Crane was already heading up the stairs. "Tell them they've got two minutes."

Jason Tate paced around the game room and slapped the eight ball from his pool table from one hand to the other and back. Outside, he could still hear muffled shouts and the crack of gunfire. The game room was windowless, a reinforced safe room designed as a defensible refuge in case of something like this.

Two nervous cartel fighters stood near the doors with heavy

automatic rifles. Esteban sat at a corner desk, listening to radio chatter through a headset he held up to one ear.

When they'd gotten Jason out of bed and hurried him in here, all Esteban was able to tell him was that a plane had landed at the airstrip, and there had been gunfire. Once they reached the compound, alarm had turned to confusion. He'd told them to expect a VIP visitor, but not the one he'd originally told Lalo was coming. So they'd prepared for that, but instead this was the rescue mission the late Detective Stratton had told them about. Everything was off course. Worse, it was because of him, for reasons that had nothing to do with the cartel.

Lalo wasn't happy about any of it, but it couldn't be helped. Tate's job was to serve as a bridge between two very different groups with different methods and agendas. The cartel was actually quite predictable. The others he dealt with were not.

Esteban listened to the radio chatter for a moment. "We've lost the workshop," he said. "That means they've got the engineers out. They'll be heading back to the airstrip. We can't let them get out."

He gave Tate a grim look and shook his head. Lalo had agreed to send up some three-dozen additional men with automatic weapons and some additional trucks. They were to wait outside the compound, ready to roll in when the rescue mission arrived and take them by surprise. But with his unexpected guest coming, he'd demanded that they pull back farther down the road from the compound. This was no time for some unfortunate misunderstanding.

So now it was taking longer to get them back in place to counterattack. Esteban listened to the radio chatter for a few more seconds, and his irritation was obvious. Then he seemed to come to a decision. He gestured to one of the men near the door. "Gerardo, take him back to his room. And make sure he's safe there."

Gerardo nodded and then gestured to Jason. "Come with me, sir."

Jason followed him toward one door out of the room while Esteban headed for the other one.

"Where are you going?" Jason asked.

"Where do you think? To chase these bastards down and kill them!"

Then Esteban disappeared out the far door, and Jason heard him barking orders into his radio handset from the hallway. Jason followed Gerardo down the gallery to his master suite. He supposed it wasn't good that someone had figured out that the cartel's radio network was built and maintained from here. In the worst case, he'd have to move somewhere else. But so what? The cartel could afford a hundred places like this one, and they needed his abilities and his connections. They'd get over it.

Ahead of him, the gallery ended at the recessed door to his suite. Gerardo went ahead to open the doors for him.

"No problem, huh, Gerardo?" he said as he followed him around the corner. "Ready for a new place, anyway, right?"

As Jason cleared the corner, his brain registered three facts in quick succession.

The man waiting there for him wasn't Gerardo.

Gerardo lay on the floor in the doorway to his room, not moving.

The man smiling at him was John Crane.

"Hi, Boz," Crane said as Jason stood there, too surprised to react. "Really sorry about the boat."

Then, just as Jason was drawing breath to shout, an electric current surged through him. Jason went rigid, trembling, and then fell to the floor.

CHAPTER 36

Crane supposed there must be other things as satisfying as dropping Jason Tate with a stun gun. But at the moment, he couldn't think of any. He moved quickly, taping Tate's mouth and securing his wrists and ankles with zip ties. Then he snatched the radio handset from the guard's belt and stuck it on his own belt. Finally, he hefted Tate up over his shoulders in a fireman's carry and headed back out into the night.

Outside, he avoided the pools of the house's floodlights and made his way toward a small gate in the perimeter wall that he'd spotted on the drone video. Then he heard engines and stopped. Two trucks rolled in from the other side of the compound, loaded with armed men. The stragglers from the house detachment ran alongside and climbed aboard. The trucks crossed the compound and headed down the dirt road toward the airstrip. Where had they come from? And why? Did the cartel get some kind of warning they were coming?

He decided those were questions he could address later. They presented a more immediate problem. Crane thumbed his mic.

"You've got incoming," he announced. "They've got reinforcements. Two trucks full of men heading your way."

There was a flurry of reaction in the channel, and then Jessie's voice cut through them. "Roger that. What's your status?"

"Got what I came for," said Crane. "On my way back now."

A few moments later, Finney's voice broke in. "Might be able to help with your truck problem."

"Finney, where are you?" Crane asked. Tate was starting to struggle on his shoulders.

"Partway back," he said. "I can cover the road from here. Give me a second."

Crane hauled the struggling Tate up the wooded slope. Suddenly the cartel radio on his belt burst out in a storm of confused shouts. A moment later, in his earpiece, Finney said, "Okay, they're on foot."

From the cartel traffic, he gathered Finney had put a couple rounds into the lead truck's engine and blocked the road. Crane heard someone giving orders to fan out.

"Good job, Finney," he said. "Now get to the plane. We've got to get out of here."

"You're one to talk," said Finney.

Crane picked up his pace. He could see the beginnings of dawn on the horizon. Tate was thrashing now and trying to shout at him through the tape. Crane put his head down and pitched Tate forward. He hit the ground with a grunt, and Crane bent down and sliced through the zip tie binding his ankles.

"Get up and move," Crane snapped.

Tate glared up at him. Crane pointed the F2000's muzzle at his chest. "Idea is to bring you back alive," he said, "but if I kill you, they'll get over their disappointment."

Tate climbed to his feet and staggered forward. He was trying to slow Crane down, but it was still faster than trying to carry him thrashing and struggling on his back.

They reached the ridge line and headed down the far slope. Crane could hear sporadic gunfire in the distance and see the lights around the airstrip. Then Jessie spoke in his ear.

"We've got a problem," she said. "The runway's blocked."

Crane's heart sank. This kept getting worse.

"Blocked how?"

"Looks like an old fuel truck, about a thousand feet from here. I can't take off in that, and we're starting to feel some heat. How far out are you?"

This wasn't going to work, he realized. Going after Tate had been reaching too far, and somehow they'd underestimated the numbers they'd be facing. Now the plane was pinned down. If they couldn't clear the runway, those superior numbers would eventually overrun the rescue team.

"Not sure it matters how far out I am," Crane answered. "Nobody's going anywhere until the runway's clear."

"If you've got an idea ..."

He had an idea. He just didn't like it.

"How are you holding up?"

"Hostages are aboard. We're holding for now, but nobody has cover to get to the truck."

"Is Finney back?"

"He is."

That meant he was the last one out. He was the one who had held things up by going after Tate. He was the only one who could get to the truck and clear the runway. It had to be him.

"Get the engines hot," he said. "I'll go for the truck."

"How are you going to make it back here?"

"One thing at a time," he said.

Tate had turned and grinned at him through the duct tape. Crane prodded him forward, and they hurried down the gentle slope through widely spaced trees. Crane listened to the chatter of the cartel soldiers on his radio. They were confident, pressing against the defensive perimeter. They moved cautiously, but they knew they were winning.

Crane kept a close eye on Tate, yanking him back on course when he strayed. They had moved around the battle zone now. The airstrip was a long void in the trees to Crane's right.

Then he saw the truck in the distance. It was an old International 4900, rusted and dented. It had been parked in a cut-out in the woods on the near side of the airstrip. Either someone had gotten the clever idea to use it to block the runway, or they actually kept it there for that purpose. Either way, it had to move.

"Hold up," he said to Tate. Tate was tired now, breathing hard with his hands zip-tied behind his back. Crane moved him to the trunk of a tall oak and sat him down with his back against it. Then he stunned him again. That part was fun. He pulled another zip tie off his belt and restrained Tate's ankles again. He could carry him from here if he needed to.

Satisfied that Tate would be here when he got back, Crane made his way cautiously through the trees toward the runway and the truck. Someone was moving near the edge of the airstrip. Crane heard tuneless humming and then saw the red point of a cigarette. He readied the F2000 and moved forward, faster now, dodging around saplings and leaping over a fallen branch.

The man heard him coming, but too late. He whirled and cried out, but then Crane slammed the rifle's heavy butt into his jaw, snapped his knee with a brutal, thrusting kick, and drove him into the trunk of the tree he'd been leaning against. As he was collapsing to the ground, Crane registered a second man on the runway standing beside the truck. He was running toward Crane, raising a weapon.

Crane cut him down with a quick burst from the rifle, and then dropped to a crouch and scanned his surroundings. There was nobody else here, and nothing to indicate that the shots had drawn any attention from the main battle, where there was already plenty of shooting going on.

Crane kept low and darted out of the cover of the trees. He crossed the runway and didn't stand until he was behind the bulk of the fuel truck. It looked intact, if aged. The driver's door was open, and Crane pulled himself up into the cab. They'd gotten it out here under its own power, at least. The keys were in the ignition. They hadn't pushed a dead chassis out into the runway. So the thing could be driven.

He dashed back into the trees and made his way back to where he'd left Tate. Again he hauled him, struggling and grunting, up over his shoulders and carried him to the truck. He dumped Tate in the passenger seat with a creak of springs and sat him up. Tate ended up sitting on his hands, with his zip-tied feet in a footwell full of crushed beer cans.

Crane climbed back into the driver's seat and closed the door. He thumbed his mic. "Jessie, I've got the truck. How soon can you take off?"

It took her a moment to reply. "Don't know," she said at last. "We've got a couple injured now. They're pinned down between the warehouses. How fast can you make it back here?"

No, he thought, *there's no more time for that*. The plane was going to be overrun very soon if he didn't do something.

"I'll find another way out," he said. "I'm going to clear the runway, and I'm going to pull some of the pressure off you. Get everyone back aboard and get airborne as soon as you can."

He listened to the open channel for a moment. He heard shouting and gunfire behind her, very close. Then she gave him a new frequency. "That channel, John. Soon as I get these people out of here safe, I'll be back for you. Keep safe. Use that channel, and I'll pluck you out of there. Good luck."

"You too," said Crane. Then, with a sigh, he reached over and ripped the tape off Jason Tate's mouth.

"You son of a bitch!" Tate immediately shouted. "I'm going to kill you slow, you mother—"

Crane backhanded him. "Save your breath," he said. "I need you to do something else for me."

He turned the key and coaxed the truck's aging, poorly maintained engine into sputtering life. Then he pulled the cartel radio he'd taken from his belt, opened the mic, and tossed it into Tate's lap.

"Tell your friends where you are."

Tate hunched over the radio and shouted, "Hey! It's me! It's Tate! Help me!"

Crane got the truck into gear and lurched forward. He turned the wheel in a wide, slow arc until he was facing away from the warehouses and the plane, and then he switched on the lights and drove down toward the far end of the runway.

The cartel radio lit up in a storm of voices, some demanding to know what Tate was doing on the channel, others reporting that the fuel truck was moving.

"Clear the channel!" someone snapped. "I see the fucking truck! Where are you, Jason Tate?"

"I'm in the truck!" Tate shouted back. "Crane has me! We're in the fuel truck!"

The channel suddenly went quiet.

"Come help me!" Tate was shouting. "You need me! We're in the fuel truck! Can you hear me?"

"They've switched channels," Crane said. "That one's compromised. Don't worry, they know where you are."

"You goddamn son of a bitch," Tate snapped. "I'm going to fuck you up so bad. You're going to beg me to kill you."

Well, that's original, Crane thought. He shifted up as the truck picked up speed.

Jessie's voice came through his earpiece. "They're peeling off. It's working."

"Get your people aboard and get out of here," he said. "While you can."

"You hang tight," she said. "I'll be back for you."

At the end of the airstrip, the runway gave way to an unpaved track of a fire road that twisted its way down a slope. Crane steered down it, and the truck threw back loose dirt. He downshifted and gave it gas. Behind him, he could see headlights following him. They weren't trucks, he realized after a moment; they were four-wheel ATVs bouncing over the rough ground and coming up fast.

The truck bumped and groaned over rocks and erosion gullies. If he could somehow lose his pursuers, he might have a chance at getting down the mountain and finding a place where Jessie could land and pick him up. But he didn't like his chances of outrunning ATVs on this mountainside in a twenty-year-old fuel tanker.

As if it had heard his thoughts, the truck bottomed out on a rock and skewed sideways into sand. They lurched to a stop, canted a little to one side. Crane gunned it, and the wheel just spun, digging the truck in deeper.

He sighed and cut the engine.

"You are so screwed." Tate laughed.

Crane got out. Someone shouted at him in Spanish. He got down on his knees, laced his hands behind his head, and waited. Through the sound of the ATV engines, he heard another sound. He looked back over his shoulder to see the Short lumber into the air and climb away toward the north. He'd managed that much, anyway.

As the plane receded into the distance and men circled him with guns aimed at his chest, Crane looked ahead into the rising sun. By all indications, it was going to be a beautiful day. But Crane guessed it was going to be a pretty bad one nonetheless.

Then something hit him hard in the back of the skull, and he fell forward into the dirt, which he took as confirmation for a moment before everything went dark.

CHAPTER 37

Josh sat in his office, looking out the windows at the rising sun and idly clicking through random Wikipedia articles on his laptop. He could have gone to the war room, but there were no windows there, and he wanted to watch the dawn break. Besides, very few people were around Myria this time of morning, and Josh didn't see much of a security issue.

The sound system was playing downtempo electronica. It was chill-out music from a compilation named after a bar in Ibiza. Josh leaned back in his chair, idly clicking links, trying to find odd Wikipedia rabbit holes to descend into. Somehow he'd gotten stuck in a series of articles on the Yugoslavian civil war.

Click euros. That will get you back out. Euros. Click it.

Fine.

Scroll, scroll ... oh! Esperantist. Awesome. That has to lead somewhere interesting. William Shatner did a horror movie in the sixties that was entirely in Esperanto. That gets you to Star Trek, and from there the world's your oyster.

Then the speakers sounded an alert tone and a dialog box popped up that read "Handshake Protocol Initiated."

His secure communications program was setting up a link

between here, Sawyer Cottrell in Texas, and Jessie Diamond's plane. Josh sat up and waited for the tone that meant the scramblers were in place and he could speak.

It came a moment later, and he heard Jessie say, "Sawyer? Josh? Can you hear me? Sound off."

"I'm here, Jessie," he said.

A moment later, he heard Sawyer. "I'm here. Talk to me, Jessie. Talk to me."

"We're airborne," Jessie said, "approaching US airspace. We've got six civilians rescued."

"My son! Is Martin there? Tell me you got him!"

Jessie paused. Josh could hear the drone of the engines behind her. He had a sinking feeling.

"I don't have good news, Sawyer."

Sawyer's voice fell. "He wasn't there."

"He was. There's someone aboard who roomed with him. He says Martin tried to escape a couple months ago. I'm sorry, Sawyer. He didn't make it."

It was almost as if he heard Sawyer take the punch to the gut. He let out a breath and then went quiet.

"Thank you for trying," he finally said.

"I'm sorry, Sawyer," said Josh.

"There's more," said Jessie. "It's Crane."

Now it was Josh who felt a cold chill grasp him and squeeze.

Crane's dead. You got him killed. How are you going to live with that?

"He didn't make the plane," Jessie was saying. "He cleared the runway so we could get out, but he couldn't make it back to the plane. He said he was going to try to make it out on his own, but there's no way."

"Don't sell Crane short," he said a little quicker than he'd intended.

"It was rough down there. The cartel had more people than we thought."

So damn cocky, aren't you? You're richer than God, so you think you can do anything. Nothing can touch you. Well, how'd that work out for you? They got to your driver, and now they've probably killed Crane.

We don't know that.

Uh huh. Sure.

Until we know, we have to do everything we can to get him out.

Whatever, dude. Whatever.

"Too late," Sawyer groaned. "Wasted. All of it. For nothing."

"It wasn't for nothing," Jessie told him. "We got six men out. That's six families who won't have to go through what you're going through now. That's worth something, Sawyer. Martin would be proud of you."

Sawyer said nothing. After a moment, Josh heard him quietly sobbing.

Josh let out a slow breath. This wasn't the morning he'd been expecting. He'd convinced himself that Crane could do anything. He expected to hear him on the radio with Jessie, telling him they'd rescued everyone and Jason Tate was aboard.

"Jessie," he said quietly, "when do you land?"

"A little under an hour," she said. "It'll be another couple hours at least before I can get airborne again."

"What's the plan? What do we do?"

"I gave Crane another radio frequency," she said. "Sending it to you now. I told him we'd be monitoring it."

His laptop pinged as a new channel was added to his favorites list.

"Got it. So we monitor it. Then what?"

"Not much we can do," Jessie said. "We've got no idea what's going on back there. If Crane can get himself someplace safe, he calls in, and we figure out where to pick him up."

But she doesn't think that's going to happen.

"We just sit and wait? That won't cut it, Jessie. There's got to be something we can do."

"If you've got an idea, let's hear it. Until we know what's happening ..."

He sighed. She was right, of course. The odds were that Crane was going to die soon, if he wasn't dead already. If they were waiting for him to get in touch on this new radio frequency, they might be waiting a long time.

"There's an airstrip about fifty minutes' flight time from the compound," she said after a few moments. "I can stage there and be ready to go. That's the best I can do. I don't have the fuel capacity to orbit over the compound for very long."

"Okay," he said with resignation. "Okay. Do what you can, Jessie. Drop off Sawyer's people and head down there. Then I guess we'll wait."

He stood up and walked around his desk and looked out across the Myria campus. The sun was up, and people were starting to arrive for work. They walked along the paths that curved through the campus to gleaming glass-and-steel buildings. They would do their jobs and go home. Today would be like any other day for most of them, but not for him. He wasn't sure if his days would ever feel normal again.

"Jessie," he said. "What else can I do to help you?"

"Nothing," she answered. "Just stand by. I'll keep you in the loop if I hear anything."

"Thank you." He sat down again, sighed, and leaned back in his chair.

There has to be something. Come on. What can I do?
You can pray it was quick.

CHAPTER 38

Crane awakened to the sound of dripping water and ripples of pale light on a cement wall. It was cool and damp. Crane hurt.

He was seated, zip tied to a metal chair. The chair was bolted into the cement floor, and plastic sheets had been rolled out all around it. He was in the middle of some underground room full of pipes and machinery. He guessed this was where the hacienda pumped in its water.

Three men lounged against the walls and the machines, calmly watching him. He suspected a fourth behind him, where he couldn't see. There were ties at his wrists and elbows, at his ankles, and some kind of leather strap around his midsection that went all the way around the back of the chair. He was almost completely immobilized. He couldn't even flex his fingers off the end of the chair's arms.

Crane knew his situation was grim. This was something he knew he might face someday; they'd even trained him for it. It seemed as though the Hurricane Group had trained him for everything. He would look for a chance to act, but it was unlikely they'd make a mistake big enough for him to work his way out of this. Failing that, all that was left was to die as well as he could.

After a bit of waiting, he heard a metal door creak open, and then footsteps. Jason Tate appeared, looking freshly showered and groomed. He stopped in front of Crane and looked down with a leering grin.

"That didn't turn out like you planned, did it?" he said. Then Tate slowly circled around him, looking down with that same leering grin. The second time around, when Tate disappeared from his field of view, Crane steeled himself for the blow. And it came just as he expected it—a hard punch to the base of his skull.

"Told you not to mess with me," Tate said. "Seriously, what is your damage? The fuck did I ever do to you?" He reached out and slapped Crane's temple, and then repeated the question.

"You get in my face out of nowhere, and you make an ass of yourself. You sink my boat!" He paced away a few steps, fists balled, as his anger overcame him. Then he whirled back, and his face was red, distorted with rage. "You sank my fucking boat, you son of a bitch!"

He charged in and threw an uppercut that caught Crane under the jaw and snapped his head back.

"And then this bullshit," Tate was saying. "The fuck is all this even about? A handful of Mexican radio geeks? I don't even want to know. Doesn't matter. Your ass was dead the moment you blew up my boat."

Crane spat out the blood collecting in his mouth. Tate looked down at it with a snorting laugh.

"We're just getting started, asshole."

Tate walked over to a metal locker and pulled out a Tyvek jumpsuit and a pair of elastic booties.

"What can I do to you to demonstrate the scale of how pissed off I am, huh?" Tate said as he unzipped the coverall and began to pull it on over his clothes. "People are some sick motherfucking animals, you know? We've come up with some shit to do to each other. You ever hear of the boats? That'd be appropriate under the circumstances, wouldn't it? You know what I'm talking about?"

Crane ignored him.

"They'd lay a guy down in a little boat, maybe a canoe or just a hollowed-out log. Then they'd put another one over top of him so they fit together real well." He demonstrated with his cupped hands.

"Seal him in there. Just his feet sticking out one end, and his head and hands at the other end. Then they'd force-feed him a whole bunch of honey and milk so he'd get massive diarrhea in there, smear more honey over his face, and float him out on a pond or something and leave him there. Let him draw flies. They'd feed him more milk and honey from time to time. Watch him sit out there baking in the hot sun, floating in milk and honey and his own wet shit. Let him feel the bugs eating him alive, burrowing into his rotting flesh. Gangrene. The smell of it. Just let him rot and get eaten up by maggots. They'd mostly go mad after a few days of this and just lay there screaming until they died. Not always, though. One guy supposedly lasted two weeks."

He finished pulling on the booties over his shoes and turned to show himself off to Crane. "Pretty fucked up, huh?"

Then he rolled a metal tool cart over beside the chair. "Don't worry," he said, "I don't have that kind of patience. But it'll feel like days before I'm done with you." He cocked his head toward the cartel guards. "I learned some tricks watching these guys. You wouldn't believe the kind of shit they come up with. Animals. Savages. Yeah, you're going to feel it, asshole."

Tate bent down to open it and sorted through the tools. He came up with a ratchet brace, considered it, and then set it down on the shelf. Next out was a draw knife, a jab saw, and a pinpoint acetylene torch.

"Fun with this one," he said as he set it down beside the others. Then he removed a pair of pliers. "This will do to start."

Crane remembered his training. He slowed his breathing, focused on his heartbeat, and went somewhere else.

He was sixteen, at a summer camp in the mountains. He'd snuck out of his cabin at night and met Suzanne Ahlborn by the lake. There was an old graveyard farther around the lakeshore, a family plot from some old farm abandoned years before. They'd dared each other to go, both knowing the dare wasn't about braving ghosts.

It had been his first time, there among the graves. It had been awkward and tentative and glorious. He went there now and held on to it, ignoring what was happening in the present. This was real. The pain was the distant memory.

But he had to admit it was a strong one.

How long it went on, he wasn't sure. But eventually he realized something was happening. He lost his grip on the night in the graveyard, the feel of her skin against his, the sound of the night birds. He was slumped against the cold metal chair. There was blood in his mouth and dripping sounds, small taps against the plastic sheet to go with the water in the background.

Tate looked irritated. One of his cartel minions was standing at his side with a phone. Tate turned away and took the phone.

"Hello?"

Crane spat blood and listened.

"Of course we're expecting you. You ..."

He listened for a long time, only occasionally saying "yes" or "that's right." Then he turned to look down at Crane in surprise.

"No, he's roughed up a bit, but he's alive. Are you absolutely certain ... ? Of course ... That's very generous. I understand. We'll have him ready when you arrive."

He handed the phone back and knelt beside Crane.

"I don't believe this shit."

He grabbed his bloody pliers from the cart, held Crane's head in place with one hand, and with the other, he seized Crane's earlobe with the pliers and twisted, hard. Crane cried out despite himself.

"Apparently you're worth a lot of money to someone," Tate said. "So we're going to have to cut this short. I admit I'm disappointed. I was looking forward to hearing you scream while you pissed yourself. But these aren't people you say no to. And she must want you real bad. So I think maybe you're going from the frying pan into the fire, my friend."

He gave Crane's earlobe a final tug with the pliers and then tossed them back into the toolbox. "Get his ass upstairs and clean him up."

Tate began stripping off the bloodstained coverall and muttering to himself.

"Hey," Crane said weakly. "Jason."

Tate stopped and whirled on him. "What?"

"Scaphism," Crane mumbled.

"What's that?"

"The thing with the boats. It's called scaphism." He laughed. "Amateur."

Tate backhanded him again, but Crane was chuckling as they cut him free of the chair.

CHAPTER 39

The household staff cleaned Crane up, bandaged his wounds, dressed him in clean clothes, and took him to a plain guest bedroom on the hacienda's second floor. It was hot and the air was stuffy. They tied him to a wooden chair and left him alone there. This was definitely what he would remember about this place, he thought. Whether the room was damp and cool, or warm and dry, whatever the décor, there was always a chair to be tied to. At the moment, though, he preferred this chair to the metal one downstairs.

Crane sat with his arms tied behind the stiff, wooden back of the chair and his wrists zip tied together. He sat watching the sunlight play through the gauzy curtains and listening to muffled voices outside.

He spent his time trying to figure out what was going on. It had sounded like someone had called Tate and literally bought him. Who would do that? Josh might try to ransom him if it was possible. But Tate wouldn't have taken that deal even if Josh had been able to get in touch to offer it. And Tate seemed intimidated by whoever was on the phone. It was possible, he reflected gloomily, that Tate was right about this chair being worse in the long run.

Several more minutes went by, and then the door opened, and a woman walked in and closed the door. She studied him for a moment. She wore an olive T-shirt with a large, red, five-pointed star on it, black BDU pants, and black boots with silver buckles. She was average height and slender, but her arms were muscled, and as she came closer, she moved with a grace and power Crane associated with martial arts training. Her hair was cut short and dyed an electric blue beneath a black beret.

She was stunningly beautiful, Crane realized. It was a shame she was probably going to do something horrible to him.

"I am Comrade Comandante Azul!" she shouted at him suddenly. "Of the Indigenous People's Liberation Front! You are a spy from the colonialist multinational corporate states!"

"Is it because of the hair?" said Crane. "Is that why they call you 'Azul'?"

She ignored him. "Our comrades in the Obregon Cartel have agreed to turn you over to us. You will be tried in a military tribunal for your crimes against the people!"

Crane sighed. Back in freshmen year, he'd seen suburban kids wearing Che Guevara T-shirts to impress girls who made more convincing revolutionaries.

"You really make a terrible communist," he said.

"What do you mean?" she asked, dropping the barking tone.

"Well, for one thing, those are Manolo Blahnik boots."

She broke out in a wide, joyous grin, whipped off the beret, and playfully swatted him with it before she tossed it away onto the bed. "Oh, John Crane, you are going to be a delight! But how in God's name did you get yourself into this mess? If I didn't have ears in places I shouldn't, I wouldn't have known you were here at all, and that jackass downstairs would have killed you by now. He really wants to, you know. Did you really blow up his yacht?"

"It seemed like the right thing to do at the time," said Crane.

"Things do tend to explode around you, don't they? Very impressive work in Brno, by the way. Even if you didn't actually kill Skala yourself."

That caught Crane's attention. Even Malcolm had assumed that he'd been the one to kill Branislav Skala. Crane had told Josh what happened. The only other person who knew Crane hadn't pulled the trigger was the man who actually pulled it, a Czech gangster named Anton Kucera. Conclusion—Kucera must have told her.

"You have me at a disadvantage," he said.

"I *do*, don't I?" she said in a flirtatious tone, and licked her lips. "Whatever ... oh, you mean that. I do know a few secrets about you. But then, you keep popping up everywhere I go. Brno. Buenos Aires ..."

Buenos Aires. He'd been following a blackmailer and gigolo that Skala's coded archive referred to as "Tamarind." Tamarind had been romancing an heiress named ... something Calvo. He looked more closely at her, replaced the blue hair with a blonde wig, the revolutionary costume with a white dress.

"You killed Tamarind!"

She shrugged. "Only because you made me. If you'd left him alone, there would have been no need."

Skala had been convinced that Crane was part of a mysterious group he referred to in his notes as "Team Kilo." Crane had no idea who or what Team Kilo was. But Skala was terrified of them. That night, after Kucera had killed Skala in the garden behind his estate, he'd told Crane that the mysterious Team Kilo had sent someone to make him an offer that involved getting rid of Skala. That meant ...

"You're part of Team Kilo," he said in amazement. What the hell was she doing here?

"That's what Skala called us, yes."

"It's kind of an awkward name," he said. "What do you call yourselves?"

She smiled. "We don't have a proper name. Whatever someone else calls us, that's what we are to them. My ... our founder didn't want the organization to become its own thing."

Whatever that meant.

"How about you?" he asked. "What do I call you?"

"Again, we're not much on names. Call me 'Swift.' It's very uncomfortable in here, isn't it?" She crossed to the French doors. She pulled the curtains back and opened the doors to let in the breeze. They looked out onto a balcony with a view across the ridge toward the airstrip.

"That's better. You're full of questions, John. You're the one tied to the chair, remember?"

It was a fair point, he supposed. "But you already know so much more about me than I do about you."

"I don't know as much as you think I do," she said with a wan smile. "You're not easy to investigate, which by itself tells me a little something. You're not US Government, but I bet you used to be. They scrubbed you squeaky clean. You graduated from the University of Virginia with a degree in philosophy." She raised an eyebrow at that. "Really, John?"

Crane just smiled and shrugged.

"And then you just drop off the map. I'm meant to believe you spent most of the intervening years working for a non-profit that helps identify organ donations for critical patients."

"I wanted to help people," Crane said with his most disarming grin. She grinned back at him. He could tell she was enjoying the give and take. He'd be enjoying it more himself, he considered, if he weren't tied to a chair in Jason Tate's guest room.

"The first time your head pops above water is in Puerto Rico, actually. So you left the government before then, but maybe not too long before. Were you Hurricane Group, John?"

"I'm sorry. Who?"

She discarded the idea with a toss of her head. "Timing could be a coincidence. Doesn't matter, really. The important question is who you're working for now. I've gone to a lot of trouble to rule out every faction we know about, and we know all of them, believe me. That's what makes you so exciting."

She threw a leg over his and sat down in his lap, facing him. Her lips were just inches from his, and he felt her taut thighs against his legs. She smelled like orange blossoms.

"You, and whoever's behind you, I mean. Providing the apparently very ample funding, choosing the missions, calling the shots. Collectively, you're a new player," she said, her voice suddenly breathy and seductive. "Nobody knows who you are, what you want. Nobody has a read on you or a mole in your organization. You're so deep under the radar that nobody even knows you're there."

Josh would be disappointed to hear that, he thought.

"I think we can help each other, John. I mean, if nothing else, I can get you out of this chair."

"I could stand to stretch my legs," Crane admitted. "What do you want from me?"

She looked into his eyes for a long moment. Crane tried to read what he saw there, but his instincts told him that wasn't going to work. This was someone who layered personas one atop another until even she didn't know who she was anymore.

"Just your complete, unthinking obedience, of course, darling," she said. "I want you to be my puppet as I conquer the world." She said it in a bantering tone, but then she immediately thought better of it. The grin faded, another layer fell away, and Crane realized she was struggling to speak the truth to him and accept the vulnerability that came with that.

"I need help," she said at last. "You can act freely. I can't. I've managed to gain a little freedom of movement, but I'm still on a very short leash. So you can do things for me that I can't do for myself."

"That actually does sound a little like being your puppet," said Crane.

She flicked his chin with a fingertip. "That's uncharitable of you! I can't pull your strings, John. But I can provide insight, and you need that. I don't think you have any idea what you're doing right now, do you? You're thrashing around at random. Skala, poor Tamarind, and now, of all the things you could be doing, you're going after Jason Tate?"

"The guy's an asshole," said Crane.

"Point taken," she answered. "But there's no shortage of those. Why this one? It makes no sense. You have no grand design."

Crane couldn't help chuckling to himself. She was starting to sound like Malcolm with his insistence that he needed a guiding vision.

She stood up and paced around him in agitation. "I have another theory. Stop me when I make a mistake. You have no idea what you've stumbled into. You came back from Brno with Skala's archive, and it blew your mind. A whole new world behind the curtains. Factions and rivalries and secret wars. But you can't make sense of it, can you? You don't have the context to translate Skala's code names and shorthand, so you're still groping around in the dark. You're not stopping me, John!"

She turned and met his eyes. Crane said nothing. She was right—spot on—and he saw no point in trying to deny it.

"Well, it's no mystery to me," she said. "I grew up in this world. Literally. I can explain every note he took, correct his mistakes, and tell you things Skala never dreamed of. I have the understanding you need, and you have the freedom that I don't. Think about it."

She turned away and went to the French doors. In the distance, Crane heard aircraft engines. Then a helicopter flew past the house, heading south. A few moments later, two airplanes appeared in the distance, climbing out of the airstrip and heading in a different direction. One was an aging DC-3, while the other was a smaller passenger plane.

Swift stood looking at them as they slowly receded into the distance. Then she turned back to him.

"Better think fast, John. We may not have much time."

"Why? What's going on?"

"They've cleared the airstrip. Everything parked there just flew out." She took a breath. "Including the plane I flew in on. My pilot wouldn't have willingly left me here."

She moved quickly across the room to stand behind him.

"Things are moving faster than I expected," she muttered. She bent down with one hand on his shoulder, and with the other, she pressed something into his hands. It was a knife, he realized. It felt like an out-the-front automatic blade. He wrapped his fingers around it, felt the release button pressing into his skin.

"I'm not the enemy, John," she whispered in his ear. "Not today, at least."

Then the doors burst open, and men with guns flooded into the room.

CHAPTER 40

Eight men were dead. The engineers were all gone. The place was shot to hell. Worse, the outside world knew where he was now. Someone knew how to find the engineers, and now they'd no doubt tell the Mexican authorities. The only good thing about it was that he'd finally gotten his hands on that son of a bitch, John Crane. And now a blue-haired woman from the only group he found more frightening than the cartel was in his upstairs bedroom right now, taking Crane away from him.

Jason Tate was not having a good day.

He stalked around the pool as the household staff cleaned up broken glass and shell casings. Esteban was on the phone with his superiors, and he kept glancing over at him in ways Tate didn't like.

He was probably going to have to move after this, and despite his earlier bravado, that was going to suck. He'd put a lot of time and effort into this place. He'd gotten used to it. And it didn't help that the cartel was angry about all this. They'd lost people, and now they'd lost this place that they'd sunk a lot of money into, and they didn't see what any of it had to do with them. But it would be all right. They might resent him, but they still needed him. If nothing else, having Turnstone's fixer show up would remind them of that. They needed the connections he could provide, and the cover.

Tate looked into the pool and shook his head. One of the cartel men had managed to get himself shot and fall into the pool to bleed out. They'd removed the body, but the water was tinted faintly pink. It would have to be drained and cleaned, and he wasn't even sure anyone would bother.

I should get a bag packed, he thought as one of the servants headed his way with a satellite phone. Who the hell knew what was going to happen next?

The servant handed him the phone, and he looked at the number on the screen. Not his cartel contact. The number was unfamiliar, and two digits too long. *Keating*, he thought, *or another of Turnstone's people.*

"Hello," he said.

"Tate?" He'd only heard the voice once before, but there was no mistaking it. He was speaking to Turnstone himself. He swallowed involuntarily.

"Yes, this is Jason. How are you?"

"I want you to listen carefully," Turnstone said. "There's a woman there from my organization."

"That's right," he said, "we're showing her every courtesy."

A shrill and discordant tone cut him off. It sounded as if Turnstone was using a touchtone phone and holding down several buttons at once. It went on for a good five seconds before it cut out. Then Turnstone spoke again.

"I want you to listen carefully. There's a woman there from my organization. Anything she may have told you, any representations she may have made, are inoperative. She is acting without authority. I'm coming there with soldiers to take her into custody. Detain her and keep her there until I arrive. Don't let her leave, and take away any communication devices she may have with her. She doesn't talk to the outside world under any circumstances. Detain anybody who came with her. Kill them if they resist. But she is to be unhurt. Do you have all that? Am I clear?"

Tate stammered for a moment. What the hell was going on? First the business last night, and now this?

"I hear you," he said at last, "but I don't understand what's going on."

"You don't need to! This is an internal matter. Do you have cartel support there?"

"Yes, yes, of course."

"Then use them. She's very dangerous. Be careful. Send one man with a pistol for her, and she'll kill him. Do you understand me? Use everyone you've got, and keep her there until I arrive."

"Yes, I understand. But what about Crane?"

"Who?"

"The man I asked you about. John Crane."

Turnstone made an exasperated noise. "Irrelevant. Kill him."

Then the connection went dead.

Tate looked at the satellite phone in disbelief. Madness. This was madness. He glanced up to the second floor where the blue-haired woman was interrogating John Crane. Kill him. Well, that's just what he was trying to do before the blue-haired woman had come along and stopped him. It sounded as though she'd gone rogue somehow. And while Turnstone might think John Crane was unimportant, the blue-haired woman obviously didn't, and Tate was inclined to side with her. He'd have to find out why she was interested in Crane before Turnstone arrived to take her off his hands.

He dropped the phone on a side table beside a chaise lounge

and looked around for Esteban. He was still standing in the open double doorway that led into the west gallery, talking to someone from the cartel in hushed tones.

"God damn it, Esteban! Get off the damn phone and get over here! We've got trouble!"

Esteban murmured something to the phone and then set it down and walked over. Tate explained his call. Esteban glanced up at the second floor just as he had done.

"Is she still up there?"

"Hell would I know? If she hasn't come down."

Esteban pulled his radio handset from his belt and summoned a pair of his lieutenants. They arrived within a minute, hurrying back from cleanup operations.

"The woman," he asked them. "How many people did she bring with her?"

"None," one of them answered. "Just her pilot. He's still at the airstrip."

Esteban considered his orders for a moment. Tate didn't like the sense he was getting that he was being ignored.

"Go take him," he said at last. "If he gives you any trouble, kill him."

"Jesus!" he cried out. "You can't do that! These people are major league!"

"These people want the woman taken care of," Estaban snapped. "She's not under anyone's protection anymore. We'll lock her down and take care of the pilot for you, but then we're gone."

He turned to the lieutenants. "Get Chago, Manuel, Hector, and Dacio for the helicopter. Fly everything out, back to Durango, before they get here."

"What are you doing?" Tate asked.

"We're locking the place down," said Esteban. "We take away

anything that flies and she's stuck here. Unless she wants to try driving down the mountain."

He may spin it that way, Tate thought, *but what they are really doing is getting their expensive aircraft out of harm's way.* As well as the one that, from the sound of things, they were planning to steal from the blue-haired woman.

"And put the men on the transports," Esteban said. "I'll clean up here and go with Dacio."

They were abandoning him, he realized. They were pulling out and leaving him here with just his small locally hired staff. Everything was coming apart suddenly.

Esteban seemed to read his mind. "This place is no good anymore, anyway. And like you said, these people are big league from the north, flying in with soldiers. My men are already on edge. Best we get out of their way, let you deal with your friends. We'll come back for you when it's settled."

He turned and clapped one of the lieutenants on the shoulder. "Go."

Tate stood there beside his expensive, bloodstained pool. A bird landed in the ivy on the archways he'd always admired. It sat there, repeating the same sequence of notes over and over again, and Tate wished he had a gun so he could blow the damn thing into a cloud of feathers.

Everything was coming unglued around him. But the basic truths of his situation hadn't changed. He could provide the connections to people and money and opportunities in the States that the cartel would otherwise have no access to. And he could still work in the other direction as well, connecting Turnstone's organization to the reach and power of the cartel.

They both needed him. Once the dust had settled, they would still need him, and somehow this would all get worked out. He would end up with a new home, which was unfortunate, but once this had been a refuge as well. He would get used to it.

In the meantime, he should be looking out for himself. Someone had to go detain the blue-haired woman, but that wasn't going to be him. He was going to check his bug-out bag and be ready to get the hell out of here if things went sideways.

One thing he'd learned about living down here was that things could always go sideways.

CHAPTER 41

After they took Swift away, they pulled a bag over Crane's head and cut him loose from the chair. But they left the zip ties on his wrists, and they didn't notice the knife he'd slid partially up his sleeve.

Two men led Crane downstairs, across a tile-floored room, and out a side door. Crane felt sunlight and breeze on his skin.

"What the hell's going on?" one of them asked as they walked.

"I don't know," said the other one. "They just left. Esteban's gone. Nobody knows where Tate is. This is fucked up."

One of them walked at Crane's side, guiding him by his right arm. The other one sounded like he was a few feet ahead, to Crane's left.

"Where you want to take him?" the one at his side asked.

"Outside the wall. He won't want it in the yard."

Crane fingered the knife, feeling the button that would trigger the blade. Tate didn't want another body dumped on his lawn. He supposed it was reassuring somehow that Tate still worried about the landscaping after the chaos of the previous night. Though he wondered why Tate wasn't here himself to threaten and gloat. He'd have thought Tate would want to pull the trigger himself.

They were taking him to the same gate he'd used last night, he realized. Now he could picture the surroundings. He heard the metal gate creak open, and then the hand on his arm turned him and shoved him through the gap in the wall. The man who had been guiding him would be directly behind him, positioned in the narrow doorway.

Now.

Crane dropped the knife into his hand and thumbed the button. The blade snapped out, and Crane sliced through the zip tie at his wrists. He yanked his wrists free and whirled, raising the knife, thrusting at chest level behind himself. He felt the impact of the point driving into flesh, and then the surprised gasp. He yanked the knife free and fell away to his right.

Crane hit the dirt and rolled over his shoulder. He whipped the bag off his head. The man behind him was staggered, blood spreading through his white cotton shirt. The other one, in front, had been surprised and was only now raising an automatic pistol. Crane sprang at him, leading with the knife, and tackled him before he got off a shot. They fell in the dirt and struggled for a moment, until Crane plunged the knife between his ribs and into his heart.

He ripped the pistol from the dying man's hand, rolled over, and saw the first man staggering toward him, trying to draw his own gun from his belt. Crane shot him.

Then he lay there, forcing his breathing to slow. He kept the pistol trained on the gateway, but no one appeared to investigate the gunshot. They'd been expecting one.

Crane was outside the stone and plaster wall that partially surrounded the hacienda. He lay on a grassy slope where the builders had brought in fill dirt to level the site. Behind him were the pine woods where he could easily evade pursuit.

Beyond the gateway were heavily armed cartel soldiers. But that was also where he would find his weapons, the radio he needed to summon help, and Jason Tate.

The dead man he'd taken the pistol from had another magazine in his pocket, and the other one had dropped a revolver. Crane took that as well and then edged up to the gateway and looked across the manicured lawn to the house. Surprisingly, he saw no one. He sprinted across the grass to the wall beside the door they'd taken him out through. He peered through a window and saw a spacious kitchen with stainless steel appliances and glass-fronted cabinets. Again, there was nobody there.

The door opened easily, and Crane slipped into the kitchen. He'd been through the other side of the house when he'd slipped in last night. But he'd been blind when his two would-be killers had taken him out this way. He remembered turning right into the kitchen after about a dozen steps down a tiled hallway. Carpeted stairs up to the second floor where the guest rooms were.

Swift probably knew the layout better than he did. Where had they taken her? He moved quietly to the door into the hallway. It was empty, but he heard footsteps and slipped back out of sight. A few moments later, two men hurried past, both carrying large Louis Vuitton suitcases. Whatever was in them was heavy. They passed by without looking into the kitchen and disappeared around a corner.

Crane went the other way and found pantries, a laundry room, and an electrical panel with breakers for the house's circuits as well as the alarms and security lights. Normally, that would be quite a useful discovery, but Crane wasn't planning to be here that long, and the time for subtlety had long passed.

He headed back the other way down the hall and nearly collided with a stocky woman in a gray maid's uniform. She shrieked, and Crane caught her wrist and spun her, twisting her arm behind her back. He showed her the gun, and her eyes went wide.

"Please!" she cried.

"What's going on?" he demanded. "Where is everybody?"

"I don't know," she gasped. "Everyone is leaving. They say Esteban sent them to the airplanes."

"Who's Esteban?"

"The narco boss. Most of them are gone. The rest just work for Mr. Tate, like me. Please."

"I'm not going to hurt you," said Crane. "What about Tate?"

"He stays," she said. "There's someone coming. He's to meet them."

"The woman with blue hair. Take me to her, and I'll let you go."

She nodded. "I know where they took her."

Crane let her lead the way, holding her arm and keeping her in front of him. She took him through a dining room to another guest wing, separated from the main living areas. They walked up a flight of stairs and to the end of a hall where she nodded toward a closed door. Crane noticed it had heavy hinges and close clearances to the metal frame. It was reinforced metal behind a wooden facade, he realized. There was no lock on the handle, but there was a separate deadbolt.

"Do you have the key?"

She took a ring from her pocket and fumbled nervously with a key before the deadbolt clicked back.

Crane moved her around him while still gripping her wrist with his left arm. With his gun hand, he pushed the handle down, and then kicked the door open.

Inside was a bare room with a tile floor and barred windows. In the center was a heavy wooden chair, and behind it, pointing a pistol at him, was Swift. She quickly lowered the gun as she recognized Crane.

"Why, John! How lovely to see you again."

She came around the chair, and Crane saw blood on her T-shirt. "Don't worry, it's not mine," she said. Then she tossed the gun away. "And that's empty, anyway."

Crane stepped in, pulling the maid behind him. He noticed two bloody bodies piled in a corner. The maid gasped in horror.

"Looks like you've got things under control," he said.

"Oh, sure. I just couldn't get out."

"This is a lot more secure than the place where they kept me," he observed.

"Jason's a lot more afraid of me. And he's right to be. Shall we go? Is she coming?"

Crane shook his head and released the maid. Then he and Swift headed back toward the main areas of the house. She noted the revolver in Crane's belt and said, "How thoughtful of you. May I?"

Crane handed her the gun. "You sure that's not overkill?" he asked. "You know, given how much more intimidating you are?"

She opened the cylinder to check the load and then snapped it shut again. "Don't be peevish, John. It's not attractive. And it's my reach that scares him, not my combat prowess. If you need a handicap, you'll notice you've got the automatic. I've only got four shots here."

At an intersection, she turned a corner without hesitation and led him down a short hallway to a closed door.

"Where are we going?" Crane asked.

"To get your things. They let me look them over before I went up to talk to you."

She opened the door, and then Crane heard her sharp intake of breath. She whipped up the revolver and fired two shots into the room.

Crane dropped into a crouch and readied his pistol. He

checked behind them in case someone came to investigate the shots.

"Come on," Swift said quietly. She led the way into the room, and they closed the door.

"Put a chair against that," she said. Then she stalked into the middle of the room with the revolver leveled.

They were in a living room in a wing of the house opposite the one where Tate lived. A huge bay window looked out past the front foyer and across the lawn to the garage. The furnishings were very expensive, hand-carved wood and coffee-colored leather. And two of Tate's staff lay wounded on the floor.

She strode quickly to the nearer of them. He was reaching for an MP-5 submachine gun on the floor.

"No!" she said, as if scolding a puppy that had done its business on the carpet. She put her foot on the gun. "Your things are in the hutch over there," she called over her shoulder.

Crane opened the cabinets and found his pack with his equipment laid out on top of it. The weapons were useful enough, but the main thing was the radio set. He pulled the headset on and switched it to the backup frequency Jessie Diamond had given him. It was a lot to ask that she was still nearby and listening on that frequency, but it was what he had.

"Zookeeper, this is Ocelot," he murmured. "Come in, Zookeeper. You out there?"

He spotted a heavy wood and velvet chair in the corner and hauled it to the door. But so far nobody had come in response to the shots. It was strange, he thought. It was as if nobody knew what to do now, so they were either panicking or just pretending everything was normal.

"Crane!" said Jessie's voice in his headset. "Crane, is that you? Are you okay?"

"I've been better, but I'm okay. It looks like the airstrip here is clear. Can you get here?"

"I'm staged about forty minutes away. Wheels up in five. Are you okay until then?"

Crane confirmed that his F2000 appeared to be in working order and checked the ammo load. "Yeah, things have quieted down. If we're lucky, I'll have a passenger for you."

"Looking forward to it," said Jessie, and Crane heard her starting up the Short's engines. "Be ready to dust off in forty-five. Zookeeper out."

Crane put his MHS pistol in his belt in place of the .45 and closed the hutch.

"So you're still after Jason?" said Swift. She'd knelt down to retrieve the MP-5 and held it in one hand with the revolver still ready in the other. The two men lay still, looking up at her in fear.

"That was the plan," said Crane. "Is that going to cause problems between us?"

"Not a one," she said. "It's not like he's on my Christmas list, and it will drive Turnstone to distraction."

"Turnstone?"

"Major player in Team Kilo," she said with a broad smile. "See, you're learning things already! I'm in the process of reducing him to ashes. So let's go find Jason."

She turned back to the nearer of the two wounded men lying on the floor.

"Where can we find Jason Tate?"

The man shook his head. "I don't know."

Swift shot him in the chest.

Crane flinched in surprise, and the other man screamed. Then he trembled as Swift turned to him.

"But I bet you know, don't you?" she said sweetly.

The man stammered and trembled. "Please," he said, "please."

Crane was going to protest, but then, through the sweeping

picture window, he saw one of the garage bay doors pivot upward. A brightly colored desert rally truck roared out on huge, knobby tires. Crane caught a glimpse of the driver before the truck fishtailed onto the gravel drive and sped away. It was Jason Tate.

Swift was looking out the window now as well. "Never mind," she said to the terrified man on the floor. "Found him."

Then she stood up and hurried toward the far door. "They keep some ATVs around the back," she said. "Follow me!"

CHAPTER 42

Crane opened up the ATV's throttle and sped down the access road toward the front gate. Swift was about fifty feet ahead, checking over her shoulder to see what was keeping him.

They shot through the gate and headed down the gravel road. The dust Tate's truck had kicked up was still settling.

Swift was a capable rider. She kept up an almost reckless pace, and Crane fell in beside her. They whipped around the first switchback in a shower of gravel and raced down a long straight that gradually descended down the mountainside.

They reached another sharp reverse, and Swift signaled for a stop. "We'll never catch him this way!" she shouted as Crane stopped alongside. She pointed down the steep slope to where the road passed by. It was a forbidding run of scree and tree trunks. Crane gave it a dubious look.

"How bad do you want him?" she shouted. Then she gunned the engine and veered off the road. Crane watched her slide down the slope, the ATV's wheels throwing off tiny avalanches of loose stone as she skidded around a pine tree.

If she could do it, then so could he, Crane told himself. He spurred the ATV forward and went over the edge of the road with a stomach-jarring drop. It was as much a fall as a controlled descent. He fought to keep the ATV under control, remembering how notoriously easy they were to roll. Ahead of him, he saw Swift gun the engine and slew her ATV sharp to the left as she bounced onto the road. A moment later, Crane followed suit. He let out a breath and sped after her.

He could still see dust in the air ahead, heavier here. They were closer. Then he caught a flash of movement in the distance as they cleared a rise in the road, and he recognized the truck. It had probably been hand built from the ground up, with a fiberglass skin of a body over a welded tube frame. It was fast too, he realized as they lost sight of it again. Tate might be a worthless human being, but Crane had to admit he was a good driver. Even after Swift's shortcut, they were going to have a hard time catching him.

Crane glanced down the mountainside and saw the road coming back below. Another switchback ahead. He assessed the slope between him and that stretch of road. It wasn't appealing, but he'd survived one run down a slope like this.

He pulled up alongside Swift and shouted, "Get close! Pressure on him!"

She grinned and nodded, and then took off as Crane slowed and looked for the best place to descend the slope.

There, he thought. Below, the road bent around a rock outcrop. It would hide him, especially if Swift was giving Tate something else to worry about. And there was a spot where the road crested a small rise and then sloped more sharply down for a few hundred feet. It would do, he decided, if he could get there in time.

Crane guided the ATV over the edge and started down the slope, more carefully this time. The trees had been thinning out as they descended toward the desert floor, but the scree was especially loose here, and he felt the rear wheels trying to slide out. He steered into it and released the throttle, letting gravity do the work. In the distance, he heard engines and then a burst of gunfire from Swift's MP-5.

Crane bounced and rattled down the slope, carefully steering into the skids as the wheels sent stone skittering down the mountainside. As he reached the road, he heard another burst of gunfire. He got off and quickly pushed the ATV across the road, looking back up at the bend and rise and choosing his spot.

When he found it, he aimed the handlebars at the crest of the rise. He left the ATV running and ran to the outcrop. From there, he could see the truck coming closer, Tate driving like a madman. He caught a glimpse of Swift close behind him now. She fired another burst at the truck. There was no way she could aim—Crane was surprised she could stay on the road at that speed while steering with one hand and shooting with the other. But she was definitely giving Tate something to think about.

Crane ran back to the ATV. He stood beside it, leaning over to hold the handlebars, and raced the engine. As Tate's truck came around the outcrop, Crane had the revs up at the redline. He put the ATV into gear and ran with it as it accelerated forward. It quickly outpaced him, and Crane let it go, sending it flying like a rocket straight into the front of the truck.

Tate must have seen just a flash of color coming at him in the corner of his eye. He instinctively veered away an instant before the ATV slammed hard into the forward quarter of the driver's side with a sickening crunch. The truck went off the road, skidding up the rocky grade Crane had just come down.

For an instant, it seemed Tate might manage to keep control of the truck as it fishtailed through the loose stone. Then the back end slammed into a pine tree and the truck slewed sideways. The tires caught, and the truck rolled up onto two wheels for a moment and then went over. It rolled once and then a second time as it tumbled back down toward the road.

Crane watched it roll as Swift braked to a stop beside him. The truck ended up on its roof in the middle of the road, the front end facing back toward them. They ran to the wreck. A roll like that in the middle of the Baja 1000 wouldn't be all that remarkable, Crane expected. The bodywork was a lot less shiny, but he expected the frame and a racing harness would have protected Tate.

As they approached, Tate pulled himself free of the wreck, crawling out onto the gravel on his back. He saw Crane coming and reached back into the truck. Swift stopped and raised her MP-5.

"Don't shoot," Crane shouted. "I need him!"

Tate brought out a scarred AK-74, twisting his torso toward Crane. The muzzle caught on the doorframe, and he was still trying to aim the rifle one-handed when Crane kicked it away. The rifle clattered off the bodywork and tumbled away as Crane bent down to catch Tate's arm and haul him out of the truck.

He dragged Tate to his feet. Tate yanked his arm free and threw a wild haymaker that Crane sidestepped.

"Going to have to do better than that," he said.

Tate shook off the effects of the crash and took a deep breath. He gave Crane an unconvincing grin and shook one hand at him. "Yeah, yeah, it's all right."

In the middle of the sentence, he exploded at Crane with a punch. Crane slid to the left and raised one forearm to blunt it. With the other, he trapped the arm with a move that flowed into a strike to Tate's shoulder that turned him around. The turn forced Tate's weight onto one leg, so Crane delivered a short kick to the back of the knee and Tate fell. Crane guided him down to the ground with his right arm now held rigidly behind him, and ended with one knee in the small of Tate's back.

Tate cried out as his cheek pressed hard into the gravel road.

"Nice," said Swift, standing back and looking on with appreciation.

"See," Crane answered, "that's how you do it without just killing someone outright."

Swift shook her head and slung the MP-5 over her shoulder as she came to join Crane. "That's just because you need him alive. If you didn't, you'd be tempted."

"Yeah, okay." He hauled Tate to his feet and slammed him face first against the side of the truck. "But this guy earned it. Back there ..."

Swift helped him zip-tie Tate's wrists and ankles. Then they dumped him on the edge of the road.

"I don't need your approval for my methods, John," she said. "I learned them the hard way. Now let's get this thing back over on its wheels, shall we? You've got a plane to catch."

The rally truck was built to take punishment. Once they rolled it back over, it started on the first try. They drove back to the airstrip with Tate lying on a pair of huge spare tires, lashed down in the back.

Now Crane stood at the edge of the runway with Swift at his side. He put the radio headset to his ear.

"Zookeeper, this is Ocelot. Ready to go here. What's your status?"

Jessie's reply came back immediately. "Couple minutes out. Glad you're ready. Radar shows four aircraft about fifteen minutes behind me. I'm thinking we want to be gone when they get there."

Crane glanced at Swift. "Keep the engines running."

"Roger that."

"So who's coming behind her?" he asked Swift.

"That will be poor Turnstone," she said, "coming to make sure I finally meet my well-deserved fate when I'm caught doing something I shouldn't."

"What's that?"

"Throwing a monkey wrench into his organization to save you, of course. I've completely wrecked his relationship with the Obregon cartel. That's his liaison trussed up in the back of his toy truck over there. All for you."

She reached out to playfully squeeze his bicep.

"My word," she said in a fake southern belle accent so thick Crane could almost see her fanning herself. "What a charmer you must be, John Crane, to seduce me so completely."

So she was using him as part of some scheme, he thought. Again. Just as she'd used him to keep the Czech underworld from realizing that she'd had Branislav Skala killed. He had to admit she was good. If this was the level of play for Team Kilo, he could see why people were so afraid of them.

The sound of the Short's engines rose in the background, and he saw Jessie's plane, a dark dot descending toward them. In a few moments it was down, and he saw Jessie in the cockpit in her baseball cap and sunglasses. At the end of the runway, she pivoted the Short to face back the way she'd come and lowered the cargo ramp. She left the engines running.

Crane dragged Jason Tate out of the back of the truck. He took Tate's shoulders, Swift took his legs, and they carried him up the plane's cargo ramp and dropped him on the deck.

Jessie shouted back from the cockpit. "You okay? We should move."

"Give me a minute," Crane called back.

Swift was heading back toward the truck. Crane hurried to catch up with her.

"Last plane out," he said. "Do you need a ride? We can drop you somewhere."

"I'll be okay," she said. "All part of the plan. I'd love to borrow that radio, though."

Crane unclipped it and handed her the radio and headset.

"Thank you," she said as she clipped it onto her own belt. "Think about my offer, John. We could do great things together."

Then she pulled him to her and kissed him, hard. Her tongue probed his lips, and he found himself pulling her closer, one hand moving up her back to run his fingertips through her short blue hair. He found himself wishing she didn't find it quite so easy to kill people.

As they broke the kiss, she suddenly darted back in for another brief coda, and then she stepped back, licking her lips as she met his eyes.

"You be careful out there, John Crane," she said. "I'll be in touch."

By the time he got Tate safely secured in the back and joined Jessie in the cockpit, the Short was at cruising height and heading north. Crane closed the cockpit door and settled into the copilot's seat.

Jessie glanced over as if to confirm that he was okay. "So. Friend of yours?"

Crane chuckled. "Not sure I'd say that."

"She certainly seemed friendly."

Crane conceded the point with a nod. "But a little too bloodthirsty for my taste."

Jessie raised an eyebrow at that, but let it drop. She adjusted something on the control panel and was quiet as the plane droned on toward home and safety.

Crane found himself remembering that kiss, the taste of her lips and the feeling of her body pressing into his. Yes, she was dangerous and not to be trusted. The wise move would be to keep his distance and not get himself snared in whatever trap she was setting.

But he already knew it wasn't going to be that simple.

CHAPTER 43

Josh and Myria Group's General Counsel met with a very polite officer from the Investigations Division of the San Mateo County Sheriff's Department. They met in a conference room at Myria with leather chairs and an untouched pitcher of water on the table. Josh was in no mood for the meeting. There was the very welcome news that Crane was all right. Jessie Diamond would have him and Jason Tate back in the United States very soon. Beyond that, though, the news was just confusing. Too many pieces moving at once.

The officer said there was still no sign of Tim. Deputies had searched the area but found nothing. Josh hadn't exactly mentioned injecting Tim with drugs of unknown legality, so they seemed to assume he'd simply walked off. Apparently there were reports of someone who might have been Tim stumbling along the road nearby.

So you didn't actually murder him outright. I guess that's something.

It also appeared that someone had hurriedly gone through Tim's apartment. It wasn't yet clear whether that was Tim himself or someone else. Either Tim was on the run somewhere, or whoever was pulling the strings had gotten to him and then cleaned the apartment to remove anything leading back to them. His fiancée had reported him missing and was frantically searching for him.

Emily. You were going to have them out for steaks one weekend. Congratulate them, give them some extravagant wedding gift, wish them a future of happiness that won't happen now.

The short version was that the detectives were inclined to agree that Tim had been induced to kidnap him by persons unknown. Josh was lucky to have escaped. When the kidnap attempt failed, the accomplices panicked. The officer spoke carefully around the subject, but Josh got the impression they weren't expecting to find Tim alive.

Is this a dagger which I see before me, the handle toward my hand? Come, let me clutch thee.

"I got him killed, didn't I?" Josh said suddenly. "It's my fault, isn't it?"

His General Counsel looked at him with alarm.

"I mean, sure, he did what he did. But he wasn't evil. This was done to him because he worked for me. If he'd never run into me, he'd still be living a normal life."

"I can't speak to that, sir," said the officer. "But the choices he made were his. They weren't your fault."

"But you're a cop. You must see this all the time. How much crime is just ordinary people and a moment of weakness? They get tempted by something, or their life's lousy and they think they see an easy way out? I think we all have that inside us if we hit just the right situation. It's just that most of us never do."

The officer hadn't come here to talk philosophy. There was a hint of disapproval in his eyes as he said, "I don't believe we're all criminals waiting to happen, Mr. Sulenski. You've got a lot of people working for you here. None of them ever tried to hurt you."

No, until someone gets to them. Maybe they'll just poison me next time. I don't see anybody drinking this damn water.

He nodded. "I'm sorry. I've just ... it's been a rough couple of days. Then this. I'm still feeling like I'm off course. It's all right."

"You've gone through something very traumatic, sir," said the officer. "It's normal to experience some aftereffects. You might want to talk to a counselor. The county offers a group program."

"Yeah. Thank you. I'll look into that."

Great. This guy's going to go home tonight and tell his wife that today he sat down with one of the richest men in the world, and he was a ragged ball of anxiety, just a wreck. And she'll say it just goes to show you that money doesn't solve all your problems and sometimes the rich have it worse than us. Then he'll tell her how his duck painting is going to be on the three cent stamp, and he'll put his hand on her huge, pregnant belly and say, "Two more months."

That's the end of Fargo, you jackass. Now? Here? You just can't help yourself, can you?

He noticed that the officer and his General Counsel had stood up. Apparently the meeting was over. He stood and shook the officer's hand, and they walked him out. The officer promised that his department would keep Josh informed of any new developments, and Josh thanked him.

It was all very businesslike and civilized.

Twenty minutes later, Josh was in the Mercedes, driving toward Hayward. It wasn't like he'd forgotten how to drive himself. He'd done it all the time when he was a normal person.

Of course you're alone out here. If someone comes after you, you've got no protection.

Shut up. Just stop thinking. Stop it.

His phone chimed through the car's speakers, and he

checked the screen. It was Laura Berdoza calling from the war room. He hit the accept button.

"What is it, Laura?"

"We found Alexander Tate," she said. "He was checked into UCSF Medical Center an hour ago."

"How is he?"

"Don't know yet. We'll know something when they do."

"Thank you, Laura. Who checked him in? Who's responsible for him?"

"Working on it."

Josh felt a rush of relief as he hung up. There was one gnawing burden of fear lifted, anyway. At least Alexander was alive and in safe hands. If his condition had been induced, the doctors at UCSF would be able to help him. If not, he'd still be getting real care instead of whatever had been done to him at Fallon Point.

Josh pulled into the Hayward Executive Airport and through a side gate to the general aviation area. He pulled up in front of the hangar where his Gulfstream waited, and got out. He walked around the car, feeling the wind through his hair, listening to the sounds of airplane engines in the distance. After he'd circled the car, he leaned back against a front fender, and for a time, things were simple. The flat black plain of the tarmac, a car, a hangar, a lone figure with the sun warm on the back of his neck. If he could shut out the rest of the world, fall back to just that, maybe he could calm the fears and the gnawing doubts that were eating him alive.

So simple when you could just play at solving puzzles, put them down when you were done, and none of it really mattered. What have you gotten yourself into?

Josh stood there for a long time and fought his quiet, inconclusive battle. After a time, the sound of propellers disturbed him, and he saw Jessie Diamond's plane taxiing toward him. It stopped, the propellers spun down, and a few moments later, John Crane stepped out. Crane looked banged up but intact. Josh noticed some bruises and a bandage beneath his shirt. Whatever he'd been through himself, Crane had had it worse, Josh reminded himself. On the other hand, he realized, he'd assumed Crane was indestructible, but this proved he wasn't.

What's going to happen if he doesn't come back one day? From something you sent him into?

"It's good to see you, John. Are you okay?"

"I'm fine," Crane said. "How about you?"

"I've been better," he admitted. "I will be again."

Crane nodded. "This is a win, Josh. It's a messy one, but it's a win. Jason's here. Is the warrant out?"

The DA's office had issued a material witness warrant for Jason Tate the day before. Pressure in the right place had greatly increased the system's interest in reviving the old case.

Another useful lesson right there. You should be taking notes.

"The warrant's out. But we're on pretty shaky legal ground ourselves, you know. We kidnapped him in Mexico and illegally extradited him. If we're not careful, we'll let him off the hook for everything."

Jessie emerged from the plane and tossed a quick salute at him as she walked over.

"Hey, Josh. Found your spy."

Josh smiled despite himself. "Thank you, Jessie. I mean it. Thanks."

"Don't thank me until you see the bill," she said. "This one wasn't cheap." Then she leaned over to Crane and said, "Ten minutes."

Crane nodded. "He's not getting away with it. Jessie's got someone coming to drive him down to the Tenderloin. There's a room waiting for him at the Ambassador. The police will get a phone tip that he's hiding out there. He can yell about illegal extradition all he wants, but it's just going to be noise. A judge isn't going to care. Unless the cartel sends someone up to testify for him."

"I want to see him," Josh said suddenly.

"You sure?" Crane asked.

"Very sure."

Crane and Jessie traded a look, and Jessie shrugged. "Come on."

They walked over to the plane, and Josh noticed bullet holes in the fuselage. They entered through the side door and went back into the cargo hold.

Jason Tate was there, trussed up and stacked on a folding jump seat like a sack of mail. He looked like hell. He was bruised and dusty, his hair was an unkempt mess, and he hadn't shaved in a couple days. He glared up at Josh and let loose a string of obscenities as Crane hauled him to his feet.

"What have you done, Jason?" he asked. "What the hell happened to you?"

"Sulenski," Jason spat. "Great. You're in this too. Great. This your trained ape? That's perfect. I'm going to have fun watching you go down."

Josh wasn't intimidated in the least, he realized. Jason wasn't something to be feared at all. He just looked pathetic.

"What happened to you?" he repeated. "Your own father."

"Fuck you, Josh. He was more father to you than he ever was to me. You can keep him. I hope you're enjoying this. It's not going to last. You have no idea what kind of shit you've stirred up."

"Why don't you tell me?"

"I've got power at my back. I'm not talking the cartel. They're nothing. The people I'm talking about, you won't even see them coming. Put me in court. I dare you. I'll walk out, and your whole world will be falling down around you before you get back to your car."

That would be a lot more intimidating if they hadn't already taken a shot at you and missed.

Josh just smiled at him. "I don't think it's going to play out like that, Jason. My legal team's been watching your little empire. Last twenty-four hours or so, things have been moving fast. Companies folding up, accounts transferred, assets liquidated. Somewhere, some lawyers have been burning the midnight oil. They're filing papers by the pound over there."

He saw Jason's face start to fall, saw fear start to rise up behind his eyes at last.

"They've cleaned you out, Jason. What they could grab quick, anyway, and that was a lot. You don't have a whole lot left to work with. And your friends won't be sending their lawyers to get you out of trouble this time."

He heard a car horn honk twice outside. Jessie's driver was here to take Jason to the next station on his little railroad to hell.

"They've burned you, Jason. They've cut you loose so you don't bring them down with you. They've tossed you off the back of the sleigh to distract the wolves. So that's how I think it's going to play out. I think you're going to go to jail for a very long time, and I think I'm going to go home and have a nice grass-fed porterhouse and a bottle of Malbec."

Jason struggled in vain against his restraints, and Josh could see the rage and fear in his face. "Kill you," he snarled. "I'll kill you!"

"First things first, Jason," he said. "Your ride's here."

Crane and Jessie walked him forward and out onto the tarmac. Josh followed and saw a black Chevy Suburban with tinted windows waiting nearby. They loaded Jason into the back, and the Chevy sped away.

"I need to get the plane out of here," Jessie said when they came back. "Are we good?"

"We're good," said Crane. "Josh?"

He nodded. "Thanks again, Jessie."

"Don't mention it." She grinned. "Try and stay out of trouble, you two. When you can't, give me a call."

"That was good," Crane said as they walked over to the Mercedes. "You handled him well. How did it feel?"

Josh laughed. "I've felt worse in the last few days."

They reached the Mercedes, and Josh waved the key fob at the car and unlocked the doors.

"I was serious about that steak and the Malbec, by the way. What do you say?"

"That sounds really good," said Crane.

CHAPTER 44

Josh's house was quiet, and its cavernous rooms were dark. Josh explained that he'd sent most of the household staff home as he switched on the lights.

"Until I figure out who I can trust," he said.

Crane imagined Josh running around alone in this sprawling mansion, going slowly mad and collecting his urine in mason jars like Howard Hughes. It wasn't an appealing thought. Josh had been through a lot in the past few days, things he apparently thought he was safe from. But he was going to have to learn to deal with them now. Crane could see him beginning that process, but he still had a ways to go.

Josh led the way into a large chrome-and-glass kitchen and found a couple steaks in the Sub-Zero refrigerator. Then they passed through a living room that looked distinctly unlived in, and outside to a tiled patio with conversation pits and a huge, gleaming grill. Josh played with his watch, and the lights came up, and hidden speakers began playing quiet music. Finally, the grill sprang to life with a hiss of gas and actual red-accent backlighting.

"Seriously," said Crane. "The grill too?"

"What do I need staff for?" said Josh.

When the grill was hot, Josh tossed the steaks on. Then he said, "This music's got to go, though. I'm going to grill—I got to have my jam."

He spoke into the watch. "Gorillaz, Demon Days ... track twelve."

The music shifted to something much more upbeat, and Josh shimmied back and forth in front of the grill, singing into his spatula. He was doing a great impression of someone for whom everything was going just right. Crane knew better.

Crane had to admit Josh could grill a mean steak without hiring some ten-thousand-dollar celebrity chef. They sat at a table in the backyard, beneath the overhanging branches of an enormous tree. They'd talked over their meal, but neither had said anything significant. The past several days hung over them like a heavy, dark stone that they were pretending not to see.

Finally, Crane said, "So where do we go from here, Josh?"

Josh stopped with his fork nearly to his mouth, as if Crane had committed some social faux pas by breaking the unspoken rule. Then he put the fork down on his plate.

"I don't know," he said. "We did everything we set out to do, but this still doesn't feel like a victory party. It feels like we blew it somehow."

"Jason's in custody," said Crane.

"Alexander's in UCSF getting the help he needs," Josh added. "Whatever happened to him was real. He wasn't just being drugged. He'll need full-time care for the rest of his life. But the court will appoint a trustee, and I'll keep an eye on them."

He drained the last swallow from his wineglass and set it down. "Your friend's daughter's okay, right?"

"She's okay," said Crane, "until the next time she goes rogue, anyway."

"Okay, that's the upside," said Josh. "But we have no idea who was behind Jason. He wasn't doing all this from his little getaway hacienda in Mexico. He was a tool, but we don't know whose tool. We're no closer to that than when we started."

"That's a problem," Crane admitted. "Especially since they know who you are, and they've already taken a shot at you."

"And they hurt people. There's still no word on Tim," said Josh. "And that poor girl he was going to marry. Her life's been smashed to pieces."

Then Josh sighed. "And I don't know what the hell's wrong with me. I go from thinking everything's fine, I can just back off and everything will be like it was, to feeling like I'm naked and alone in the wilderness and predators are stalking me. I don't know what to do. I don't know whom to trust. I don't know how to be safe."

Crane knew the feeling. One of the first things he'd done in training for the Hurricane Group was a counter-surveillance exercise. He'd been tailed through downtown Washington while trying to identify the people watching him and make it to an objective unobserved. He'd eventually figured that they'd done this particular exercise early on precisely for the sense of creeping paranoia it created. It had stripped away all his confidence and his preconceptions, left behind only uncertainty, a foundation they could build on. The agent they'd built on that foundation had been more focused and more capable. Eventually he'd been ready for the field.

"Two things," he said. "Tomorrow, we'll start revising your security protocols. And we'll get people who can back them up, and who you can trust. Some of it won't be fun, but if you listen to me, I can give you the tools you need to keep yourself safe."

Josh looked at him thoughtfully. "I understand," he finally

said. "Deal." Then he stood up and started collecting plates and silverware. "What's the second one?"

Crane pushed back his chair, stood up, and helped gather up the rest of the dishes. "Second is something a couple people have brought up lately, in very different circumstances. We need a plan. Right now we're just groping around in the dark and whatever we find, that's what we work with."

"There's a lot to find, John," said Josh. "Everywhere I look, I see something that needs to be done. I see people in trouble. I see problems we can solve."

Crane smiled as they walked back into the house. "Cats in trees. I know. I'm not saying we leave them up there. But we need more of a guiding strategy than just doing good, and right now, we don't have one, do we?"

"Not much more than that," Josh admitted. He led Crane into the kitchen, and they stacked the dishes beside the sink. "Kind of think we need a better map if we're going to figure out where we're headed."

"Not saying we have to have it settled tonight," said Crane. "But we need to think in that direction."

Crane felt his phone buzz in his pocket. He took it out and found a text message on the screen. "Skala's 'tesař' = 'carpenter' = Gordon Carpenter. Shady money guy from NY. Dinner at Hashiri says he's on the team bleeding Tate. Text me when you're ready to pay up. XOXO - S"

So apparently Swift had survived whatever this Turnstone had planned for her. Crane was relieved, and a little surprised at how pleased he was to hear from her. He smiled, shook his head, and put the phone back into his pocket. "I've already got someone who's more than happy to lend us her map."

Josh raised an eyebrow. "Would it take us someplace we want to go?"

Crane considered that as Josh left the kitchen, and Crane

followed him down a hallway. Of course, Swift had her own agenda, and he'd seen firsthand how ruthless she could be in getting what she wanted. On the other hand, she knew things they didn't. The question was how much information could they get out of her without compromising themselves. It would be tricky to walk up to that line without crossing it.

"I wouldn't follow it blindly," he answered finally. "But if we keep our eyes open and don't jump off any cliffs, we could learn a lot about the landscape."

"Keep me posted on that," said Josh. "Lot to think about in the meantime. But when we're ready, let me know what you've got."

Josh opened a pair of double doors and revealed an enormous home theater with a curving screen wrapped around one wall.

"You got plans tonight, John?" he said. "Still got the new Batman. I mean, it's out now. Not really that big a deal anymore. But with all that's been going on, I still haven't seen it. You want to check it out? Unless you've got things to do ..."

Crane imagined Josh sitting alone late into the night in his huge, empty house, watching his movies and imagining noises in the darkened corners. That couldn't be good for him, especially in the state he was in.

In fact, Crane suddenly realized, that was why this had all hit Josh as hard as it seemed to. He felt isolated, adrift, facing a strange new reality alone. That was why Tim's betrayal had shaken him so badly, and why he felt responsible for whatever had happened to him. Josh was alone and looking for a friend.

"No!" he said. "I'm up for Batman. Let's do it."

"Awesome," said Josh, and Crane could see the relief break across his face. "You're going to love this setup. Go grab a seat down front. You want popcorn?" He looked suddenly bashful as he gestured over to a stainless steel setup sunk into one wall. "I've got a thing ..."

"Let me guess," said Crane, "you can make popcorn with your watch."

"Yes," said Josh, "yes, I can, and I make no apologies for it."

"Fair enough."

Crane headed down to the front and chose a seat in the middle. Before long, Josh followed with a tub of hot popcorn and sat down beside him. "This is going to be awesome," he said.

"Well, there's probably going to be a lot of camera tricks and stunt doubles, though, right?"

Josh looked over. "What do you mean?"

Crane gave him a dubious look. "I mean Adam West has to be pretty old by now, right?"

Josh's jaw dropped. "What?" He stammered for a moment and then landed on, "You don't really think that ... No. No, you're screwing with me, aren't you?"

"Yes," said Crane, "I was screwing with you. I'm not completely detached from popular culture. I know there have been many Batman movies and TV shows since then. Some involving Superman. I know Jack Nicholson and Heath Ledger both played the Joker, though Mark Hamill did his voice for the animated shows, and many consider his to be the definitive portrayal of the character."

Josh threw a piece of popcorn at him. "Nerd."

Crane snorted back at him. "I'm not the one with the watch that makes popcorn."

Josh waved that off. "Just shut up and watch the movie. Wait, are you one of those people who talks about stuff during the movie?"

"No," said Crane. "God no. The government trained me to kill people like that. Save it for post mortem."

"Good," said Josh, "good. I don't want to have to kick your ass right here in my theater."

"Yeah, that's probably best for both of us."

Josh turned away for a moment and murmured furtively into his watch. The lights went down and the screen lit up. Crane felt his phone buzz in his pocket once again. He slid it out and saw another cryptic message from Swift. He would have to figure out what he was going to do about her sometime soon, and he didn't expect that to be easy.

But not tonight, he thought. *Not tonight.* He held down the button until his phone powered down, and then slid it back into his pocket. Tonight he was going to hang out and watch Batman with his friend.

The End

John Crane returns in *Shot Clock*.

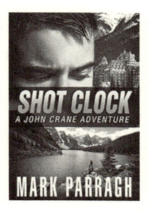

Available now at:
Amazon

Want even more?

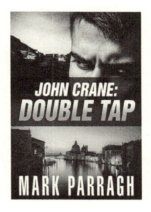

John Crane: Double Tap collects two novella-length adventures that expand John Crane's world and flesh out what happens between the first three novels.

And you can get it **free, right now**, when you join Mark Parragh's VIP email list. You'll get updates on new releases, sneak previews, and free bonus material available nowhere else, starting right away with your free copy of *John Crane: Double Tap*.

Join us at MarkParragh.com

Contact Mark Parragh

Mark Parragh's web site is at markparragh.com. There you can find a complete list of his books and much more. You can also find him on Facebook at facebook.com/MarkParragh, or email him at inbox@markparragh.com.

———

If you enjoyed this book...

...please help someone else enjoy it too. Reviews are hugely important in helping readers find the books they love. Reviews help me keep writing and they make sure the books you enjoy keep coming. Just a few moments to leave a review of this book pays off in so many ways. I'd really appreciate your help.

Thank you!

— Mark Parragh

Made in the USA
Monee, IL
20 January 2022